I0681884

BLOOD GOLD

BY WILLIAM NIKKEL

SUSPENSE PUBLISHING

OTHER BOOKS BY WILLIAM NIKKEL

Jack Ferrell Series
GLIMMER OF GOLD
NIGHT MARCHERS
CAVE DWELLER
MURRIETTA GOLD

Max Traver Series
DEVIL WIND

BLOOD GOLD
By
William Nikkel

PAPERBACK EDITION
* * * * *
PUBLISHED BY:
Suspense Publishing

Copyright 2014 by William Nikkel

Cover Design: Shannon Raab
Cover Photographer: iStockphoto.com/Sisoje
Cover Photographer: Shutterstock.com/bodnarchuk

PUBLISHING HISTORY:
Suspense Publishing, Print and Digital Copy, 2014

ISBN-13: 978-0692327890 (Suspense Publishing)
ISBN-10: 0692327894

All rights reserved. Without limiting the rights under copyright reserved above, no part of this publication may be reproduced, stored in or introduced into a retrieval system, or transmitted, in any form, or by any means (electronic, mechanical, photocopying, recording, or otherwise) without the prior written permission of both the copyright owner and the above publisher of this book.

This book is a work of fiction. Names, characters, businesses, organizations, places, events, incidents are the product of the author's imagination or are used fictitiously. Any resemblance to actual events, locales, or persons, living or dead, is coincidental.

For my brother Ray and his many contributions to this story.
Also, a special thanks to Greg Laskowski, retired Criminalist with the Kern County District Attorney Forensic Science Division in Bakersfield, California, and Diana Trent, owner of Trent's Bookshelf in Elk Grove, California, for their contribution.
And as always, for my wife Karen who has stuck by me from the beginning, and my mother Shirley for her unconditional love.

PRAISE FOR WILLIAM NIKKEL

"Brings plenty of wild action to an exotic setting."
—Thomas Perry, *New York Times* bestselling author of "A String of Beads"

"Settle in for an action-packed adventure that grabs you and never let's go. Jack Ferrell, William Nikkel's intrepid biologist hero, is back. This time, he's in South America, where the jungle is an impenetrable wall of green humidity and the river flows with the toxic runoff of that ancient human sin, greed. It's a powerful setting for a powerful page-turner, peopled with tough men, smart women, and villains who just keep going from bad to worse. Does Jack Ferrell beat the bad guys and make things right? Read and find out.
But beware. You may want to read it in a single sitting."
—William Martin, *New York Times* bestselling author of "The Lincoln Letter"

"William Nikkel swings for the fences and hammers a home run in this superlative eco-thriller that will make you think twice before your next dip in the ocean. 'Blood Gold' shines in all respects, a book that's one part cautionary tale and two parts perfect pacing and unrelenting suspense. This is Carl Hiassen without the laughs, a story that shows what happens when we start taking the environment for granted, as Nikkel stakes his claim to ownership of this particular sub-genre."
—Jon Land, *USA Today* bestselling author of "Strong Darkness"

"Frantic degrees of fast and furious action erupt as the mastermind behind an illegal mining operation in Guyana, South America cares more about an ounce of gold recovered than the river of innocent blood lost throughout nearby villages. Only someone like Jack Ferrell can stop the slaughter. Nikkel's 'Blood Gold' is intense with pacing that will leave you breathless."
—Sandra Brannan, author of the *Liv Bergen Mystery* series

BLOOD GOLD

BY WILLIAM NIKKEL

PROLOGUE

The Upper Mazaruni River
Guyana, South America

The oppressive heat and dripping foliage closed in on Samsundar Balgobin like a sodden veil of despair. He splashed into a puddle and lost his footing in the mud. A ropy tentacle snagged his ankle, sending him to his hands and knees in the yellow-brown muck.

He drew in a deep breath and let it out. The rainforest had always been his home. Now the jungle felt like an impenetrable barrier of exposed tree roots and clinging vines that clawed at his body, and ankle-deep mud that sucked at his boots, refusing to let him go.

The rain that threatened began to pelt the already saturated ground around him. He lifted a muddy hand and clutched his red shirt where it was tucked into his pants at the waist. His fingers closed around the cloth bundle concealed next to his skin. It was still there.

This was not how he pictured himself, running like a hunted animal. He'd risked so much for a chance at a better life. He couldn't let them catch him.

Gerard Gourde's reputation for brutality was well known among the workers. No one crossed him.

And no one stole from the mine.

He gained his feet and pushed himself hard. Never had he known a more intense fear than what he felt right now.

He chanced a glance behind him. Only the tangle of jungle he'd passed through met his gaze. But the voices were there. Louder now. *Closer.*

He stumbled, righted himself and pushed through the dense undergrowth, no longer sure of the direction he was heading. There were no paths for him to follow. Only more impenetrable growth and clinging vines slick with water.

And his determination to make it to the coast and Georgetown.

With each step he took, the steamy jungle dampness threatened to drag him down. The persistent downpour of rain only added to the oppressive humidity sucking the life from him. Still, he refused to lie down and die. No more than a kilometer or two ahead of him lay the Mazaruni River.

He sloshed through knee-deep water and up a muddy rise. Not slowing down, he pawed aside vines blocking his way and ducked under a limb that snagged and tore his shirt. Once again, he gripped the bundle and drew renewed strength from its weight.

Gold that would pay his way out of the pits.

More undergrowth, more vines and exposed roots, more mud, then the leafy canopy above him opened up letting a gray light penetrate the jungle gloom. Pausing to catch his breath, he glanced at the thick clouds overhead and scanned the limbs high in the trees. Pairs of blue and red and yellow macaws and colonies of howler monkeys sat huddled against the wet, staring down at him.

The monkeys began their howling. The birds squawked and took flight.

The creatures of the forest had betrayed his position.

He imagined seeing his family again—of being far from this place. Those thoughts kept him moving steadily toward the river. Always forward.

He heard voices clear and loud above the sound of the rain.

The men were in the clearing.

Frantic to put distance between him and his pursuers, he scanned the forest hoping he was headed in the right direction. He pushed through vines, ignoring the fatigue that threatened to drag him down.

Have to make it to the river.

His chest heaved with one labored breath after another. Exhaustion and dehydration robbed him of strength to keep going. He collapsed onto his hands and knees in a puddle halfway to his elbows and scooped up a handful of murky water that he greedily sucked down. The acrid taste rose in his throat and made him gag.

The gold he carried no longer provided him motivation to keep moving. Instead, the weight of it tugged at his soul as if some ancient curse would not let him escape the jungle it had been dug from.

He straightened and clawed at the bundle concealed beneath his shirt, desperate to free himself from the evil pressed against his skin. But he didn't have the will to throw the small bar of gold away.

The lure of all that it could bring was too strong.

* * *

Chester Abbott and Tyler Cartwright watched the huts come into view in a clearing on their left. The sight of a village came as a great relief after weeks alone in the dense jungle upstream. A sign that they were nearing civilization.

"Put us ashore next to those canoes." Cartwright pointed.

Abbott steered their eighteen-foot skiff in that direction. "Smell that?"

Cartwright pressed the back of his hand to his nose and scanned the bloated fish carcasses floating belly-up in the weeds. "What do you suppose killed them?"

"Maybe the villagers dumped them there."

"So many? I'm thinking something in the water killed them."

Abbott cut power to the outboard motor. The skiff coasted the last dozen feet to the sliver of beach and wedged its bottom in the mud. Cartwright climbed out over the bow and pulled the boat high enough onto dry land so that the craft wouldn't drift away. Abbott leaped over the side onto shore and walked in the direction of the village.

"I've got a bad feeling about this," Cartwright said. "Maybe we should just keep going."

"Nonsense." Abbott continued up the riverbank.

"You sure about this?" Cartwright followed close behind.

Abbott topped the rise and stiffened. "Holy mother of God."

Cartwright stopped next to him. "Jesus." He stared in disbelief at the half dozen corpses that stopped Abbott in his tracks. Men and women whose half-naked bodies faintly resembled something human.

"Come on." Abbott gripped Cartwright's shirtsleeve.

"You're not serious," Cartwright wrenched his arm free from Abbott's grasp. "We don't know who or what killed these people."

"And there might be someone alive who needs our help."

"Help?" Cartwright glanced around. "There's nothing we can do for these poor souls. Everyone's dead."

"We don't know that. Let's check inside the huts."

Cartwright peered down at the lifeless figure of an Amerindian man maybe thirty years old. Next to him lay a bare-breasted Amerindian woman of about the same age. Both bodies were twisted and bloated in a way that led him to believe they'd died writhing in pain. Their eyes and mouths were wide open, their tongues blackened and swollen. The victims clutched their necks as though struggling to breathe.

"We'd best be quick about it," he said, fighting off a wave of nausea. "I don't like this one bit."

The first two huts were vacant. Everything of use to anyone was gone from inside. Cartwright got the feeling the villagers—with the exception of the six dead near the river—had fled deep into the rainforest, taking their belongings with them. There were animal pens made of sticks and wire but no goats or pigs or chickens to be found.

Then he saw the dead woman curled into a fetal position on the ground at the forest's edge, the lifeless body of an infant clutched in her arms.

"Let's get out of here," he said.

"What's the matter?" Abbott chuckled. "Afraid a dead body is going to rise up and grab you?"

"You kidding? This whole place is dead."

Abbott pointed at the next hut. "Relax. We'll go as soon as I check in there."

"Make it fast."

Abbott nodded and took a couple of steps, slower this time. He reached toward the door at the same time a ragged man in a red muddy sweat-stained shirt burst through the doorway in a demented rage.

Cartwright watched in horror as the crazed man's machete sliced the air in a vicious hatchet stroke that cleaved Abbott's head in two. Blood and brains spilled onto his feet a second before his lifeless body crumpled in a gory heap on the ground.

For what felt like an eternity, Cartwright didn't move.

He couldn't.

Then he turned and ran toward the river. Fleeing for his life.

The crunch of the man's shoes grinding on soil pounded after him. And then he felt the blade slice his back.

He stumbled, but kept his feet moving. In the next instant, he heard a heavy thud and gagging and choking. A sickening gurgling followed by silence.

It was as though the madman had suddenly fallen dead.

Cartwright didn't stop. He didn't turn and look. There was only one thought on his mind.

Survive.

CHAPTER 1

Bartica, Guyana
The Lower Mazaruni River

Ahalya Pillai stood on the bank of the Mazaruni River, the ten thousand or so residents of Bartica were oblivious to the threat facing them. Nor were they aware of the importance of her work.

She dipped the specimen jar into the vast expanse of water, screwed the lid on tight, and held the glass container up in front of her. The sample looked innocent enough, although she feared it was far from pure. Mercury and other toxins used to separate gold from the gravel beds in the mines upriver had been finding their way into the water at an alarming rate. How serious the problem was and how much of those toxins were being absorbed by the aquatic life in the rivers and the ocean was something she and the other members of her research group would find out.

Before it was too late and people died.

So far, their findings revealed dangerously high concentrations of mercury and cyanide in the water . . . and many of the people in Guyana depended on the fish and shrimp for livelihood. To date there hadn't been any human deaths directly linked to mercury poisoning, but she was afraid it was only a matter of time.

A splash drew her attention to the water in front of her. Bringing her fingertips to her cheek, she brushed back a lock of long, shiny black hair that had fallen across her eye, and caught sight of a gray-brown dorsal fin a second before it disappeared under water. The boat sitting fifty yards offshore had been there when she climbed out of her Jeep and walked down to the river. But she hadn't paid attention to the shirtless, tall, muscled, dark-haired man in it...until now. He held what looked like a spear of some type. Not a harpoon for killing, something else.

Seeing the shark swimming in fresh water this far inland didn't surprise her. She recalled hearing there was an increase in bull shark attacks on swimmers. But what was the man in the boat doing?

Despite his dark tan and rugged features, he didn't look like a local fisherman. So who was he?

And more importantly, was he there for a reason other than sport?

Suddenly she felt him looking at her. He was too far away to know for sure, but she could see his gaze was focused in her direction. Had he noticed her watching him?

A nervous shudder brought goose bumps to her arms. Strangely, it wasn't out of fear or embarrassment. Even at this distance there was something about the man that attracted her.

He stared at her with such openness it reached into her mind and mesmerized her. Part of her wished he would look away and part of her wished he would race ashore and take her in his arms and kiss her.

Always the kiss . . . .

So much can be learned about a person from the way they kiss.

A breeze off the water stirred the muggy air. She welcomed the relief from the heat of day and the desire smoldering inside her. And was even more thankful when she saw him turn and go about his business. To have been immediately and so intimately attracted to a stranger was disconcerting. She'd been drawn to men before, but never like this.

When she turned to walk back to her Jeep, she noticed a Guyanese man striding toward her. She thought for a second he had been sent to escort her back to the lab. But then, she'd met all the locals who helped out at the research lab, and couldn't recall meeting him.

His expression was not at all friendly.

She glanced up and down the shoreline. There was no one else in sight. Only the stranger in the boat.

The man walking towards her was close enough now for her to see his eyes. Black and lifeless, but then they didn't have the look of unquenchable lust that she would have expected to see if he was a sexual predator.

Perhaps she had misjudged him.

She offered the guy a polite smile and continued walking, cradling the specimen jar in her hand as she climbed the bank to her Jeep. She heard him pass behind her, and let her thoughts return to her work. Then all at once he was on her, his strong arms wrapped around her chest in a bear hug that pressed her arms to her sides.

Her hands went limp. The jar slipped from her fingers and broke on the ground at her feet.

"Get off me," she yelled, struggling to free herself from his grasp. She screamed.

His hold on her tightened. A cold fear rushed through her as she felt herself being dragged toward the water.

"Let go of me," she groaned and lashed back with her foot.

Her heel struck the man's leg. A feeble blow.

It was all she could manage before she felt her breath being squeezed from her lungs. She tried desperately to pry herself loose of the unrelenting pressure on her chest, but she was pinned; helpless in the man's clutch. She wanted to scream and scream and scream, she wanted to yell for help, but couldn't.

Blackness closed in on the edges of her vision. *Do something*, she told herself. Desperately holding on to consciousness, she felt her life slipping away. He was going to kill her.

A moment before she was enveloped by the black void that preceded death, she heard a crunching sound like someone stepping on a dry stick.

A sickening awful sound.

Then darkness.

CHAPTER 2

Pillai gasped and blinked her eyes open. She breathed in and coughed. She took another breath . . . and with the next, she became dimly aware of the tall, dark-haired man in cutoff jeans standing over her. His broad shadow blocked the hot sun from her face. When the fog began to clear from her mind, she thought he was the most beautiful sight she could imagine.

She groaned and sat up. All at once, her eyes opened wide in fear. She glanced around, desperately searching for the person who attacked her.

The assailant was gone.

She relaxed and peered up at the stranger: the man who had been watching from his boat. He had kind eyes and a concerned expression.

She asked, "What happened?"

"You were attacked."

She hadn't forgotten. Her arms and chest still hurt from having the breath squeezed from her lungs. "I meant the horrible man who assaulted me. Where did he go?"

"You mean the man who tried to kill you?"

"Murder me?" She felt her body slump.

He nodded. "I fed his body to the sharks."

"You killed him." A jolt of panic made her stare.

A furrow formed in the center of his brow. "Broke his neck. He wasn't a nice man."

An unexpected chill made her shiver. She rubbed her upper arms reliving the brutal attack. A tear welled and broke loose. For a second she thought she was going to be sick. Quickly putting her hand to her mouth, she fought back a wave of nausea. Slowly panic gave way to apprehension.

She wasn't sure how she felt.

But I'm alive.

"My name is Jack Ferrell." The stranger squatted and offered her his hand.

"I'm Ahalya Pillai."

"Ahalya," he stumbled on the pronunciation, "that's a nice name."

"Please feel free to call me Pillai."

He smiled. "Pillai, that's a nice name, too."

She took his hand in hers and felt oddly flustered by his touch. She recalled feeling the smolder of desire stir inside her as she now studied his rugged features—schoolgirl fantasies shattered by the savage assault. Even so, there was an undeniable sincerity about him that removed the trepidation she'd felt only a moment before.

"Thank you, Jack." She gazed into his alluring eyes. "Thank you for saving my life."

"I'm glad I was here to be of assistance."

"When I screamed," she rubbed a bruise forming on her right arm, "I was afraid no one heard me."

"You've got a good pair of lungs."

"Fortunately."

He grinned, and added, "And I was watching you gather your water sample when I noticed the man walking toward you. That's what you were doing, wasn't it, taking a water sample?"

She felt a twinge of uneasiness hearing him say he had been watching her. But the awkwardness she felt was quickly replaced by a feeling of relief. His awareness and quick response had saved her from a violent death.

"I was," she admitted. "And I saw you staring at me from your boat. Lucky for me you weren't distracted by whatever it was you were doing out there."

"Sharks," he said. "I work with American and international marine agencies—NOAA primarily."

"The National Oceanic and Atmospheric Administration— you're a marine biologist?"

He gave her a wink. "Among other things."

She couldn't avoid the lure of his deep blue eyes—as blue as the sea. "Sharks are your specialty?"

"Apex predators actually—I'm here because of the recent influx of bull sharks into the river system."

"So that's what you were doing?"

"Working, yes. And I was looking at you."

She felt her face heat with a wave of embarrassment.

He grinned. "The answer's no."

She furrowed her brow in puzzlement.

"You were wondering if I'm married," he added. "The answer is no. How about you? Is there someone in your life?"

She shook her head, feeling a bit foolish. "Not even close."

"Good." He steadied his tone. "Now that we got that out of the way, why do you suppose that man wanted to kill you?"

All she could think about was the man's arm locked around her. The anger she felt. And then the helplessness that overtook her when the breath was being squeezed from her lungs.

"Robbery, I guess. Or . . . ?"

He shook his head. "I don't think rape was what the guy had in mind. He was dragging you toward the water, not forcing you to the ground. And he made no effort to pull you into the undergrowth or tear off your clothes. My guess is he intended to drown you."

She remembered being dragged toward the water. His theory made sense. "Why would anyone want to murder me?"

He shrugged. "Only you can answer that."

"This is positively crazy."

"You were collecting a water sample. What type of work is it that you do?"

"I'm a biochemist. Certainly I'm no threat to anyone."

"I wouldn't think so. How long have you been in Guyana?"

"Only a couple of weeks. I'm part of an international research team documenting the level of toxins in the country's water system."

"I'm aware of your group. Doctor Fredericks, the Deputy Director of the Office of Marine and Aviation Operations at NOAA, informed me your team was working here in Guyana. Concerns about recent influx of wildcat mining that's going on, if I remember correctly."

"Only the contaminants finding their way into the water system."

"And that's what you're checking for?"

"That's all."

He frowned. "Hardly a reason for murder."

"As I said, it's crazy." A tear formed and she swiped it away with the side of her hand. "We're here to help the Guyanese people not hurt them."

"Well you've made someone pretty damn mad at you, that's for sure."

"I can't imagine who. Perhaps it was a case of mistaken identity."

She saw him look her up and down, his gaze settling on her eyes. It was obvious what he was thinking.

"Doubtful," he said.

Aware of her unique beauty, she realized she'd been grasping for an explanation no matter how remote. She simply could not accept the reality someone tried to murder her.

She sighed. "It's all so ridiculous."

He gave her a long look. "Perhaps you can give it some thought."

"I plan on reporting this to the authorities as soon as I get back to the lab. I'll let them figure it out. That's their job. Me, I'd like to forget it happened."

"There could be consequences."

"I did nothing wrong. We're here by invitation from the government."

"I wasn't referring to consequences for you. What will you tell the police when they ask what happened to the man who attacked you?"

"That—"

She stopped herself in mid thought. She hadn't for even a second considered the trouble she would make for Jack if she told the police a stranger broke the man's neck and fed him to a hungry bull shark. Still, she had to report the assault. It was the right thing to do. Bjornson would insist on it.

"I'll tell them I screamed and he ran off."

"You'd be half right." He smiled and asked, "Would you care to have dinner with me tonight? I'd like to talk a little more about the research you're conducting. It's quite possible there's a connection to my work."

CHAPTER 3

Raoul Billaud stood in the mud at the top of the creek bank and peered into the widening gulley. A steady late-afternoon rain pounded the leaves of the trees and undergrowth, and pasted his khaki shirt to his shoulders, chest and back. Rivulets of water trickled from the broad brim of his straw hat. Twenty feet in front of him the surge of brown sludge streaming out of the tailings pond continued unabated. A serious setback he'd hoped to avoid.

He turned at the sound of bulldozers and massive wheeled tractors with huge buckets operating in the clearing beyond the line of trees. Plumes of black diesel smoke spewed into the air as the heavy-equipment operators worked to close the breach in the dam around the tailings pond.

A futile attempt to stop the escaping cyanide waste from reaching the Mazaruni River.

Gerard Gourde pushed through the dripping foliage next to Billaud and entered the small clearing. "We've plugged the initial break," he said. "But a second one has opened up. And it's getting larger."

Billaud noticed his construction foreman's clothes, arms, hands, and face were stained with mud streaked by the rain. "Do we know what happened?"

"I can't say for certain."

"But you have a theory?"

"The blasting we did this morning weakened the dam. There was simply too much pressure for it to hold."

"And this other leak?"

Gourde swiped the rain from his eyes and took a breath. "It opened up an hour ago."

"And?"

"The equipment can't keep up."

Billaud scowled, and bit back a surge of anger. The worst possible news. But he knew there was nothing to be gained by losing his temper.

He asked, "And you can't plug it?'

Gourde's shoulders slumped. "We're trying."

"But?"

Gourde turned to leave. "I'd best get back to work."

Billaud placed a hand on Gourde's shoulder to stop him from walking away. They had worked together for a long time. He knew when his friend had something preying on his mind.

"You have something you want to say?"

Gourde paused. "It's of no consequence now."

"Possibly." Billaud maintained his resolve. "But I want to hear what's on your mind."

Gourde sighed. "For months we have been releasing large amounts of poisonous leach wastewater into the stream, exactly as you ordered. But we simply couldn't keep up with the increased ore production. The tailings pond was filled to capacity, and then some. Plus this rain isn't helping."

"There is something else you want to tell me?"

Gourde hesitated and said, "We should've treated the leach waste instead of letting it sit in the pond to break down the cyanide naturally."

Billaud turned his hard, deep-set dark eyes on Gourde. He didn't like being second guessed.

By anyone. Not even Gourde.

Gourde didn't press. Obviously, he'd realized he had overstepped his bounds. Billaud considered his silence a wise move.

"A regrettable circumstance," he admitted when his temper cooled. "But as you said, it's of no consequence now. When will the auxiliary pit be ready?"

"A day, maybe two. Every spare man and piece of equipment is working on it."

Billaud stood a moment in silent contemplation. He had only ordered the pit dug at one o'clock that morning when the first leak was discovered. There was no one he trusted more to get the job done in the least amount of time.

"The moment it's completed," he instructed, "begin pumping over the effluent from the tailings pond."

"I'll inform the men." Gourde turned to leave, hesitated, and asked, "You've notified the Mines Commission?"

"No." Billaud had little tolerance for mining regulations. "And I won't unless it becomes absolutely necessary."

"I think that is a wise decision. The commission would shut us down for sure. The cyanide level in the tailings pond is three hundred times the accepted level of point two parts per million. A level that high is bound to create far greater problems in the river than we already have."

"Do you think I care about a few dead fish," Billaud asked coldly.

"You do not." Gourde's expression tensed. "And neither do I. But we are no longer talking about a few dead fish."

Billaud considered what Gourde was telling him and dismissed the concern. "For now, time's on our side. This rain will swell the river and dilute the concentration. If we get the leak stopped before government officials arrive to investigate, the level should be well within an acceptable range. Besides, the government needs their five percent of the gold we produce here—not that they'll get it. But they don't know that, and I'm sure that even if they do come snooping around, they'll be eager to downplay the incident."

"And the OMG office in Toronto?"

"No one will have to be told anything if your men get this damned leak stopped before those stupid bureaucrats in Georgetown find out about it."

Gourde puffed out his chest. "I'll see to it that doesn't happen."

"Make sure of it," Billaud said. "I will not tolerate any further failings."

"There won't be."

"Very well," Billaud said. He wasn't finished. "And, Gourde, keep in mind that the next time you speak your thoughts, I might not be so understanding."

"You're the boss. But may I remind you we are in this together."

"Then I suggest you do your part. There is too much at stake."

"I assure you I will." Gourde turned and walked away.

Billaud tempered his anger and redirected his attention on the expanding brown wave of toxic sludge surging into the creek. He could practically smell death riding the tide. But a few more dead fish in the Mazaruni didn't bother him. His concern was that officials at the Ministry of Health had already grown suspicious of high quantities of toxins in the river. A problem he'd taken steps to eliminate.

"Before you go," he called out. "Those scientists your men in Bartica told you about, they've been dealt with?"

Gourde looked over his shoulder at Billaud and nodded. "They won't cause you any further problem."

CHAPTER 4

Philip Bjornson sat at his desk inside the military surplus Quonset hut that served as the research team's lab. The metal building sat at the edge of a dirt clearing that had been carved from the surrounding jungle. The lot was used for vehicle parking at the marina, and at times the noise from cars and trucks coming and going could be distracting. Today the traffic was quiet.

He tented his fingers and pressed them to his lips as Pillai described the attempt on her life. The news of the violent assault was clearly disturbing and difficult for him to believe. But he listened without interruption until she finished explaining what happened.

When she was done, he relaxed his hands. After a moment he asked, "There is no doubt in your mind the man tried to kill you?"

"None," she answered.

"And you don't think he mistook you for someone else?"

"I can't see how that could be possible."

Bjornson took a deep breath and let it out. "You say the man was Amerindian and that he was unarmed?"

"I said the man looked Guyanese." She shuddered, still upset by her nightmarish scrape with death. "I honestly believe he intended to drown me."

"There are other possibilities," he said in a tone of concern. "Can you describe him?"

"I'll never forget him. Dark skinned, black hair, stocky, and a

28

face that reminded me of my cousin's bull dog."

"And his clothes?"

"Cutoff jeans, filthy red t-shirt."

"No scars or tattoos?"

"He ran off before I got a good look at him," she lied. "Which was fortunate for me."

"Fortunate, indeed." Bjornson settled his forearms on his desktop. "Rape is an ugly word, and forgive me for saying this, but you're a voluptuous woman and I can't believe there is any other reason he would attack you."

"Murder was on his mind, Philip, not sex—robbery either." She had purposefully held off mentioning Jack Ferrell, the stranger who'd saved her life. She carefully weighed her words and added, "There was a man who saw what happened. He thought the same thing."

Bjornson straightened in his chair. "He witnessed the attack?"

She nodded. "From his boat. His name is Jack Ferrell. He's a marine biologist sent here by NOAA to conduct research on bull shark attacks."

Bjornson rummaged through a stack of papers on his desk and held up a sheet the size of a large postcard. "I received a wire that he was going to be here. Strange that he was there at the exact moment you were."

"Lucky is what I presume you mean."

She watched Bjornson look at her. He had no reason to doubt what she was telling him. But she could tell he struggled to make sense out of the details; just as she had. She was a harmless biochemist doing her job, not an international terrorist threat. What possible reason could anyone have to want her dead?

"Okay," he said after a long moment. "Let's say the guy's motive was murder. Why didn't he use a knife or gun or some other weapon? Dragging a person into the river and drowning them is a rather erroneous way to commit murder."

She looked at him with the same disconcerted expression he had given her. "Is there a right way to commit murder?"

He shook his head and sighed. "I think it's possible he only wanted to scare you."

"He certainly did that. But it wasn't what he'd come there to do. He wanted me dead."

"But—"

She wasn't surprised Bjornson still had a difficult time believing what she was telling him. He was a scientist, like her. A laboratory and data sheets were the focus of his daily world, not violence and murder.

The breeze from the overhead fan dislodged a wisp of her long black hair and dropped it across her face. She tucked the stray lock behind her ear with a stroke of her hand. "Think about it, Philip. When people get shot or stabbed or bludgeoned to death, it's without a doubt murder and the police get involved. People drown in rivers so often it doesn't routinely arouse suspicion or initiate an investigation."

"All right," he said with a tone of exasperation. "We're back to why."

She knitted her thick dark brows together in thought.

"You have a theory?" he asked after a moment.

"I do," she said. "Maybe it has something to do with our research."

"I guess it's possible," he admitted.

"It's the only answer."

"That we have come up with," he pointed out. "But I have to say that it's highly unlikely since there are five of us conducting research here and no other member of the team has been attacked. The others are out in the Zodiac now. And there's been no problem."

"Maybe I was the first, possibly because I was a woman and they thought I'd be an easy target. Or perhaps my death was to serve as a warning to the rest of you to abandon the project."

He pulled his forearms from the desktop and shook his head. "We were invited into this country to gather data on toxins polluting their waterways. We are certainly not a threat to anyone."

"Those were my thoughts, too. But we must have made someone nervous or upset enough to kill."

"The only affect our findings will have on this country, or anyone in it, is to prompt the government to institute tighter controls on the indiscriminant dumping of hazardous waste."

She nodded. "And most of that comes from mining along the river."

"It does," he agreed. "That and logging. Which reminds me; officials from the Guyana Geology and Mines Commission and the Guyanese Ministry of Health have asked us to conduct further research upriver. There have been reports of fish kills, and they feel an increased level of toxins in the river may be responsible."

"And you're making preparations to go?"

"I planned to send Alec Soukis to act as team leader, you—if you're up to it—and Martin Fletcher."

"Martin? Why not Colton?"

"Colton will assist me here. Is there a problem?"

She huffed. "Only that Martin undresses me with his eyes every time he looks at me."

Bjornson sighed. "Perhaps he's a bit of a pervert, but you've handled him so far. And he's a damned good chemist; he knows the equipment."

"Is that a compliment for me or him?"

"Does it matter?"

"I just hope I don't have to put him in his place again."

Bjornson smiled. "I'm confident you can deal with him."

She could and would—a slap on the face if need be. Letting the issue drop, she rested her elbows on her knees and leaned closer. "You know this research project is important to me."

"To all of us," Bjornson readily admitted. "I'd be leading the team upriver myself if I didn't have pressing responsibilities here."

She locked gazes with him. "That's why I don't want to report the assault."

"It's your right," he pointed out. "Maybe it's even your duty to report a crime as serious as this."

"Is it?" she asked. "If we go to the police and tell them someone tried to murder me they'll most likely postpone the trip upriver . . . maybe even put a hold on the entire project. I'm not ready to go home."

She noticed Bjornson furrow his brow. He was obviously concerned. In spite of her resolve and dedication to the project, she had been emotionally scarred by the attack that almost took her life, and he knew it. Undoubtedly, he worried about her safety.

The next time she might not survive.

She waited.

"Perhaps," he said with regret, "it would be better if you stayed here until this is sorted out and I send Colton along instead."

No way would she let Colton take her place.

She stood and gripped the edge of his desk. "You wanted me to go, I'm going."

He rose to his feet behind the desk. Without question, it was his decision. She hoped he could read the resolve showing in her eyes.

"Very well," he said, with a hint of uncertainty. "You and the others leave at first light day after tomorrow."

She breathed a sigh of relief.

"You're worried about me," she said. "I appreciate that. But we'll be all right."

CHAPTER 5

The Brazil restaurant sat on the corner of Front Street and Fourth Avenue. Jack was standing on the walkway out front when Pillai walked up at seven-thirty sharp. She wore a clean pair of khaki bush shorts and a blue sleeveless blouse. He smiled as she approached.

"Punctual," he said, glancing at his Seiko dive watch. "I like that."

"And you look much better cleaned up," she answered. "When I saw you last, you looked a little ragged."

"I only dress like that when I'm rescuing beautiful black-haired maidens from fire-breathing dragons."

He looked at her through the bluest eyes she'd ever seen. His voice had a deep mellow quality that reminded her of the sound an oboe makes. And he smelled clean and fresh and masculine, not as though he'd been doused with a pungent department-store perfume.

"Do you do that a lot," she asked. "Slaying dragons, I mean?"

"Some," he said. "You appear to have recovered from that unfortunate incident this morning."

"I'm working on it." She appreciated his tactfulness in referring to the deadly assault as an 'unfortunate incident'. She could still feel her assailant's arms forcing the breath from her lungs and did not need unpleasant reminders.

The memory would always be there to haunt her.

"What you need is a good dinner and a couple of cold beers."

She smiled. "That may very well do it."

"Then let's not waste time." He took her gently by the arm and asked, "Inside or out?"

"Outside," she said. "I enjoy the night air."

"If you insist." He motioned with his hand. "Your table awaits you."

They were seated with a view of Front Street all the way to the Mazaruni. The sun was low in the sky and cast long shadows, but it hadn't yet set. She could see the river and imagined her head being forced under water and held there.

For eternity.

Averting her gaze, she forced the nightmare from her mind. But the thought of having her head held under until her oxygen-starved body forced her to take a breath of air that would never come, wouldn't fade. She shuddered to think what it would feel like to struggle and fight and gag as her lungs filled with water. And all the time, be completely helpless to stop what was happening. She hugged herself, and rubbed her upper arms to dispel the chill of fear that swept through her with the realization of death.

Perhaps, she told herself, she should just pack it in and go home.

"Your arm hurt?" He pointed. "Looks like you'll wear a bruise for a while."

His question brought her back. "What? No. I'm fine. I want to thank you again for saving me from that creep."

"It was my privilege. I can't stand men who go around assaulting women."

"Any woman?"

"Especially the defenseless ones." He smiled and added, "Particularly mature, intelligent, beautiful, raven-haired, East-Indian biochemists."

His voice was sincere and unthreatening. She felt herself flush and unconsciously peered down at her hands. Had any other man made the comment, she might have been upset. She thought about Martin Fletcher. Jack was nothing like him.

Fletcher was a lecherous dog.

She brought her gaze up and met his. "Do I take that as a compliment?"

"Absolutely," he said and smiled. "Now how about I order us a couple of beers?"

Waving a server over, he ordered them each a Banks. The server walked away and he asked Pillai, "You like Guyanese beer, I hope?"

"As long as it's cold," she said. She liked a man who took charge.

"It's cold," he reassured her. "And if you haven't already tried the food here, I'm sure you'll find the Brazilian cuisine quite satisfying. We can order whenever you're ready."

"I'm in no hurry."

"I hoped you wouldn't be."

"Oh . . . and why is that?" She had an idea why and wanted to hear him say it.

He made a sweeping gesture toward the street. "There are a lot of dragons out there."

"And you think I need protecting?"

"You might." He winked. "Mostly it's because I think it would be nice to get to know you."

She smiled. "It's a fine evening."

"It is at that."

The beers arrived and she noticed him glance around. "Those dragons you mentioned?"

"It's something to think about. Perhaps it would have been better if we'd sat inside, out of street view."

"Here?"

"Never know." He took a swig of his beer.

She considered the likelihood there could be a second attempt on her life. Several rough looking men roamed the sidewalks in front and to the side of the restaurant and across the street. A few men stood and stared. Any one of them could be waiting for the right moment to make a move on her. It might happen and it might not; there were no guarantees one way or the other. She wasn't going to hide.

"Like you said, it's something to think about." She smiled. "But it'd be an awful shame to waste this fine evening."

Their gazes met and she peered into his blue eyes.

"I like an adventurous woman," he said, lifting his bottle in salute.

She touched her bottle to his. "Do you really think someone

will try again?"

"I hate to think so." He took another look around. "If you don't mind, I'd like to talk about the work you're doing here."

Discussing work wasn't what she had in mind. But it might help. *Anything to put this ugliness behind me.*

"Earlier today, you mentioned your research and mine might be connected in some way?"

He nodded. "I believe there is a strong possibility they are. But we won't know until we compare notes."

Scooting her chair back, she and stood up. "First, excuse me while I use the ladies room."

CHAPTER 6

Jack watched Pillai's walk when she returned to the table a few minutes later—confident and sensual, not flirtatious. He stood, and pulled her chair out for her. She retook her seat and he sat down in his. While she was gone, he had repositioned his chair so that he had a better view of the street and anyone approaching. It looked as though she had brushed out her hair and added a fresh layer of red gloss to her lips.

"You look nice," he said, admiring her.

"You're full of compliments tonight."

He grinned. "You make it easy to say nice things."

"And I think you've been out in the sun too long."

They both laughed.

"I hope you don't mind," he said, when he gained his composure. "I took the liberty of ordering tonight's special."

"Thank you." She took a sip of her Banks, then settled her hands in her lap. "Everything has been about me. Let's talk about you."

"If that's the case," he said, "I'm going to need another one of these."

"I'm fine," she told him.

"Indeed you are."

He raised his beer bottle to the waiter, extended his index finger in a signal for another, and refocused his attention on Pillai. "This afternoon, I told you I'm a marine biologist. My field of study—as you know—is apex predators, primarily sharks—the hunters of the world's reefs. Most of my research time is spent in the Northwest Hawaiian Islands where there has been a notable deterioration in the reefs. The effect is an appreciable decline in the population of fish larger predator's feed on, which has directly resulted in a decline in the number of giant jacks, groupers, barracuda, and of course, sharks."

"How is it you're into sharks?"

"I don't exactly consider myself *into* sharks. I just study them. When you saw me earlier I had just finished tagging an eight foot bull shark."

"That explains it."

"What's that?"

"The splash I heard. That's what drew my attention to you out there in your boat."

"Destiny," he joked.

"If that's the case we owe that shark a lot."

"We do at that."

In more ways than one.

He smiled inwardly at the thought. "Now you know all there is to know about me."

She arched her brow. "I doubt that."

He let her comment hang a moment. "Okay. Maybe not everything."

She stared into his eyes and he peered into hers. He thought perhaps she was trying to read his mind. And maybe she was.

Whatever the case, he really was glad she was sitting there with him.

"But that's what's happening to far too many of the reefs," he said, getting back to the subject of his work, "all around the world."

The corners of her lips curled into a satisfied little smile.

"Pollution," she said. "That's what it sounds like?"

He nodded, and couldn't keep from sighing in disgust at the sad truth. "As I'm sure you know, the sea is a dumping ground. I feel like I'm singing to the choir here, but people need to understand they're killing our oceans. Bottom line is reefs around the world are dying off at an alarming rate. And so are the fish that inhabit them."

"You're passionate about your work. I like that."

"It's been known to get me into trouble now and then."

"Me too, it seems. But we're talking about you." Her eyes were peering into his again. "When you're not on the water studying sharks, what do you do? You have a home somewhere, I suspect."

"I sold my condo in Oregon, recently. When I'm not on my sixty-foot catamaran *Pono*, I live in a friend's guesthouse on Oahu. In fact, they're flying in tomorrow. Great people—I'd love to introduce you to them."

"I'd be delighted," she said. "Your boat, *Pono*, that's an interesting name."

"It's Hawaiian," he explained. "Short for *ho'oponopono*—means 'making things right.'"

"Like today?"

He played the scene over in his mind. It angered him to think about what the asshole would have done to her.

"I told you," he said, "I can't stand men who go around assaulting women."

She gave him a long appraising look. "You mentioned you're here in Guyana because there has been an increased number of bull shark attacks inland. What's that all about?"

"As you know, much of my work is with NOAA. The Guyanese Government asked them to look into the problem and they sent me. I've been here a couple of days."

"What have you discovered so far?"

His beer arrived and he waited for their server to walk away. There was nothing sensitive about his research, but he had learned it paid to be cautious. It seemed to him someone wanted Pillai dead. Whoever that person was, he was still out there.

When the waiter was out of earshot, Jack answered, "All sharks, by nature, are voracious scavengers. They take advantage of a free meal whenever they can get it. Bull sharks—more than the others—have an irrefutable reputation of venturing long distances in fresh water when searching for food. Without getting too technical, they possess several organs which maintain an appropriate salt and water balance in their system: the rectal gland, kidneys, liver, and gills. They are extremely territorial and attack animals that enter their territory. Since bull sharks often dwell in very shallow waters, they are more dangerous to humans than any other species of shark."

"The fish kills," she said, as if suddenly making the connection. "Doctor Bjornson told me there have been reports of fish kills upriver and that an increased level of toxins in the river may be responsible."

"Isn't that why you're here in Guyana?" Jack had already concluded fish kills were likely attracting the bull sharks. She and her team were measuring toxins in the water. It made sense.

"Not entirely, but yes. Our research team was invited here by officials from the Guyana Geology and Mines Commission and the Guyanese Ministry of Health. They're under a lot of pressure from international environmental organizations, like the World Rainforest Movement. Groups who have grave concerns about the destruction of the country's rainforest and high concentrations of mercury and other toxins leaking into the river system and on into the ocean. There is a lot of mercury used in the gold mines with no regard to damage done to the watershed."

"Mercury is nasty stuff," he said. "But I don't think mercury alone would account for the massive fish kills that are attracting the sharks."

"Cyanide," she said, as though thinking aloud.

"From the mines?"

"Five years ago, a tailings dam at a gold mine on the upper Essequibo breached, releasing up to a hundred thousand cubic meters of cyanide wastewater per hour into the river. The effluent was reported to have a cyanide concentration of twenty-eight parts per million. Point zero two parts per million is the maximum allowed by World Health Organization drinking water standards. In that case, mine owners reported the leak and the Guyanese government intervened."

"But the damage was already done," Jack was quick to point out. He could easily imagine the death toll on the river's aquatic life.

"It was," Pillai agreed. "Despite warnings delivered by helicopters and the media, residents on the Essequibo continued to depend on the river for survival. Potable water was distributed to some of the affected areas, but people depend on the rivers for more than drinking water. A man, his wife, and two children downstream from the mine were hospitalized with suspected cyanide poisoning four days after the spill. It turned out the family hadn't received potable water; they had cooked with river water and eaten fish and shrimp they'd caught."

"So no one died?"

"Luckily, no. An investigation into the spill revealed a failure on the part of the company to build a second tailings dam in spite of an increase in ore output. The initial dam simply could not hold all the effluent, and it collapsed. Environmental Protection Agency officials shut down the mine and it remained that way for two years. As a result, lost tax revenues seriously impacted the government and caused a lot of criticism of the agency's decision. Guyana remains committed to effective management of the country's natural resources, but government officials tread lightly when it comes to a potential loss of revenue."

"And you suspect a similar situation has occurred?"

"A massive leak, or an intentional release of huge amounts of leach water into the Mazaruni, are the only answers that make sense. We've already found dangerously high concentrations of mercury and cyanide in the water around here, and even as far away as the coast. Day after tomorrow, two team members and I are traveling upriver to run tests on the water there and the effect toxins are having on the aquatic life. I'm betting we'll find even higher concentrations of both. If cyanide *is* responsible, we'll know for sure in a few days."

A few days . . . how much damage can be done in a few days?

He lifted his beer. "To a safe, productive trip."

CHAPTER 7

Jack spent the morning drinking coffee and studying a map of Guyana. Most mining in the Amazon rainforest revolved around alluvial gold deposits in river channels and on the floodplains where rivers once ran. There was a lot of mining activity occurring deep in the jungle on the upper Mazaruni. And from the articles he had read, the deposits were actively mined by large and small-scale operators who relied heavily on hydraulic mining techniques—blasting away river and creek banks with high-pressure hoses, and clearing floodplain forests with heavy machinery to expose the vast gold-yielding gravel deposits.

What he found particularly disturbing was the estimate that close to three pounds of mercury was being released into waterways for every two pounds of gold produced. If that wasn't a serious enough threat to the environment, there was the cyanide used to separate gold from sediment rock. After talking to Pillai, he was sure a toxic level of cyanide in the river was responsible for the fish kills that were attracting the bull sharks. But that meant a mine upstream had to be dumping large amounts of the chemical into the water.

The answer, he knew, was somewhere on the upper Mazaruni.

At eleven, he locked the door to his hotel room and hoofed it to the marina to meet Robert and Kazuko. He considered taking a taxi, but the entire town was little more than a mile square, and a cab ride cost three hundred dollars Guyana. He could easily afford the fare, but it was hardly worth the expense. Plus, the walk would stretch his muscles.

And with luck he'd see Pillai.

On the way to the marina, he took the long route and walked past the Quonset hut that housed Pillai's research team's lab. Between courses of freshly barbecued meat and fish at dinner the night before, she had told him the Quonset hut was located at the far edge of the dirt parking lot up from the boat launch. He had no trouble locating the building, and hoped he'd catch a glimpse of her through a window. But he wasn't going to intrude on the team's work. Robert and Kazuko had flown into Georgetown on the redeye and chartered a jet boat to make the eighty-kilometer trip inland to Bartica. They would arrive any time. He continued walking and stopped at the edge of the parking lot up from the dock.

The Mazaruni flowed as it always had, joining with the Essequibo River on the way to the sea. Innocent in appearance, but it was more than a broad expanse of water. With it…came death. An invisible killer.

"You're waiting for your friends?" Pillai asked from behind him.

He turned at the sound of her voice. She was dressed in stained khaki shorts and a worn khaki shirt that didn't flatter her shape. Her hair was tied back and she wasn't wearing lipstick. His faded blue shirt with sleeves rolled to the elbow and Khaki bush pants were no better.

She looked great.

"I hoped I might see you." He scanned the river for approaching boats. "They'll be here any minute."

"I had a nice time last night."

"Me, too," he said, taking in the full allure of her dark eyes.

She held him in her gaze as if she had something to say and was having a difficult time choosing the words.

He wanted to kiss her. "You're leaving tomorrow morning, right?"

"First thing," she said. "When I saw you walk by the lab a minute ago, I was busy inside assembling the equipment we'll be taking with us."

"I figured you were and didn't want to interrupt your work."

43

"That would have been all right." A breeze dislodged a lock of long black hair and wisped it across her face. She finger-combed it back behind her ear. "I remembered you were meeting your friends today, and was hoping you'd drop by and say hi."

He stared into her big brown eyes. The day was getting even better.

"Great," he said. "How about joining us for lunch at Hack's Café? They serve a decent burger and you can meet Robert and Kazuko."

"I'd like that. You're staying at the Pegasus Hotel across the street from there, right?"

"You do have a good memory."

She smiled. "I should be able to break away from here in an hour or so."

Making the date, he watched her walk away, wishing she could have stayed. The distant sound of an approaching boat drew his attention to the water. It'd feel good to see his friends. He dug his phone from his pocket and called for a taxi, then hurried onto the dock, eager to greet them.

Five minutes later Robert and Kazuko handed Jack their luggage and stepped onto the pier. Robert was tan, looking fit, and smiling. Kazuko was as beautiful as ever. A great beginning to a week of fun.

Jack didn't feel guilt; he knew he'd find a way to fit time in for work.

"I don't know about you, but I'm ready for a cold beer," Robert said. "And you're buying."

"First things first," Jack said. He wrapped his arms around Kazuko and gave her a squeeze. "Ready to run away with me yet?"

She chuckled. "Just as soon as I can dump this bum."

"And I thought you loved me." Robert gripped his chest as though his heart had been broken.

"Haven't lost your sense of humor, I see." Jack offered his hand to Robert. "Gosh it's good to see you two."

Robert grinned and gripped Jack's outstretched hand. Pulling him close, he clapped him on the back. "And I'm glad to see you're as ugly as ever. Otherwise, I might think Kazuko was serious."

Jack groaned. "Remind me again why I asked you to come here."

"I'm sure it was to see Kazuko," Robert joked. "You reserved us a suite, right?"

"Right next to mine. The best room the Pegasus Hotel has to offer. Let's get you two settled in, then we'll walk across the street to Hack's and eat us a burger and drink us that cold beer you wanted."

"Just so they don't serve Kool-Aid."

"That was Jim Jones in Georgetown. There's no Kool-Aid in Bartica."

"That's comforting."

"It is," Jack agreed. "And before I forget, there's a lady I want you to meet. She'll be joining us for lunch."

"A lady," Kazuko said, offering up an eye-roll. "It figures."

Jack laughed. "Glad I didn't disappoint."

"And I wouldn't have expected less," Robert added. "The girls can talk, and you can tell me all about that self-defense course you went through. Hopefully, it did you some good."

"Some good . . . ?" Jack grinned. "I'm a trained professional."

"You're neither trained nor professional."

"Trust me; that school was worth the money."

"Taught you some things, did it?"

"You have no idea. But I'd rather talk about it when it's just you and I. The girls might find it a bit distasteful."

"Your lady friend's not into that sort of thing?"

"Let me just say, a lot has happened since I got here."

"You've only been in town two days."

"Three actually—four, counting today."

They walked side by side into the parking lot in search of the cab. A dozen feet in, Kazuko stopped and pointed at a yellow and white De Havilland Beaver floatplane tied to a small finger of floating pier in the backwater section of the marina. The vintage aircraft looked to be well maintained.

"There's your plane," she said to Robert.

Jack and Robert stopped walking and looked in the direction of her pointing finger. Robert appeared to study the plane a moment.

"Looks familiar," Jack said.

Robert took several steps closer to the plane and stood there. An obvious sparkle showed in his expression. "A DHC-2. It's even the same color."

Jack was as surprised as Robert was. "I'd swear on a stack of bibles that plane wasn't sitting there yesterday when I brought the boat in."

"No?" Robert looked at Jack. "Maybe it's there now for a reason."

CHAPTER 8

Jack led the way across the street to Hack's Café. It was close and had decent food. Here, there weren't a lot of choices.

When they got to the restaurant, he discovered the few tables inside the small, wood-sided establishment were occupied. His only option was an outside table under the shade of a large umbrella. He asked to be seated back away from the road. Had it been just the three of them, he wouldn't have cared where they sat. But his anxiety was still present. Even though Pillai wasn't there yet, she would be joining them.

He worried about her safety.

They took their seats and Jack requested a round of Banks in bottles for them to drink while they waited for Pillai to arrive. Robert let Jack sit facing the street so that he could see her approach.

Once the beers were ordered, Kazuko pushed her chair back. "If you boys will excuse me, I need to use the ladies room."

Jack knew there was more to her exit than a trip to the restroom.

He and Robert watched her walk away. She was giving them a few minutes to guy-talk.

"So," Robert said, "tell me what you learned in that school you went to?"

Jack huffed. "How to not get my butt kicked by that woman instructor, that's what." He asked, "You ever heard of Krav Maga—a close-quarters fighting technique used by Israeli commandos?"

Robert shook his head. "Can't say I have. What's it all about?"

Jack thought a second, and said, "The three A's: attentive, avoid, attack."

"Which means?"

"Mostly"—Jack groped for the right words—"the importance of split-second decision making. Good/bad, life threatening/non-life threatening, run/fight—the most effective element of dealing with any conflict is speed in making a decision. Then a person's fighting skill comes into play. If you stop and think: this is going bad, what am I going to do? You've already lost the fight. You have to make the decision to run or stand and fight, instantly. And then you react swiftly and without inhibition. We both know there is no such thing as a fair fight; there are no rules. You react fast and without restraint."

Their bottles of beer arrived, and he stopped talking. Kazuko returned a minute later.

She took her seat, and asked, "Did you boys get caught up?"

"Some," Jack said.

He saw Robert pick up his beer bottle and stare at it. He wore a pensive expression Jack had seen on more than one occasion. No doubt Robert was thinking back on the deadly confrontations he'd encountered during their dicey adventures together.

Jack gave his friend a moment of introspection and slipped into thought himself. It hadn't been that long ago since he'd come within inches of being killed. So had Theresa Montero, the woman with him. But they rescued his brother, Deacon, and found Joaquin Murrieta's buried gold. Luck had been with the three of them that day—and later in the hospital. Afterward, he and Theresa had spent an unforgettable time together sailing the Hawaiian Islands—rehab for both of them.

He'd not forgotten her.

Robert set his bottle down and glanced from Jack to Kazuko, and back at Jack. "So size really doesn't matter?"

"Robert." Kazuko gave him a playful jab on the shoulder.

Jack looked at them both. "What was that all about?"

Robert rubbed his arm. "In a fight, size does matter."

Jack chuckled. "It helps."

"Tell me about your friend," Kazuko asked.

"Ahalya Pillai?" She was turning out to be special, too. He peered up the road in the direction of the marina, hoping to see her walking towards him. "She's a biochemist here in Guyana, part of a research team documenting concentrations of toxins in the water. So far they have discovered high levels of mercury and cyanide in the river. When I heard there had been reports of fish kills on the upper Mazaruni, it was easy for me to connect the carcasses from those kills with the recent influx of bull sharks."

"Makes sense," Kazuko said.

"Until I find another explanation, I'm going with it. I should know more in a couple of days. Pillai and two other researchers from her team plan to go upriver tomorrow morning to conduct further testing."

"And while you're waiting for confirmation?"

"I'll continue tagging as many as I can. I've attached transmitters to a half-dozen that have staked a claim on the mouth of the Mazaruni. And, of course, I'll monitor their range and activity."

"You've got that look," Robert said.

"What look is that?" Jack asked. Robert knew him too well.

"There is something else going on here."

"It shows?" Jack felt like a fox cornered in a henhouse.

"It does. And that usually gets me into trouble."

"And usually it involves a woman you've just met," Kazuko added. "Ahalya Pillai?"

Jack realized he had to tell them. "A man tried to kill her yesterday."

"Let me guess," Robert said. "You rushed to her rescue."

Jack looked his friend in the eye. "If I hadn't, she'd be dead."

They slipped into silence. Robert and Kazuko exchanged glances.

"You're talking murder," she said. "That's not something you just assume. You're sure that was his intention?"

Jack inhaled a slow, deep breath and let it out. He was glad his friends hadn't pressed him to explain exactly how he'd intervened. He wasn't sure how he would tell them he'd killed the man.

Maybe they figured as much.

"Pillai was on the beach," he explained. "I was about fifty yards offshore in my rented boat. I'd just finished tagging an eight-footer when I noticed a man walking towards her. He didn't pause and look around. He didn't dilly-dally. He walked up to her with purpose and grabbed her in a bear hug from behind; then he started dragging her to the water. There was absolutely no doubt in my mind he intended to drown her. And that he'd come there to do just that."

"Seems strange, trying to drown her," Robert said. "If he wanted to kill her, you'd think he would have used a gun or a knife, some sort of weapon."

"Not if he wanted it to look like an accident."

"I don't doubt your powers of observation, Jack. But why would someone want to kill her?"

"I've given the question considerable thought. She's not a spy or an international terrorist that I can tell. And from the way she talks, there's nothing special about her life that would cause someone to want her dead. That only leaves her work."

"You said she's a biochemist," Robert reiterated. "What could there possibly be about her work that would drive someone to murder?"

"Listen to Jack," Kazuko said. "I think he's onto something."

"I believe I am," Jack said. "The toxins that find their way into the country's river systems come from logging and mining—mainly the mining operations' indiscriminant use of mercury and cyanide to separate gold from sediment. In this case, I believe a toxic level of cyanide is killing the fish. And that the dead fish carried downstream by the river are attracting the sharks. The Guyana Geology and Mines Commission and the Guyanese Ministry of Health think so, too. They haven't come out and said it, but my guess is that's why I'm here. And that's why Pillai's research team has been asked to run some tests upriver."

"But wouldn't the poisoned fish kill the sharks?" Robert asked, stopping Jack before he could explain further.

"Certainly, but so far it's only the fish that are being killed. They're small by comparison. It would take a higher concentration of toxins to kill the much larger sharks. Apparently, it hasn't gotten to that point yet."

"Makes sense," Robert admitted. "What I don't understand is why those agencies haven't stepped in to stop whoever is dumping the cyanide into the river?"

"My guess is they want to be sure before they take official action."

"Like shutting down the mine," Kazuko said.

"Tax revenue generated from the gold mined here is vital to the government's economy."

Kazuko scoffed. "Enough so that they would look the other way?"

"Let's just say governmental intervention and shutting down a mine is a last resort."

"It's always about money," Robert said.

"In this case gold, even diamonds."

"Revenue all the same," Robert said. "And that brings us back to why someone would want your lady friend dead."

"Which is what I was getting to. I believe the reason that man tried to kill Pillai, is because his boss is afraid of what the tests will show. Killing her or any other member of her team would suspend testing, or stop it all together. She just happened to be the one who provided them with an easy target."

"Until you showed up."

"Exactly."

Jack heard a vehicle break to a stop and saw Pillai climb from behind the steering wheel of the war-surplus jeep she'd been driving the day before. She was dressed in the clothes she had on earlier; but he couldn't help notice she had brushed out her hair and added a layer of red lipstick.

She looked fabulous.

He waited for her to approach the table. When she was a few feet away, he stood next to his chair to make the introductions. "Robert, Kazuko—this is Ahalya Pillai, the woman I wanted you to meet. Ahalya, these are my friends."

CHAPTER 9

Jack pulled a chair away from the table for Pillai and remained standing while she took her seat. When she was sitting, he waved to the server to bring her a Banks. The waiter stepped inside the building and reappeared a half-minute later balancing a beer bottle on a serving tray.

"I've been telling my friends about your research and the unfortunate event yesterday," he said, retaking his chair. "I hope you don't mind."

She scanned their faces. "Not my best moment, I'm afraid."

The waiter set the bottle on the table in front of Pillai. His gaze swept over the women, and he smiled wide.

"That will be all for the moment," Jack said. "We'll let you know when we are ready to order lunch."

"Take your time," the waiter answered and walked away.

When he was gone, Kazuko leaned toward Pillai. "I know what it must have felt like. It's understandable you're upset by the ordeal."

"I have to admit I considered just packing it in and going home." She looked at Jack. "Last night at dinner it hit me just how close I came to suffering a horrible death. It scared me."

He nodded. "I noticed."

"But you didn't say anything."

"I knew you would work it out."

"Ignore Jack." Kazuko leaned forward in her chair. Her tone

softened, "I can't imagine anyone blaming you if you *had* gone home."

"Perhaps no one would," Pillai agreed. "But I want you to know that I no longer consider leaving an option. I'm not going to let this unfortunate incident keep me from completing my work here. Tomorrow, I'm going upriver."

"You're not afraid."

"I didn't say that. But I'm not going to let it stop me."

Kazuko settled back in her chair. "Jack mentioned you're a biochemist."

Jack noticed her shoot him a quick glance before facing Kazuko. He thought he saw her lips curl up slightly at the corners.

She said, "I did my undergraduate studies in New Delhi and my graduate studies at Stanford."

"I find it interesting you chose the U.S. to do your graduate work."

"My parents insisted."

"I studied at the University of Hawaii," Kazuko explained. "Initially, the focus of my research was invertebrates. Now, my specialty is dolphin behavior. I take it Jack didn't tell you I'm a marine biologist? "

"He didn't." Pillai looked at Jack.

He smiled. "I had to give you ladies something to chat about."

"With you around," Robert chimed in, "There's no shortage of sordid topics for them to talk about."

His comment made them all chuckle.

"Are they always like this?" asked Pillai.

Kazuko slowly shook her head from side to side. "Ahalya, believe me, they're much worse. My suggestion is that you don't pay any attention to either one of these guys. They're incorrigible when they're together."

"I'll keep that in mind. And please, feel free to call me Pillai. Most everyone with the exception of my family does." Pillai offered her hand to Kazuko. "We started talking and I never did tell you how nice it is to meet you."

"I'm very happy to meet you, too," Kazuko said.

"So you've known Jack for a long time?"

"About ten years. He and Robert were friends when Robert and I met. Now we just kind of watch over him."

"Mother hens, both of them," Jack said, before Pillai could question Kazuko further. "What do you say we order something to eat?"

Pillai was grinning at him again. He got the feeling she was enjoying herself.

She said, "The conversation was just getting interesting."

"And I'm hungry," Jack insisted.

"Hungry?" Pillai held Jack in her gaze. "Or avoiding?"

"Both," Jack said. "Now can we order?"

"Jack's just being Jack," Robert offered. "I'm curious; biochemistry is a broad scientific discipline with a wide range of applications. My guess is you returned to New Delhi and went to work for the university there?"

"It was expected of me," Pillai answered. "I enjoyed the analysis work I did in the lab there. That is, until 2004, when waves as high as thirty meters swept through the Indian Ocean killing two hundred and thirty thousand people in fourteen countries. That was my first opportunity to work outside of the lab. It was hard for me to go back. Now I jump at the chance to conduct research in the field—especially as a member of an international team like the one I'm on now. I truly enjoy interacting with scientists and specialists from other fields."

"And I'll drink to that," Jack said. He drained the remainder of his beer and raised his hand to the waiter. He noticed Robert, Kazuko, and Pillai glance in his direction and look away.

Robert turned to Pillai, and said, "You and Kazuko are a lot alike."

Pillai nodded. "She's a lovely lady."

Kazuko reached next to her and gripped Robert's hand. "A thought just occurred to me." She turned to Pillai. "I don't really have any obligations keeping me here. It'd be fun if you let me tag along with you and your team."

CHAPTER 10

At six the next morning, Jack stood next to Robert on the weathered wooden dock. The jet boat ferrying the research team thirty kilometers upriver to Marshal Falls was twenty feet long and made of fiberglass. It had a small cuddy cabin and a high windshield—lots of open space for passengers and equipment.

A stable, safe boat.

Pillai had convinced Bjornson it would be beneficial to their project to have Kazuko travel upriver with the team—not only because she was an experienced marine biologist, but because it would be good to have another woman along. Bjornson hadn't been able to argue with her reasoning, and agreed.

Jack thought maybe it was because of the attack on Pillai, and in part because he was there on a NOAA sanctioned project that had proved to be connected to Bjornson's team's research.

He and Robert waved to Pillai and Kazuko as the boat accelerated away from the pier.

Have a safe trip, not good-bye.

Jack already anticipated their return.

The women understood what they were getting into. He hadn't said anything to them, but he harbored misgivings about their trip, even with two men along. Still, he knew he was in no position to demand that they stay back. Pillai was adamant about going, and Kazuko was just as committed. Robert had already resigned himself

55

to the certainty she was going along.

There was nothing either of them could do now, but wait.

* * *

The two women stood at the stern of the craft and waved to Jack and Robert.

"They both think a lot of you," Pillai said.

"And there is nothing I wouldn't do for them," Kazuko answered. "But they weren't just waving at me. Jack has taken a real liking to you."

"Really?" Pillai stared at the two men a moment longer, then took a seat.

"Did you find that surprising?" Kazuko asked, when she settled onto the seat next to Pillai.

"I'm not hard to look at," she admitted.

Kazuko envisioned her own beauty and the looks she got from men. "Believe me when I say I understand what you are getting at."

"I'm sure you do," Pillai agreed.

"So you weren't surprised?"

"That he was attracted to me, not at all. But, I don't know. He seems different, in a likable sort of way. When I was a child I imagined what it would feel like to have a handsome young prince rescue me from an evil sultan. I kind of feel that way when I'm around him."

"That's Jack all right," Kazuko reassured her. "The white knight to the rescue."

Pillai glanced at her hands as if embarrassed to have admitted her feelings. "I've been afraid I was misreading him."

"You haven't misread him at all." Kazuko chuckled. "He feels a need to protect each and every one of us. Why, I don't know. He just does."

Her gaze remained fixed on her hands. "He saved me."

"And you're attracted to him."

Pillai's gaze came up. Her eyes confirmed Kazuko's observation. "Am I making a mistake?"

"Don't take this wrong," she said. "Jack likes women. Women

like Jack—for obvious reasons. When it comes to that he's an open book."

"That's not hard to figure out," Pillai answered. "What I want you to tell me about is the other side of Jack; the side that's not an open book."

Kazuko gave her a long appraising look. Pillai was not some love-struck bimbo. She was intelligent, mature, and focused. She deserved the truth.

"You've seen the congenial, unpretentious Jack his friends know and love," she said, "his humorous, impulsive, easygoing, always quick-to-help side." She paused, envisioning some of the questionable things he'd done. "There's a cold, efficient Jack, as well."

"Don't I know," Pillai admitted. "He killed that man to save me."

Kazuko hadn't expected to hear that Jack had killed the man. She was a little taken aback by the news, but not especially shocked by what he'd done. Jack had killed men before, when they needed killing and when he had no choice. What surprised her was that Pillai had chosen this moment to tell her.

She placed her hand caringly on Pillai's arm. "Let's keep that our little secret."

Pillai fell quiet and Kazuko watched the last vestiges of urban life give way to lush jungle. On both sides of the river a thousand species of trees and countless number of plants and vines formed the Guyanese rainforest that covered seventy-seven percent of the country's land mass.

Soukis, the team leader on the excursion, made his way along the gunwale to the stern and took a seat close to her.

Kazuko asked, "What do you know about this village we're going to?"

"Marshal Landing?" he shrugged. "English speaking. It's in the Amerindian territory of Kaburi—primarily people of the Akawaio and Patomona tribes with a lot of Dutch influence. It's frequented by tourists visiting the falls, and miners and loggers traveling the Mazaruni."

She eyed the stack of aluminum cases holding the team's test equipment. "So, do you think we have enough supplies?"

"We have bottled water and food for a week waiting for us in the village," he said. Pointing at the aluminum cases, he added, "The portable GC-MS, the ICP-MS, laptops, and enough beakers and jars to hold half the water in the river. Are you concerned we might need more?"

"Just a thought," she told him. "I like to be prepared."

"What's a GC-MS and an ICP-MS?" The question came from the shirtless, black-haired boy stepping around the stacked cases.

Kazuko smiled—Tony Melvin, the captain's son. He was tanned dark, and all of eleven or twelve years old. *Still a kid*, she thought, *but old enough to help his father on the boat.*

She asked, "Are you interested in science?"

Tony shrugged his bony shoulders. "I like to learn."

"Do you know about bad things in the water?"

He nodded. "Things that can make you sick."

"That's right," she said. "Or worse—it's very bad stuff. If there is too much it can kill you if you drink from the river or eat the fish."

His eyes widened. "And that's what this stuff is for?"

"A GC-MS," Soukis explained, "is a device called a gas chromatograph/mass spectrometer. It identifies chemicals in the water that are highly toxic to fish and animals. We will use it to make sure the river is safe for you and your people."

"How does it do that?"

"We will take a water sample from the river, place it inside the machine, and push some buttons. The machine will analyze the water and tell us the level of cyanide in the river."

"And the other one?"

"The ICP-MS is an inductively coupled plasma/mass spectrometer. It's basically the same type of device as the gas chromatograph/mass spectrometer, only the ICP-MS uses different technology. It will tell us which metals are present in the water. We are especially worried about high concentrations of mercury."

Tony grinned. "From the mines."

"That's right."

"But not everything in the river is bad?"

Soukis nodded. "Only in sufficient quantities."

Tony quieted in thought. Kazuko sat back and watched his gaze move to the aluminum containers stacked on the deck. No doubt, the boy's mind processed the information he'd been given.

She gave the boy a gentle pat on the shoulder, happy to see his young mind work. "You're a fast learner."

He straightened and puffed out his small chest. "My father says I'm smart enough to go to the university when I grow up."

She couldn't keep from smiling. He was not unlike many of the young boys back home in Hawaii. He was growing up in a place where everyone in the family worked to survive. Eager. She hoped he got his wish.

"You'll make a great scientist."

"When I grow up?"

"You're already a big boy," she reassured him.

"But not big enough."

"You will be," Soukis interrupted. "Remember, in science there are no toxic compounds, only toxic levels."

Kazuko leaned back in her seat, further admiring the boy's spunk. He reminded her of herself at his age. She had owned the same confidence; self-assurance that earned her a Masters Degree in Marine Science, and a rewarding career that allowed her to watch over the oceans' creatures.

Her true passion.

She felt the boat slow and saw Tony's gaze shift to his father presiding over the helm.

"I have work to do now," Tony said.

She watched him hurry off toward the bow of the boat, then scanned the surface of the water stained brown from suspended silt, sand and mud. The Mazaruni flowing from its source in the remote western forests of the Pakaraima Mountains the way the river had since the dawn of time. Marshal Falls came into view and she settled her gaze on the cascading water.

A popular tourist destination—a wonder of nature.

She couldn't help but worry about what they would find on the other side.

CHAPTER 11

The pilot settled the skids of OMG Enterprises' Sikorsky helicopter onto the landing pad at the small airport on the outskirts of Bartica. Gerard Gourde climbed from the cockpit and walked to the rusted silver Toyota sedan sitting on the tarmac fifty-feet away from the twirling blades of the corporation's private chopper. He pulled open the passenger door, settled his bulk on the worn seat, and slammed the door closed.

Cheddi Norton, the skinny, black-haired, narrow-faced man with the hawk nose, sat attentively behind the steering wheel. He'd been trusted to make sure the results of the research team's analysis of toxins in the river did not find their way into the hands of Paulette Sukhai, the Deputy Minister of the Guyanese Ministry of Health.

Gourde was interested in one thing. He turned his hard eyes on Norton, and spoke, "Drive."

Norton started the car and drove away from the airport without question.

Gourde leaned forward and adjusted the dash vents so that the weak blast of cool air flowing from them blew directly on his sun-baked skin. Confident he had every degree of comfort the small car's air conditioner had to offer, he leaned back in his seat.

"So," he said after a moment, "tell me our problem has been taken care of."

"You were right about the scientists," Norton explained. His nervous gaze shifted back and forth between the roadway and the big man in the seat next to him. "There are five of them working out of a Quonset hut at the marina, and as you suspected, they have been collecting water samples from the Mazaruni."

Gourde shifted uncomfortably on the exposed springs in his seat. The deplorable ride did nothing to brighten his mood. He'd come to look into Norton's eyes and hear what he had to say. Talking on the radio was simply unacceptable—a conversation too easily overheard. And the man's eyes would betray his lies.

"Do not tell me what I already know," he said.

"I was only—"

Gourde waved him off. "Just tell me you have taken care of the problem."

Norton's Adam's apple bobbed as he swallowed hard. "There is a pretty woman scientist with them. My cousin at the marina tells me her name is Ahalya Pillai. Merano and I had been keeping an eye on her, hoping to catch her alone. We thought she would be easiest to get to. Two days ago Merano followed her to the river. I have not seen him since. And the woman is still alive."

"The other members, too, I presume?"

"Regrettably, yes."

"Your assignment was simple." Gourde fought back a surge of anger. The failure of Norton to neutralize the situation frustrated him. "And yet you were unable to carry out my orders."

Norton remained quiet behind the wheel, his eyes fixed on the road ahead.

"You have nothing to say for yourself?" Gourde demanded.

"You were specific in your instructions." Norton sighed. "But it is not always simple to make a death look like an accident."

"And it is no great feat either," Gourde said smugly. "I do not tolerate failure."

Norton took a deep breath, clearly searching for an acceptable explanation.

Gourde was growing even more impatient.

"Something must have happened to Merano," Norton said after a moment. "That is the only answer."

Gourde sighed in frustration. "Merano is of no concern to me.

The man is a fool. I care that you did not succeed in eliminating this threat."

"Honestly," Norton glanced back and forth nervously between Gourde and the road, "I do not know how our plan failed."

Gourde fought to control his anger and stared out the side window. "Did I not tell *you* to see to it the matter was handled?"

"You did. And it should have been."

Gourde clenched his teeth.

He glared at Norton. "But it wasn't."

Again, Norton's Adam's apple bobbed.

"Merano must have been killed," he said. "Otherwise, he would have returned to tell me what went wrong."

"Do you want me to believe that woman—a *scientist*—killed him?"

"Not her. But someone must have. There is no other explanation."

"Excuses, Norton."

A pot hole in the road bounced Gourde in his seat. He was hot, uncomfortable, and exceedingly irritated at Norton's incompetence. For months, Billaud had ordered the systematic release of cyanide wastewater into the river. But health officials would have had a difficult time tracing the source of the toxins to the mine unless they were caught in the act. The leak in the tailings pond had changed that. Hundreds of thousands of gallons of cyanide wastewater was spilling unabated into the river despite their efforts to stop the flow. A leak of that magnitude would not go unnoticed if someone went looking for it. It was even more imperative the research team was stopped before that happened.

Gourde noticed Norton swallow as though he was choking down a sour lump that had suddenly lodged in his throat. The man was obviously holding something back.

"What else do you have to tell me?" Gourde asked.

Norton cleared his throat as if to stall. After an uncomfortable moment, he answered, "Early this morning, Pillai and two men from the research team left here to conduct further testing at Marshal Landing. They were joined by another woman who arrived just yesterday."

"This other woman," Gourde demanded. "Tell me about her?"

"She is in her thirties, mixed Japanese descent, pretty, her name his Kazuko; she arrived in town along with a tall man with blond hair named Robert. I do not know their last names."

"What is their reason for being here?"

"The man they came to see arrived in town about a week ago. I believe he is here because of the bull sharks."

"Do you know his name?"

"Jack Ferrell. He was on the Mazaruni in a boat he rented from my cousin the day Merano went missing."

Gourde quietly considered the information. He'd worried something like this would happen. The threat was getting worse, not lessening as planned. Norton had been instructed to stage an accident that would direct attention away from toxins in the river. Instead, the research team was moving closer to finding the source of the deadly pollution poisoning the waterway. And now someone else was in town that could cause trouble for OMG. He wasn't concerned about management in OMG's main office in Toronto or the mine's shareholders, but he didn't want anything disrupting Billaud's and his plan.

Too much was at stake.

"Billaud will not be happy when I tell him what went on here," he said. "I don't need to remind you what will happen if Deputy Minister Paulette Sukhai gets her hands on that information."

Norton shifted nervously in his seat. "I understand completely."

"For your sake, I hope so." Gourde locked gazes with Norton. "Do not take Jack Ferrell lightly, or the blond-haired man with him. I find it ironic that Merano went missing shortly after Jack Ferrell's arrival in town. It is possible there is more to this man than an interest in sharks."

"How do you suggest I handle the problem?"

"I leave that up to you; just see that it is handled. But remember there are also the scientists to worry about. Too many accidents will arouse suspicion. The situation is already out of control thanks to your incompetence. I do not want the police involved as well."

Norton puffed out his chest. "I will not fail you this time."

"See that you don't," Gourde warned. "Now turn this car around and take me back to the airport. I have urgent matters to attend to at the mine."

CHAPTER 12

Jack peered through the side window of the yellow and white De Havilland Beaver and watched the spray of water stream off the pontoons as Robert pulled back on the yoke. He hoped the plane didn't come apart.

He swallowed. "Maybe we should rethink this half-baked scheme of ours."

All he got for a reply from Robert was a chuckle.

The twin floats lifted clear of the river, and at fifteen hundred feet Robert leveled off and put them on a heading that followed the Mazaruni upstream. The river below was a reddish brown ribbon snaking its way through a sea of green.

"Handles like a dream," he said to Jack in the seat next to him.

Jack relaxed, but kept his seatbelt tightened. He had complete faith in Robert's flying ability; they had flown together many times over the years. It was the reliability of the vintage aircraft he worried about. At least for now he could put his concerns to rest.

"Just like old times," he said. "I still don't know how you talked that guy into renting you his plane."

"Finesse, Jack. Something you lack."

"More like a gift of bullshit," Jack shot back. "Something you have plenty of."

"If you say so." Again Robert chuckled. "But it got us this plane."

"It did," Jack admitted. He scanned the surrounding horizon.

"Looks like mostly clear skies. If a gold mine upriver is dumping toxic sludge into the water, we should be able to see a noticeable change in water color that will lead us straight to the source. Especially if we're flying low and slow."

"We can skim the tops of the trees if we need to," Robert assured him.

"It may very well come to that."

Jack had confidence in what they were doing. He just held onto the hope that finding the leak accomplished what they wanted—that exposing the source of the toxins would remove the threat against Pillai and the members of her team.

Anything to keep her and the others safe, and put a stop to the poisoning of the river.

He saw the white water of Marshal Falls come into view ahead of them. Kazuko and Pillai and the other two members of her research team had been gone close to six hours. They should have already hiked past the falls and be in the process of setting up shop at the village a half kilometer upstream.

Providing nothing had happened to them.

He pointed at the cascading water. "That has to be Marshal Falls. The women should already be in the village on the other side."

"That'd be my guess." Apprehension showed in the tone of Robert's answer. He asked, "Did you know there was a massacre in Bartica in 2008 when the town was attacked by a heavily armed gang led by a man named Rondell Rawlins? Twelve people, including three policemen, were shot dead when the gang terrorized shop owners and townspeople for over an hour before fleeing."

"What's with the history lesson? Were you on the computer last night?"

"No, before we left the house on Oahu. You know me; I like to know as much as I can about a place before I go there."

"Like local massacres?"

"And that Dutch fort down there." Robert pointed. "Or what remains of it."

Jack sighed inwardly. The local history was interesting, but his thoughts were on Kazuko and Pillai and the toxins poisoning the river. And that someone had tried to kill Pillai for no apparent reason other than her research. But even as his mind mired in images of the two women and the danger they faced, his gaze swept the skeletal ruins of the fortress at the confluence of the Mazaruni and Cuyuni Rivers. He knew he was about to hear the history behind the Dutch stronghold whether he wanted to or not.

And he knew why.

"I'm sure you're going to tell me anyway," he said, looking at Robert. "So go ahead and tell me about the fort. Just try to refrain from giving me the long-winded version."

Robert clutched his chest, feigning a heart attack. "I thought you enjoyed my anecdotes."

"And your jokes," Jack assured. Even as he said it, he knew Robert harbored deep-seated concern. "But that's not what's on your mind, is it? You're worried about Kazuko. So am I."

"You could tell?"

"I've known you a long time."

"And I can tell you're concerned about Pillai."

"Sure I am." Jack wasn't going to deny he was worried—but not just for Pillai, for the entire team. And for every person living along the Mazaruni.

"Still want to hear about the fort?"

Jack peered through the windscreen at the falls below, wishing he could catch a glimpse of the two women so that he could convince his overactive imagination they were all right. He sighed. "Think it will relieve some of the angst?"

"Probably not."

"Right," Jack agreed. "Tell me anyway. It'll give us something else to occupy our minds."

"The fortress"—Robert began, with a hint of reluctance—"was built in 1616 and named *Kyk-Over-Al*—Dutch for *See Over All*—because of the commanding view of the river. In 1665, the fort fell to British control until the Dutch Commander of Berbice, a settlement on the Berbice River, was able to march overland with a group of soldiers and recapture it. Then, in the early seventeen hundreds, there were several failed attempts by French and Spanish privateers to march on the settlement."

"Pirates . . . now you've got my interest."

"I knew you'd like that part. The first pirate attack came in 1708 when Captain Ferry led French privateers up the Essequibo to the Mazaruni to plunder the settlements on both banks. Kyk-Over-Al, unfortunately, was of little help to the colonists because the commander refused to come to their aid, saying that he had to protect the fort. It wasn't until Captain Ferry was paid a ransom of 50,000 guilders that he agreed to leave with his privateers."

Jack thought about the movie *Pirates of the Caribbean*. His mind filled with images from the scene where Captain Barbossa and his scurvy crew—having stolen Captain Jack Sparrow's ship the *Black Pearl*—attacked Port Royal.

But that was fantasy.

"All right," he said. "Back to reality, Captain Sparrow."

Robert shot him a look. "Were you somewhere I wasn't?"

"For a moment," Jack said. He leaned toward the windscreen and peered past the engine cowling to get a better view of the river ahead. "We're coming up on Marshal Landing. Take this thing down nice and low and let's see if we can see the girls. They should be settled in by now."

"Probably already working, if I know Kazuko," Robert added.

He pushed forward on the yoke and took the plane down to five hundred feet. There were no power lines or skyscrapers for him to worry about. He kept the plane at that altitude and throttled back to 60 mph.

Flashing Jack a grin, he asked, "How's this?"

Jack didn't know what the stall speed was for a De Havilland Beaver, but was afraid they had to be close to it. He didn't want to end up in the drink or on the top of a tree. He'd trust his friend to know what he was doing.

"If they're out in the open I'll see 'em," he said. "But I doubt they'll know it's us in the plane."

"Probably not," Robert said. "But at least we'll know they made it here safe."

"Yeah, for now." Jack turned his gaze on the side window and peered down at the shoreline.

"Relax," Robert said. "I'll give them a wing-wag for luck."

"Good idea," Jack answered without turning his head. "Who

knows, they might put two and two together."

"I'm pretty sure they will."

The village slipped by on the starboard side of the aircraft providing Jack the best view. Kazuko and Pillai stood on the bank a few feet up from the water. He saw them look in his direction. Obviously, they had been attracted to the sudden appearance of the noisy floatplane. He waved and smiled even though he doubted they could see him clear enough to know who was waving at them. At almost the same instant, he felt the wingtip dip and rise, dip and rise.

Robert doing his thing.

Just as fast, the village was behind them. Robert leveled the wings, maintaining an altitude of five hundred feet. As they continued on a westerly course, the sun began to dip below the upper edge of the fuselage. Jack slid on sunglasses to lessen the glare; he noticed Robert do the same.

Below them the Mazaruni continued on a windy course: innocent, unabated. The jungle closed in on the river's banks. And somewhere up ahead, toxins poisoned the water.

He settled back in his seat, relieved to have at least seen the two women. Now it was up to Robert and him to find the source of the deadly pollution.

Before anyone died.

He exhaled his angst in a long breath, and said, "The women are safe. Let's find that leak."

"If it's there, we will."

"Believe me. It's there." Jack turned his gaze on the river.

The drone and vibration of the 450 hp Pratt & Whitney radial engine filled the cockpit and for a minute they flew without talking. The lull broke when Robert said, "I have to ask you something."

Jack faced his friend. "What's that?"

Robert's expression turned taught and serious. "Be honest with me, did you kill that guy?"

CHAPTER 13

Kazuko stood on the bank of the Mazaruni taking in the village. Marshal Landing was a small cluster of crudely-constructed plank buildings sitting in a clearing next to the river. Some of the dwellings were little more than shacks. Windows, for the most part, were large rectangular holes with wood shutters and no glass or bug screens. What glass there was in the windows, was stained and cracked. Pigs and goats were corralled inside fences made of sticks. Chickens roamed free. The air was heavy with humidity, increasing the stench of rotting vegetation and animal waste.

She refused to let it bother her.

The sound of an approaching plane drew her gaze skyward. The deep grumble of the engine told her it was flying low and slow. A sound she was quite familiar with. One that conjured up an image in her mind.

And brought a smile to her face.

She turned to Pillai who stood next to her, searching the sky. In her hand, she cradled a specimen jar filled with river water. Their fifth sample since arriving at the village. Each one from a different location in the river.

"Maybe we have a visitor?" Kazuko said. She refocused her attention on the approaching aircraft.

Pillai shrugged. "Some kind of vacation tour, more likely."

The yellow and white De Havilland Beaver came into view. They both shaded their eyes with the palms of their hands and watched the vintage craft approach. Low and slow, tracing the course of the river upstream, exactly how Kazuko pictured it in her head.

Pillai lowered her hand to her side. "It looks like the plane from the marina."

"I believe it is." Kazuko felt a shiver of exhilaration at the thought of Robert flying the vintage machine with Jack sitting in the seat next to him. But the craft was too high for her to make out who was in the cockpit.

The floatplane flew on by, leaving Kazuko with a tinge of disappointment. Then she saw the wings dip and rise the way she'd seen Robert do on numerous occasions. Whoever the pilot was, he was saying hello. She waved back, but too late. The plane was already past.

She turned and saw Fletcher striding toward them. His long, blond ponytail bounced from side to side as he walked. He anxiously scanned the sky upriver. It was obvious he'd been drawn to the sound of the plane.

"Did I miss something," he asked.

"Only a plane flying upriver," Pillai answered.

He looked both women up and down, then pointed at the jar in Pillai's hand. "You've got another water sample?"

She nodded. "If you're ready we can run it."

"Soukis finished running that last sample a few minutes ago. He was calibrating the GC-MS when I walked out here to see what was going on with that plane."

"Nothing's changed?" Pillai asked.

"Cyanide concentration varies depending on where you collected the water sample. But they are all significantly higher than ones we found at Bartica."

"Just as we figured."

"Appears so."

Kazuko was taken aback by what she was hearing. "Is there any chance we're getting false readings?" She didn't honestly believe there was, but had to ask.

"None," Fletcher answered.

She saw the grim resolve in his and Pillai's expressions.

The river was dying.

She followed Pillai and Fletcher back to the board hut the team was working out of. As they walked, she noticed Pillai stay a few strides behind Fletcher. He had that effect on both of them. Pillai more than her, she realized. But that was changing. She had quickly understood what it was about the young man that was so distasteful. His eyes had a way of stripping away a woman's clothes.

Men did that—the straight ones anyway—whether they would admit it or not. She knew they couldn't help themselves. Men were men. It was no big deal. But not when it came to Fletcher.

He took special pleasure in making sure women knew he was undressing them.

She doubted he'd ever had a lasting relationship.

When she stepped inside the work-shack, she saw Soukis sitting on a stool in front of the team's portable GC-MS. He appeared to be concentrating on a series of narrow peaks on a graph displayed on the video monitor. Fletcher and Pillai stood a few feet behind Soukis, looking over his shoulder at the screen in front of him. Pillai still held the water sample she carried into the hut with her.

Soukis turned in his seat, removed his wire-rimmed spectacles, and massaged the bridge of his nose. Replacing his glasses, he faced the group. Fletcher and Pillai took a step back and waited. Kazuko joined them.

Their gazes focused on Soukis, as they remained silent.

"Apart from the country's indifference toward sanitation issues," he began, "I'm finding cyanide concentrations exceeding those we observed in our test run at Bartica. The level varies from sample to sample, but what we're seeing is an average free cyanide concentration in the range of six parts per million. The ICP-MS is showing traces of zinc, copper, gold—pretty much what you'd expect to find—as well as a high level of mercury. But nothing near as alarming as the concentration of cyanide."

"Six parts per million certainly would account for the fish kills," Fletcher pointed out.

Soukis nodded at his observation. "A level that high is bound to have a disastrous effect on all the aquatic life, not just fish. Possibly even some of the smaller animals who drink from the river."

Kazuko exchanged a knowing glance with Pillai.

"Maybe not so small," Pillai said. "Kazuko and I saw a goat carcass float by us when we were in the canoe collecting this last sample."

"That *would* imply—" Soukis let his comment hang.

"Excuse me for speaking up," Kazuko said. "Seems to me there is some sort of a cover-up going on here."

"I can't say I disagree," added Pillai.

There was silence as they all looked at each other.

Soukis tented his fingers and tapped his thumbs against his lip. After a moment, he continued, "So far there have only been sketchy reports of massive fish kills from people on and along the river. No one from any of the large gold mines upstream has stepped forward to report a leak in their wastewater holding ponds, or claim responsibility for the damage done to the eco system."

"Why would they?" Kazuko asked. "I'm sure it would cause all sorts of problems for them if they did."

"You're right about that," Soukis said. "They wouldn't. Likely as not, officials from the Guyanese government would levy heavy fines and move to suspend mining operations, or even shut them down completely."

"Which is why there is a cover-up," Pillai offered.

"And why we have to keep looking," Soukis said. "By all accounts, we need to be running test samples from farther upriver."

Pillai nodded. "The same thought crossed my mind."

"Mine, too," added Fletcher.

There was an exchange of glances. Pillai straightened. "In the morning I'll take a boat upstream and bring back water samples from various parts of the river. Then we'll know."

"And I'll go with her," Kazuko said, without hesitation.

CHAPTER 14

Jack kept his eyes focused on the river, but not to avoid his friend's question. There was no reason for him to make any effort to hide what he'd done. He'd killed men in self-defense before and it was no secret. Robert had seen him do it. But he did find it a bit odd Robert was only now pressing for an answer.

"Does it bother you?"

"Not in the least," Robert answered. "It's just that you failed to mention that part and I wondered why?"

Jack looked at him. "I didn't think I needed to explain. And then Pillai showed up, and well . . . me killing that man shook her up and I saw no reason to remind her of it."

"Sparing her feelings?"

"Exactly."

"Then I don't have to worry."

"Worry?"

"Yeah. I thought there might be a trust issue between us."

Jack had to chuckle at the absurdity of Robert's comment. "Not trust *you*, now that's a laugh. You're the one person I trust with my life."

"We've always had each other's back." Robert's dour expression didn't crack. "I want you to remember that."

"We're solid, bud. No worries."

They were covering a lot of ground, even flying as slow as

they were. Their talk dropped off to an occasional comment as they concentrated on the water below. Dense jungle continued to dominate the landscape on each side of the river. A fine mist began to fall. Rivulets of water trailed off the windscreen.

They'd traced another forty kilometers of waterway when Jack straightened in his seat. The drizzle had given way to a mostly clear sky leaving a more unhampered view. He pointed at the river. "What does that look like to you?"

Robert craned his neck. "Looks like someone stirring caramel into a latte."

"Close enough," Jack said. "I could be wrong, but I believe it's runoff from that mine over there. We can swing in close and check it out, but I'd say their tailings dam has sprung a leak."

"That's a good three miles from the river," Robert pointed out.

"Nowhere else it could be coming from. The stuff's probably flowing into a creek that feeds the river."

"And the color?"

"Mud and silt from mine tailings."

"Sounds reasonable," Robert said. "Hang on. Here we go."

Jack did as instructed, as Robert banked the plane into a long gradual arc that would take them over the mine. The engine growled as he increased power to make the turn. With the sun at their backs, he leveled the plane off at two hundred feet and eased back on the throttle. The course he put them on would take them directly over the site.

"Big operation," Jack said as the mine came into view.

Robert shook his head in clear amazement. "I'd say a lot of gold comes out of this place."

"And a lot of revenue for Guyana. Not that that's bad."

Robert chuckled. "I'd say the country needs it."

The appearance of the floatplane over the mine drew a lot of attention from the workers. And not just the men toiling in the muddy pits. Or the guards armed with automatic rifles. Jack noticed a man in clean clothes and a white straw hat step from a building and peer up at them. He didn't have a happy look on his face.

Jack didn't bother waving. Nor did he crack a smile. There was no reason for him to feel particularly cordial. His gaze focused on the tailings pond which looked more like a small lake than a pond. Reddish-yellow water covered what he figured was every bit of sixty acres. There was no way for him to tell the depth of the wastewater, but a breach in the earthen dam containing it was visible. As were the tractors working unsuccessfully to plug the break.

He turned his attention on Robert. "I'd say we found the source of the cyanide that's killing the fish. Let's head back."

Robert met his gaze. "Sounds good to me." He nodded toward the windscreen. "Besides, we have company."

Jack turned his gaze in the direction of Robert's nod. A helicopter that looked like a monstrous dragonfly was bearing down on them off the starboard side of the plane. By all appearances, the two aircraft were on a collision course. Clearly, the chopper was headed for the mine.

Robert maintained his course.

So did the chopper.

Jack doubted they would collide, but the thought did cross his mind. "You don't think they intend to ram us, do you?"

"Not likely," Robert said.

The two aircraft were no more than fifty-feet apart when the helicopter buzzed by in the opposite direction. Both men in the chopper were visible through the bubble-like windscreen. So was the scowl on the big man's face who sat in the co-pilot's seat.

"Another unfriendly soul," Jack said.

Robert increased power. "My guess is he's some sort of big shot at the mine who doesn't like us sticking our noses into their operation."

"I'd say you're right."

"And I say we've overstayed our welcome."

Jack turned in his seat, and took one last look at the helicopter. "Let's get our asses back to Bartica while we still can."

CHAPTER 15

Billaud stood waiting for Gerard Gourde when the Sikorsky helicopter settled onto its skids. Gourde was met by a gust of rotor-wash when he opened the door and climbed out of the cockpit. Ducking under the whirling blades, he hurried to meet with his boss, who did not look happy.

"What was that plane doing?" Gourde asked as he approached Billaud.

"Putting their noses where they shouldn't," answered Billaud. "It would be a grave mistake to not move fast in containing this problem."

"I agree. Unfortunately, Cheddi Norton—he's the man in Bartica I paid to make sure the research team no longer presented a problem for us—failed to carry out my orders as directed."

"I trust he was dealt with?" Billaud's eyes held a flinty coldness.

Gourde regretted he had let Norton go with nothing more than a grim warning. Had circumstances been different, the man would not have been so lucky. And no explanation would have been necessary.

Only that he was dead.

Gourde's gaze held firm. "Unfortunately, I had further use of him."

"And you think he will do better a second time?"

"I did not have a choice." Gourde swallowed his mounting

frustration. "There is a man in town. His name is Jack Ferrell. He's here because of the bull sharks. And just yesterday, a man with blond hair—Robert—and a woman of mixed Japanese descent whose name is Kazuko, joined him."

"You believe this Jack Ferrell could make trouble for us?"

"I do." Gourde continued to explain, "Cheddi, and his cousin Merano, had been keeping an eye on one of the scientists—a woman, Ahalya Pillai—hoping to catch her alone. They thought she would be easiest to get to. Two days ago, Merano followed her to the river. He has not been seen since. And the woman is still alive. Jack Ferrell was in a boat on the Mazaruni the day Merano went missing. I can't say for sure, but I believe he was in some way involved in Merano's disappearance."

Billaud gave Gourde a hard stare. "This man of yours is going to see to it he's dealt with?"

"Him and his friend Robert."

"How about the woman?"

"I'm afraid there is more bad news." Gourde took a deep breath and let it out in a sigh he wasn't able to conceal. Billaud was not going to be happy. "Early this morning Pillai and two men from the research team left to conduct further testing at Marshal Landing. The other woman joined them."

Billaud's jaw muscles noticeably tightened.

"We have been going about this the wrong way," He said after a moment. "From the beginning, we have been too cautious in our methods to handle the matter. That is no longer an option. The risk of exposure is too high. I want these people eliminated and their bodies disposed of somewhere they will not be found. And I'm holding you responsible."

Gourde gave Billaud a callous smile. "They will be taken care of permanently by whatever means possible. And no one will look for them under a hundred tons of sand and gravel."

"A most efficient means of disposal."

"Indeed. And no matter how they die, their bodies will never be found."

"Now we must think about the people in that plane."

Gourde glanced at the sky, visualizing the yellow and white float plane. "I did not see any government markings on it when we flew by them," Gourde said. "It's possible someone was just being nosy as you suspected."

"We don't know that," cautioned Billaud. "We have yet to repair the breach in the dam. And the auxiliary holding pond is still not ready. A hundred thousand cubic meters per hour of effluent is spilling into the river. Even someone not looking for it could grow suspicious of a leak that size and report what they saw to the Ministry of Health. There is only so much that money can buy."

"Regrettably," Gourde said. "We were fortunate to be able to bribe that clerk, otherwise we would not have been able to stay a step ahead of Deputy Minister Sukhai. It's too bad she is not as greedy as her staff."

"Indeed." Billaud slipped into thought. "Unfortunately, the game has changed. I'm going to take immediate steps to sell the gold we have."

Gourde knew what Billaud was thinking. They shared the same thought. It was no longer a matter of dealing with a few nosy scientists. The breach in the holding pond, the plane—it was time to rethink their plan.

Still—

He had faith in Billaud's judgment, but hated to think what they would be giving up. "I would never question your decision, but with the mine's increased production we can double our take in a month."

"And the situation is close to spiraling out of control."

Gourde straightened. "And we are taking steps to make sure that doesn't happen."

Billaud visibly swallowed his growing frustration.

"Another day or two is all my men need," Gourde said. "You can give them that much time."

Billaud held his response.

Gourde waited.

"They simply cannot fail." Billaud said. He narrowed his eyes in resolve. "News of this leak mustn't reach the deputy minister's desk."

Gourde straightened to his full height. Failure was not in his plan.

"I'm sure we can take care of the problem before that happens."

Billaud nodded. "Do you have an idea where the plane is headed?"

"I do," answered Gourde. "And my men will be waiting when it lands."

"Very well, but I want you there, too." Billaud's tone was laced with the sharp edge of a threat. "And no slipups this time."

CHAPTER 16

Robert maintained their heading, taking them in a northeasterly route across the jungle and back to the Mazaruni. When they approached the water, he banked the floatplane into a turn at five hundred feet and proceeded in an easterly direction, retracing their flight path from Bartica. With the sun at their backs, the blinding glare they had endured on the trip upriver was gone.

"I'm not a guessing man," he said, "but I'd venture to say it would be a good idea to not cross paths with those men."

"And I'd say you're right." Jack thought about the attempt on Pillai's life. It had some connection to the indiscriminant poisoning of the river. He was certain of it now, more so than he had been, and wondered if one or both of those men were behind the attack.

The big man in the helicopter certainly fit the profile. So did the man in the white straw hat.

He had a feeling he and Robert would be seeing them again.

"You okay?" Robert asked.

Jack saw his friend looking at him.

"Just thinking," he said.

He refocused his attention on the brown ribbon of water and noticed they were approaching Kaburi rapids about five kilometers east of the location where the cyanide-laced effluent was spilling unabated into the river. The white water ahead looked just as daunting. And then he saw something he failed to see when they first passed over the area.

A canoe . . .

The dugout sat edged against the riverbank about fifty yards downstream from the rapids. It was nosed into the dense plant growth on the north side of the river as if it had been pushed there by the swift current. He didn't know if the boat had drifted there unnoticed after they had passed, or if it was visible now because they approached that stretch of the Mazaruni from the opposite direction. What he did know is there was a person lying face down inside the log boat, and the person wasn't moving.

"See that dugout in the bushes next to shore?" He pointed.

Robert turned his head, peering through his side window as the plane flew past. "There's a man in it. And if I'm not mistaken, his shirt is blood-soaked."

Jack craned his neck to see through the side window across the cockpit from him. All he could see was water and jungle. The canoe was behind them.

Gripping his friend's arm, he said, "Take us down so we can get a closer look."

"I'll have to circle around." Robert applied power and banked the vintage aircraft into a tight turn that brought them back on a direct line with the Mazaruni two hundred yards downstream from where they saw the canoe. The moment the plane was centered on the river, he engaged the wing flaps and pushed forward on the yoke.

Jack didn't need an explanation. It was clear what his friend was doing. "You're sure you have enough room to land this thing?"

"A De Havilland Beaver can land on a swimming pool if you need it to."

"I'll trust you on that one."

The pontoons touched the water with expert precision. Robert eased off on the throttles and taxied them to an area on the riverbank void of vegetation, easing the tip of the floats onto dry land. The canoe was twenty yards west of them on the other side of a dense growth of plants.

"Go," Robert urged. "I need to make sure the plane stays put."

"Don't leave without me." Jack had no intention of staying put. He unbuckled his seatbelt, and took hold of the door latch.

Robert waved him off. "I wouldn't dream of it."

Jack was already on the move out of the cockpit. A second later, he pounded along the aluminum pontoon toward shore. A prodding from deep within his gut urged him to hurry. It took a couple of minutes to bust through the undergrowth, but when he pushed the last limbs aside, he found the canoe sitting half submerged a foot from the bank. And inside, the bloodied man lay face down with his chin an inch above the water line.

A good sign.

Jack waded into the water and wrestled the canoe farther onto dry land where it wouldn't drift away. He had no difficulty seeing the gash in the guy's back. Nor did he have a problem finding the man's pulse.

Alive . . . but barely.

"Dead?" Robert asked, slightly out of breath.

"Close to it," Jack answered, looking up at his friend. "But I doubt he'll make it unless we get him to a hospital, fast."

"What happened?"

Jack gently lifted the flaps where the guy's shirt had been slashed. "By the looks of this cut on his back, someone took an extreme disliking to him."

"Stabbed?" Robert asked as he squatted next to Jack.

"More like he was sliced."

"With a knife?"

"Possibly even a machete or a hatchet."

Robert looked around as if he expected to see someone standing nearby, watching. "I wonder who did it?"

Jack took a quick look around—more from reflex than concern.

The attack most likely happened upriver.

He motioned at the injured man with his hand. "You can ask him if he survives."

CHAPTER 17

Robert and Jack gently laid the man facedown across the back seats and belted him in the best they could. That done, Robert turned to climb into the cockpit while Jack hurried to untie the rope securing the plane to a tree. Jack paused at the end of the pontoon when he heard the familiar sound of helicopter rotor blades beating the air in the distance. He noticed Robert step from under the wing and scan the sky.

"A helicopter," he said.

Jack knew what it was he was hearing, and straightened to look. It only took him a second to search out the dark speck a mile or so from their location. The chopper was speeding away from the mine.

"The bird we passed," Robert said.

Jack kept his eyes focused. "Most likely."

"Think they see us?"

"If they're looking for us, they do." Jack's intuition told him the situation was about to turn ugly. "But why would they be?"

Robert's gaze remained fixed on the chopper. "Appears we're going to find out."

"Maybe it's a social call?" Jack hoped he was wrong about the foreboding that hollowed his gut.

Robert shot him a doubtful look, but didn't answer.

The approaching helicopter made a course adjustment. It was flying directly toward them now. There was no way the people inside the aircraft could not see the brightly colored plane sitting on the water. The question bouncing around in Jack's mind was why were they interested?

"You asked me if they saw us," he said. "I'd say the answer is a definite yes."

"A 300 series Sikorsky," Robert pointed out when the craft was closer. "It's unquestionably the same one we saw earlier."

"I have a bad feeling about this."

"You're not the only one."

Jack trusted Robert's intuition as much as his own. He kept his eyes focused on the helicopter and the two occupants inside. As it drew closer, he couldn't help thinking the pilot might have altered his course simply to offer assistance if needed. But then, a finely-honed sense of self-preservation told him that was not the case.

He suddenly felt naked and vulnerable standing out in the open.

"You wanted to know if they're friendly, we'll know soon enough," Robert said. "The bird's slowing down."

Jack studied the riverbank and the dense jungle foliage beyond. There were no clearings in sight large enough for the chopper to land in. And it wasn't equipped with floats.

When he refocused his attention on the helicopter, he noticed the big man in the co-pilot's seat.

The same cold look plastered on his face.

Robert must have made the same observation. "That's the guys we saw earlier, all right."

"It is," Jack answered. "And that big sonofabitch doesn't look any friendlier."

"What do you think?"

"Think . . . ?" Jack studied the big man. "I think that whatever Grumpy has in store for us, he's going to have to do it from up there. There's no place close for them to land."

Robert's gaze shifted from the chopper to Jack. "Remember, that water is poison."

Jack knew what Robert was getting at. Again he scanned the forest fringe. The trees and vines beyond were bathed in shadow.

Their best bet. If they had to make a run for it, he sure wasn't going to dive into the river. Not in that sludge. Winding up with a mouthful of poison was the last thing he wanted.

He'd take his chances in the jungle.

The helicopter was close now. Jack could feel the rotor-wash press down on him. He turned to look. And just in time, he realized. The door to the bubble cockpit swung open and the big man's hand appeared. He held a black semi-automatic pistol, pointed straight at them.

"Look out," Jack yelled. At almost the same instant three rapidly fired bullets struck the water in a tight group near Jack's feet.

He wasn't waiting around to see if the big man's aim improved. Neither was Robert, because he was already hurrying along the pontoon in the direction of shore. Nothing needed to be said as they exchanged worried glances. They both raced toward the jungle with a single objective in mind.

Cover!

A fallen tree as big around as a fifty-five gallon drum presented itself, and Jack dove behind it. He was followed closely by Robert.

"Shit," Jack said. He raised his head just high enough to peer over the tree. The helicopter crept forward. No doubt the big man hoped for another shot.

"What are they doing?" Robert asked without raising his head.

"Wanting to finish what they started, I reckon."

Jack scanned the jungle canopy. Only tiny patches of sky showed through the thick foliage. If they stayed put, they had a chance.

"Keep down," he said. "I don't think they can see us."

Taking his eyes off the chopper, he pressed his body close to the log. Two bullets slammed into the thick wood a few feet away.

To move now would mean certain death.

The Sikorsky hovered at the jungle fringe, like a bird of prey ready to drop and kill an unsuspecting creature. There was no doubt in Jack's mind the big man with the gun was searching for them. The blur of the tail rotor moved back and forth in the air as the pilot worked the controls in an obvious effort to keep the helicopter steady and the copilot's open door facing the jungle. Rotor wash whipped the plants as if struck by a hurricane.

It was all Jack could do to stay put.

"What did Krav Maga teach you about a scenario like this?"

Robert asked.

"Sometimes it's better to run than fight," Jack answered. "And sometimes it's better to hide and wait. In this case, I think both apply."

Four rapid loud cracks made Jack press his face to the ground. The bullets were swallowed by the forest. Wild harmless pistol shots fired in desperation.

They hadn't been seen.

The Sikorsky held its position a moment longer, and then peeled off to the east. The clop, clop of the rotors faded and died away.

For a full minute, neither Jack nor Robert moved from their hiding spot.

"Sounds like they've gone," Robert finally said.

Jack gained his feet and brushed himself off. "I don't think they liked us poking around their claim."

"Apparently." Robert stood up and pulled a dead leaf from his hair.

Jack slapped his friend on the back. "You ready to get out of here?"

"The sooner the better," Robert answered. He shot Jack a concerned look. "I just hope they don't hold a grudge."

CHAPTER 18

It was close to three o'clock when Robert set the plane down on the wide expanse of water bordering Bartica. Dark clouds had moved in to block the mid-afternoon sun. The gloom added to their dour moods. The injured man draped across the back seats had moaned a couple of times during the flight to town, but never totally regained consciousness.

"So we agree we don't need to mention that incident back there on the river?" Jack said as Robert taxied the plane toward the dock.

"We've already talked about this."

"I just want to be sure we're on the same page."

"All the police or anyone else needs to know is the part about us finding the guy and bringing him here," Robert assured Jack. "Besides, we don't know what happened to him."

"We don't," Jack agreed. "And if the police are interested, they can ask him when he wakes up."

Robert gave Jack a long, questioning look. "You haven't said a word for the last half hour . . . until a moment ago, that is. What's working in that sullen mind of yours?"

The deadly attack on Pillai. Kazuko. The two women unprotected upriver. He and Robert being shot at. He had a lot on his mind.

And a lot to worry about.

"Maybe I just wanted some quiet."

"Bullshit. I've seen you like this before. Something is bugging you. And I don't think it's having been shot at."

"That, too. But you're right," Jack acknowledged. "I've been shot at before."

"So what is it?"

"A lot's happening, and fast."

"You saw those men with guns at the mine. They're there to guard against theft. Perhaps the owner was concerned we might be after their gold."

"Possibly, but I doubt it. We were three miles away and on the opposite side of the river when that guy shot at us."

"And missed," Robert quickly pointed out. "At least we don't have to explain a bunch of bullet holes in the plane."

Jack chuckled even though the incident was far from funny. "That certainly would have presented a problem."

"An expensive one to boot. We're just fortunate that guy was a bad shot."

But was he, or had they just been lucky? Jack wondered. The bullets hit the water next to his feet. A tight group and close to the mark.

Too close.

"Not that bad," he said.

"Perhaps it was just a not-so-friendly warning to stay away from the mine."

"And the river."

"Makes sense, since they're dumping that shit into the water."

"It could have been a warning," Jack said, "and then, maybe not. More likely they were worried we'd report the leak to Guyanese officials and wanted us dead."

"So why didn't they finish the job?"

"The same question crossed my mind. I don't think they expected to see us sitting there."

"Meaning they weren't prepared."

"That would be my guess."

"I'm not sure if that's good or bad," Robert said.

"We're alive." Jack felt compelled to point that out. "That's what's important. And at least now we know what to expect."

"Which is?"

"Good question."

Jack climbed onto the pontoon outside his door and stood ready with a mooring rope while Robert taxied the plane to the dock. By the time they got the plane secured, a gentle rain had begun to fall. No more than a steady drizzle, but it was enough to wet their shirts and drive the humidity off the charts.

Jack scanned the parking lot. "You sure the police were going to be waiting for us?"

"A police car and an ambulance," Robert answered. "That's what the control tower told me when I radioed in."

"Then they should be here."

"Maybe they got lost."

"And cows can fly, too." Jack was anxious to shed the injured man. He needed emergency care, and fast. It might already be too late.

The guy deserved a chance.

"Relax, they'll be here," Robert said.

"Yeah, when?"

Jack did not have a lot of faith in Bartica's emergency services. The faith he did have in them was diminishing by the moment.

They had no choice but to wait.

A few seconds later, flashing lights appeared on the road at the entrance to the lot. An ambulance pulled in, followed closely by a police car.

"There they are now," Robert said, pointing.

Jack blew a sigh of relief. "Let's get this guy out of the plane and onto the dock. I want to be done with this."

Robert got the door open while Jack stood a second longer, watching the police car and the ambulance roll up to the narrow pier. Emergency lights flashed, but there was no shrill wail of sirens. He was glad the drivers had refrained from announcing their arrival on scene.

Sirens attracted crowds. The last thing he wanted. Until he had some answers, he preferred that everyone in Bartica not know he and Robert were back in town.

They'd already been shot at once.

* * *

Sightseeing tours were common and the police hadn't questioned Jack's explanation as to why he and Robert were upriver in the plane. It was all perfectly logical. That, and the condition of the injured man's wound being at least twenty-four hours old, made for a short interrogation.

"That went well," Jack commented when the police and ambulance drove away en route to the hospital.

"Better than we hoped," Robert said. "So what do we do now?"

"The chief scientist on Pillai's research team is a man by the name of Philip Bjornson." Jack faced Robert and added, "We tell him about the leak and let him notify the Ministry of Health."

"That was your plan?"

"I didn't say it was a good one."

"*Good* . . . ?" Robert huffed. "If that was your intention all along, why didn't we tell the police about the breach in the mine's wastewater pond and that sonofabitch shooting at us from the helicopter and be done with it?"

"Think for a second," Jack said. "This entire mess stinks of a cover-up. That spill was too obvious, which leads me to believe Guyanese officials have to be involved, even if only to the point of slow-playing the seriousness of the pollution problem. Maybe even local law enforcement. I don't need to remind you third-world police departments have a history of corruption."

Robert scoffed. "We don't know that they're involved. Besides, Pillai and her team were invited here. You're here. It doesn't make sense to me the government's attempting to cover anything up."

"Maybe they just want it to appear they're doing something about the problem while all the time hoping it will somehow go away."

"It's happened. But we could be entirely wrong about this."

"Sure," Jack agreed. "But why take the chance. Someone tried to kill Pillai and that guy from the mine tried to shoot us. I'd just as soon keep that part quiet until we know more about what's going on."

"You're putting all your eggs in one basket, aren't you?"

"It's better than trying to sort them out and miss one."

"So you intend to keep digging?"

Jack considered the question. It was one he asked himself, and one he had still not answered. "Let's talk to Bjornson and see what happens."

CHAPTER 19

Jack stood at the top of the parking lot above the marina. He could see the lab where they had left Bjornson and his assistant. He wondered if Bjornson had made the call to the Ministry of Health yet.

Directing his attention on the street in front of him, he watched the pedestrians wander the walkways. No one seemed to be paying any particular interest in him and Robert. They didn't look like locals, but they did look like the tourists roaming the town. And there appeared to be enough of them milling about. He figured Robert and he could walk back to their hotel, inconspicuously.

"Ready," he asked.

"Let's grab a cab," Robert said.

"Nonsense, we can be there in the time it takes for a cab to get here. We'll walk it and grab one along the way if we see one."

"Seems a bit chancy, don't you think?"

Jack read the apprehension in Robert's voice. "Piece of cake."

Robert placed a cautioning hand on Jack's shoulder. "Really, a cab would be better."

Jack glanced around. His gut told him they needed to get moving. It was the same feeling of dread he had on the river right before they were shot at. Standing there debating the issue wasn't helping.

"You're still worried about the guy who shot at us. Me, too."

"I have a feeling he's not going away."

"That'd be my guess," Jack said. "Let's go. It's not that far."

Robert sighed and motioned with his hand. "After you. But I'm telling you, I have a bad feeling about this."

"And I hope you're wrong."

Jack fought the urge to glance around nervously—Robert, too, he suspected. They walked casually and with purpose. The way most everyone else around them did. Even the tourists appeared to have some place to go.

Halfway to their hotel the foot traffic thinned out. For whatever reason, luck had abandoned them.

Jack chanced a quick look around them. They were the only people on the walkway for fifty-feet in any direction.

And the only two white men walking together.

He leaned close to Robert. "You ever feel like you're trying to blend into a crowd of two?"

"Yeah," Robert said. "And that crowd of two is you and I."

They quickened their pace, but had to stop for traffic at the next intersection. Only two vehicles—a car brush-painted at least six colors and a beat-up old pickup—but the rust-buckets kept them standing at the corner.

Jack's gut tightened. He wanted to keep moving.

The seconds felt like hours. Finally, the cars continued on and he stepped into the street. Robert walked a half-step behind him. He could see their hotel no more than a city block ahead.

Luck was with them after all.

And then a van cut them off—the panel type. No windows. The side doors swung open

Jack steeled himself to run. Getting away from there was the best course of action.

Robert . . . ?

At once, Jack realized his concern for his friend had cost them. If they had fled the instant the van stopped, they most likely would have gotten away safely. But the side doors had swung open. And with three men pointing pistols at them standing there in the middle of the street flat footed, they had no choice but to comply.

"Into the van," ordered the man closest to the open doors.

Jack locked gazes with the gunman. He was a skinny, black-haired, narrow-faced man with a hawk nose. The man standing next to Hawk Nose had one eye, the right. A pale line of puckered flesh stood out like a vicious slash across his left socket. The lid had been stitched shut. The third gunman was a little taller and thicker than the other two. He had a flat nose and a scar above his left brow. All three kidnappers looked to be Guyanese. None of the men were especially powerfully built as far as Jack could tell, nor were they particularly large. But the huge bores of their .45 caliber Colt semi-automatic handguns were.

The muzzles of the two guns pointed at his forehead convinced him to move.

He weighed the odds.

Robert was already being manhandled toward the waiting van by One-Eye. He shoved Robert inside the rear cargo area and turned his gun on Jack.

No choice.

"You're making a mistake," Jack said as he climbed in.

Hawk Nose snorted. "There's no mistake. Now hurry up."

One-Eye gave Jack a shove that sent him stumbling to the floor. He tripped over Robert's legs and slammed the top of his head into the metal panel on the far side of the compartment. One-Eye climbed in a second later, followed by Scarface. Hawk Nose pulled open the front passenger door and jumped in. There was a driver sitting behind the steering wheel, waiting. The interior reeked of sour body odor and dead fish.

The van sped away.

Jack massaged his scalp and rolled into a sitting position with his back against the wall of the cargo compartment. He examined the tips of his fingers and noticed a smear of blood. Not a lot, but enough, and a bump to go with it.

He caught a worried glance from Robert who sat across from him. When he looked toward the front of the van, he saw One-Eye and Scarface sitting on milk crates, their backs to the driver and passenger seats. The lips of both gunmen were curled into a cold snarl. Their Colt semi-automatics were leveled with the hammers cocked. The index finger of each man rested on his gun's trigger.

A simple squeeze is all it would take.

If the guns weren't cocked, Jack thought, they'd have a chance. This way there was nothing he or Robert could do to stop what was happening. Not without the extreme likelihood of one, or even both of them dying.

An option Jack wasn't prepared to take.

Not yet.

CHAPTER 20

Jack flashed Robert a thumbs-up for luck and resigned himself to wait and see what happened next. At least they hadn't been killed outright. In his mind that meant there was a chance the situation could be resolved without Robert or him getting hurt . . . or worse.

And they hadn't been bound and gagged.

The van rumbled along the street before making a right turn. Toward the water, Jack thought. A second later the driver put on the brakes and stopped.

Hawk Nose turned in the passenger seat and aimed his pistol. "Your hands," he ordered. "Hold them out in front of you."

Jack could see the bore of the .45 was pointed at his chest. One-Eye and Scarface still had their guns leveled. He glanced at Robert and got a worried look back.

"So what now," Jack asked. "You clap the irons on us?"

"Something like that."

"I knew it." Robert cracked a thin smile. "Pressed into labor on a tramp steamer bound for the Orient."

Jack had to grin. Robert was talking. Better yet, he was joking. A good sign. They needed to remain cool.

"I see you're back to your old funny self," Jack said. "For a minute there, you had me a tad worried."

"What's there to worry about?" The look on Robert's face wasn't convincing.

Jack winked. "Hang in there."

The sound of metal clacking against metal drew their attention forward. Jack had a good idea what he was hearing. His suspicions were confirmed when Hawk Nose tossed two pairs of rust-pitted handcuffs onto the rear floor.

"For us," Jack said. "Thanks, but we'll pass."

"You might not think you are so funny when we get to where we are going." The gunman's eyes narrowed into a cold hard stare. "Cuff yourselves. But first give me your cell phones."

Jack had hoped they'd forget about the phones. He dug his from his pocket and tossed it to Hawk Nose. "My bill is due if you'd like to pay it."

"You like telling jokes. Save them." He pointed his gun at Robert. "Your phone, give it to me."

Robert tossed his phone forward. "Choke on it."

Hawk Nose used the bore of his gun for a pointer. "The cuffs now . . . *tight*."

Jack picked up one of the pairs and eyeballed the rusted metal. Standard police issue. Worn, but they appeared strong enough to do the job. He tossed the cuffs to Robert, picked the other pair up for himself, and ratcheted them on with his hands in front of him. He was relieved when Hawk Nose didn't object.

Their second mistake.

Robert nodded as if he understood and snapped his cuffs on with his hands in front of him as well.

"Satisfied?" Jack asked, holding his wrists up for Hawk Nose to see.

"For now."

The driver eased the van forward and gained speed. Once again they were on the move. But where to? Jack wondered.

And who or what awaited them at the other end?

"Why is it, Jack," Robert asked, "the only time this kind of thing happens to me is when I'm with you?"

Jack scoffed. "You think it's me?"

"If the shoe fits . . ."

Robert seemed to have a point.

"You just might be right," Jack whispered. "And I'm afraid it's going to get a whole lot worse."

The slow-and-go ride took them across town. And perhaps a little further, by Jack's reckoning. He still had his watch. They'd only been in the van fifteen minutes. Cooped up in back in the oppressive jungle humidity and stench of their captors' sweat, it felt like hours.

Stifling . . . almost as if he were drugged.

Had it not been for the anger-infused adrenaline fueling him he would have been tempted to rest his head on his knees and think about anything more pleasant than the situation they were in.

But he would never let that happen. He'd die before he let Robert down.

Or the women.

And that wasn't in the plan.

He'd find a way. Just as soon as they reached their destination. *Where . . . ?*

He considered the possibilities. Someplace remote, most likely. A place they could do their dirty work without interference.

"Any idea where they are taking us?" Robert asked in a hushed tone.

Jack's best guess was they had to be near the river. Or were they? They had made several turns. Straining to see past One-Eye and Scarface, he observed patches of sky through the windshield, and the green of tropical foliage as the forest closed in around them.

The jungle, but where in the jungle?

"Could be any place," he said, craning his neck for a better look. "One thing's for sure; we're not in Kansas anymore."

Robert lifted his head higher and peered toward the windshield. "It doesn't look like the Emerald Forest to me."

"You're right. No Tin Man." Jack nodded. "Only these four monkeys."

"Enough talk." One-Eye extended his gun hand.

Jack wasn't ready to force the issue.

A long minute later, the van bounced through a couple of holes and rolled to a stop. Both front doors opened up and the driver and passenger climbed out. One-Eye and Scarface did not move to exit. Instead, they raised their semi-automatics as if they expected trouble. They obviously weren't taking any chances. That much Jack understood. He'd wait.

But he wouldn't allow himself to be led like a lamb to slaughter. He'd already made his mind up that he wasn't going to be executed on some jungle back-road without a fight. And he didn't have to say anything to Robert to know he'd be right beside him. They'd been in situations like this before. The two of them would make it out alive, or they would go down trying.

When the cargo doors were pulled open from the outside, Jack tensed, ready to make his move. What he saw was Hawk Nose and the driver standing five feet in front of him with the sights of their guns lined up on his chest. He glanced to each side of him and then stared straight ahead. They had stopped on a dirt road in the jungle as he had guessed, but the van was parked in front of a plank shack. Standing in front of the crude structure was the big man from the helicopter; his own semi-automatic pistol pointed straight at them.

The same gun he had shot at them with.

Jack conceded to curiosity and stepped to the ground.

Scarface climbed out next, followed by Robert and then One-Eye. One-Eye moved to his right and Scarface took up a position to his left.

"Good to see you again," Jack said in a tone that implied they were old friends. The big man was bigger and hairier than he appeared in the helicopter. He didn't look at all cordial. "You need to work on your hospitality, though."

"And you are becoming a nuisance." The big man waved his pistol in the direction of the shack. "Bring them inside."

Jack looked for an opportunity to make his move. If he and Robert could get to the cover of the jungle they'd have a chance, but there were too many guns pointed at them. To try something now would be suicide.

They had no choice but to do as they were told.

And be ready.

CHAPTER 21

Still, Jack didn't move. There had to be something he could do to put an end to the nightmare they had gotten themselves into. He stared at the ramshackle cabin a moment longer, buying himself extra seconds of precious time. It wasn't difficult for him to imagine what would happen to them once they were inside.

Out of the frying pan and into the fire.

The old saying fit. He and Robert were out of the van, but their chances of survival were no better than when they were seated on the grimy floor of the windowless cargo compartment with One-Eye and Scarface pointing pistols at them.

And they were about to get worse.

"You heard Mister Gourde," Hawk Nose said. "Inside, *now*."

Jack cast Hawk Nose his best 'fuck-you' look. But regardless of how good it made him feel to make his feelings toward this cockroach of a man known, there was little he could do to stop what was happening—except die. And he wasn't ready to do that. Not until every option had been exhausted.

He steeled himself for what would come next. Expecting the worst, he conjured up contingency after contingency. Each one canceled out by the next. Besides having the guns to worry about, they were handcuffed. The cuffs needed to come off. But at least they were in front. A rookie mistake.

But would it be enough to make a difference?

He could hope.

And for now, do what his captors' told him to do.

But not for long.

He started to take a step and stopped when One-Eye shoved Robert forward. Cyclops appeared to be enjoying the game. At almost the same moment, Jack felt Scarface's gun muzzle press against the back of his head. Then he was pushed into line behind Robert.

Jack wasn't impressed by the gunman's display of bravado.

Little men with big guns.

They filed into the shack, one behind the other. Inside, he and Robert were ordered to sit on the wood floor with their backs to a cast-iron stove that looked as though it hadn't been used for quite some time. Jack got the same impression looking at the interior of the one-room cabin. Shack was more like it. A couple of scarred, hard-backed chairs, and a small square table served as the only furniture. Other than that, there were at least two months of newspapers scattered about, and a couple of dozen empty beer bottles that he could count.

The big man stood in the middle of the room. His gunmen stood to either side of him. Jack watched Hawk Nose hand him the cell phones.

"You will not need these." The big man dropped them on the floor and stomped them into shards.

So much for being able to call for help, Jack thought. He waited.

"My name is Gerard Gourde," the big man continued. "I want you to tell me what you know."

"I know a lot of things," Jack answered.

"For instance?"

"For instance, the migratory pattern of the Pacific humpback whale."

Gourde looked at Jack with cold, black, empty eyes. A long moment later, his gaze shifted to Robert. "How about you?"

"Sorry, I only know how to fly a plane."

"I see." Gourde stepped to the table and retrieved a four-foot length of chain and an open padlock. He tossed the items on the floor at Jack's feet.

Jack felt their chances slipping.

"Chain yourselves to that stove," Gourde said. "Then the two of you will tell me everything."

Jack picked up the chain and looked at it.

There's still a chance.

As if to emphasize the order, Gourde's thugs aimed their .45 semi-automatics at his head. They looked eager to pull the triggers. To do the big man's bidding . . . and to satisfy their tiny-pecker egos.

He got the feeling he was being singled out as the troublemaker.

"Since you insist," he said. He threaded the chain through his and Robert's arms and then through a metal handle on the stove. That done, he pushed the padlock closed, dropped the ends of the chain on the floor next to him, and waited.

Gourde nodded approval. "You were wise to do as you were told."

"Look, Gerard," Jack slid his feet up against him and rested his forearms on his knees, "if this is an attempt to keep your government from finding out about that leak at your mine, you're too late. By now they know what's going on."

The big man smiled. "Of course you are talking about your scientist friends."

A statement, not a question. Jack didn't like what he was hearing.

He furrowed his brow in concern. "And if I am?"

"I'm afraid they met with an accident shortly after you left their lab." Gourde's lips curled into a thin, mean smile. "Robbed and killed. It is a shame what this country is coming to."

Jack felt his anger boil.

Robert was already moving, attempting to stand but held down by the chain through his arms. "You piece of shit," he yelled. "You killed a couple of innocent scientists over something like this?"

"They mean nothing to me."

Robert continued to strain against the chain. Jack saw the thug's gun muzzles come up. They surely itched for an excuse to pull the trigger.

He wouldn't give them one.

Fighting back his own anger, he said, "I suppose it was your man who tried to murder the woman the other day?"

It was Hawk Nose who answered. "You killed Merano, didn't you?"

Jack felt better about having dispatched the thug at the river. And he was tired of Hawk Nose; he was tired of them all.

But he wouldn't allow himself to be provoked.

He nodded, offering a simple shrug. "I don't like men who prey on innocent women."

Hawk Nose stepped forward—his face flush with hate—and lashed out with his foot in an obvious attempt to kick Jack in the teeth. His thrust was fueled by anger and carried most of his weight behind it. His pinched expression turned to one of surprise when Jack caught his foot in midflight.

Jack held on, making Hawk Nose balance on one foot. Then he shoved the irate thug backward onto his butt.

Stunned silence filled the room. But only for a couple of seconds.

Hawk Nose scrambled to his feet and aimed his pistol. His mouth was a taut line. His gun hand shook. When he could at last speak, he narrowed his eyes. "I will kill you for that."

Jack matched Hawk Nose's cold, hard stare with a glare of his own. "I'm sure you will try."

"I will more than try."

Jack peered into the muzzle of the .45 thinking this was it. His death would come quick and deliberate.

…And then Robert's.

Hawk Nose's index finger tightened on the trigger.

Jack didn't turn away. A millisecond before his head exploded in a spray of blood, he saw Gourde push down on the gun just enough to send the shot into the floorboard.

"I'm going to kill him," Hawk Nose swore at Gourde.

"In due time," Gourde told him.

"But—"

Gourde raised his hand dismissively. He turned his attention on Jack. "Let's start over here. We can begin with your names."

Jack did not shy from the game. "I'm sure you already know who I am."

"Humor me."

Jack could see no reason to not tell the man. "Jack . . . Jack

Ferrell."

"And, your friend?" The big man's gaze shifted to Robert.

Robert didn't blink. Nor did he hold back. "Robert Foster. A name you will not forget."

Jack smiled inwardly at his friend's contempt.

"Your names will mean nothing to me when I have disposed of you," Gourde said. "Now again, what was your reason for being upriver?"

Jack spoke up. "I think you know the answer to that."

"Then there is nothing more to say."

"An apology from you would be nice."

Gourde's expression went rigid. He turned to Hawk Nose. "Let them sit here until they are mad with thirst, then kill them. But take your time doing it. I want them to suffer."

CHAPTER 22

Jack clenched his jaw to contain his anger and watched Gourde walk out the door with the man who had driven the van. He knew it was useless to fill the room with curses that would get them nothing. It was hot and humid, and for the first time since their capture, he found himself craving a drink of water. Perhaps it was because he couldn't have it. But most likely it was because thirst had not been an issue. That was no longer the case.

"Tell me you have a plan," Robert whispered.

Jack shrugged. Then he dropped his gaze knowingly to the links of chain heaped on the floor between them. The lock was closed. He hoped that Robert could see the shackle was turned to the side and not secured in the locking mechanism. Gourde had been so sure of himself he had failed to see the sleight of hand.

The way Jack played it: no display of indignation, no refusal. *Complete and total compliance.*

Robert looked down, then brought his gaze up and nodded.

"We wait," Jack whispered.

He studied the men as they moved about the cabin. They looked to be close to the same age: around thirty—a good ten years younger than him. And not very smart—or they wouldn't be in this kind of game. Common street thugs for hire, not trained killers.

All to Robert's and his advantage.

He figured the men would not be content to sit in the heat and humidity of the shack without something cool to drink. Probably beer by the number of empty bottles scattered around. When they did, they'd have to take a leak. There was no bathroom inside the hut, which meant they would have to go outside. Men being men and beer being beer, most likely one gunman would be left to keep watch while the others stepped outside for a pissing contest.

Men did that sort of stuff. He doubted these guys would be different.

And when they did, Jack decided, he would make his move.

Now he hoped the driver returned with the beer. The whole plan hinged on it. That, and men being men.

The scheme went as Jack hoped it would. Better, even. The driver returned an hour later with two cases of beer, several bags of chips, and four to-go cartons of food. He also carried in the two milk crates from the van to serve as chairs. The four of them then sat around the table and drank beer over a game of dominoes.

Except for an occasional peek at the men seated at the table, Jack kept his head down and his ears alert. He did not want to give his captors any reason to get nervous; nothing to make them check the lock and chain.

Subservient and cooperative, that's how he wanted to appear.

Until the time came for him not to be.

The sun dipped below the forest canopy bathing the room in gloom. Scarface retrieved a gas lantern from a hook on the wall and lit it. That called for another round of beers which he passed out to the men. They were on their fourth.

Jack was glad they had plenty.

He watched them suck down the beer. Each man taking long gulps from his bottle. Eventually they would have to get rid of all that liquid.

He hoped that would be soon.

And it was.

No more than ten minutes later, Scarface stood up and announced he was going outside to pee. Men being men, One-Eye and the driver of the van said they were joining him. The three of them headed for the door.

"Go ahead, play with yourselves," Hawk Nose called out. "I will watch these two pieces of shit. Maybe I will have some fun with them while you are gone."

"I would be careful if I was you," said One-Eye as he stepped outside.

"These men are nothing," Hawk Nose bragged, as he followed the other gunmen to the doorway.

Someone outside laughed. That must have enraged Hawk Nose because he stormed outside and cursed the man face-to-face. Jack picked that moment to unshackle the chain and slip it through his arms. He was still cuffed, but he was no longer tethered to the heavy stove.

Hawk Nose was still cursing his friends when he stepped back inside the shack a few seconds later. He closed the door and faced Jack. "I think it is time I teach you who is boss here."

Jack did not like what he saw in the man's expression.

He and Robert wouldn't get another chance.

"What's the matter?" he asked, subtly working his feet under him. "Is your dick too small to piss with the others? Is that why they made fun of you?"

He was sure that would do it.

It did. Hawk Nose jammed his gun under his belt and withdrew a large folding knife from his pants pocket. Flipping open the blade, he stepped close to Jack. "Perhaps it is time I cut out your tongue and quiet you the way I did that professor and his friend?"

That was the opening Jack had waited for. In an instant, he used the chain on his cuffs to lock Hawk Nose's wrist in a vise-like grip. And just as quickly, he gave the gunman's wrist a violent twist, snapping bone and tendon. Even before the knife hit the floor, Jack had the cuff chain across Hawk Nose's skinny neck. The thug—his reflexes dulled by shock and drink—was too late going for his gun.

Robert gained his feet and jerked the .45 from Hawk Nose's waistband. Then he bent and scooped up the knife.

"Be done with him," he said. "We've got to go."

"Don't wait on me."

With the cuff chain pulled tight across his throat, Hawk Nose wasn't able to yell out. Jack let him hang a moment, his eyes bulging and his good hand frantically groping to free the stranglehold.

"Come on," Robert pleaded from the door.

"I'm right behind you."

Jack didn't hesitate another second. He snapped Hawk Nose's neck and watched his body drop. "That's for the professor."

Robert showed no revulsion at the taking of the man's life. Jack would have been surprised if his friend had.

They had journeyed this route before.

Robert tossed him the semi-automatic and kept the knife. "Ready?"

"Ready."

Jack hurried to Robert's side and pointed his pistol. He hadn't forgotten about the three gunmen outside. He gambled on surprise and a drunken haze making the difference.

He jerked open the door.

CHAPTER 23

The sun had set by the time Billaud heard the helicopter approach the mine. The only news Gourde could give him that would brighten his mood was that the problem had been taken care of. The auxiliary holding pond was completed; the breach in the tailings dam had been repaired. Within a week, the Mazaruni would dilute the cyanide enough that it would not raise concern within the Ministry of Health. But there were still the researchers and their findings to deal with. The results of their current tests could spoil everything if they were allowed to wind up in the hands of Deputy Minister Sukhai.

Billaud stepped out of the administration hut eager to hear what Gourde had to tell him. Gourde ducked under the spinning blades of the Sikorsky and strode directly to him. Confidence showed in the way he walked.

"Tell me I have nothing to worry about," Billaud said.

"The threat is being dealt with most decisively," Gourde explained. "Jack Ferrell and his friend were the men in that floatplane. They flew to Bartica just as I figured they would."

"They saw everything."

"It is of no consequence. They're both dead. So are the two scientists they spoke with."

"Excellent." Billaud's mood began to brighten. "And the others?"

"Unfortunately, I was not able to deal with the scientists at

Marshal Landing. But I assure you they will be dealt with."

Taken aback by the news, the smile slipped from Billaud's lips. There had been too many mistakes and too many excuses. He was in no mood to hear more. "I was under the impression I made myself clear when I said I wanted them eliminated and their bodies disposed of. You simply cannot fail to do your part."

"I did not think it wise to land the helicopter in the middle of the village and start shooting people."

Billaud did not like admitting he was wrong. But he could see shooting up the village would have been the worst possible mistake. He would not hold Gourde accountable for failing to carry out his orders.

"Indeed, that would not have been wise."

"Like I said, they will be dealt with."

Billaud gave the matter a moment's thought before speaking, "Perhaps there is little for us to be concerned about. The scientists at Marshal Landing, they know nothing of what happened in Bartica?"

"It's doubtful the news has even reached them yet."

"Then we have time."

Gourde waited.

Billaud did not expect an answer. He clasped his hands behind him and paced back and forth as he carefully thought through their next move. "In the morning, send Bakker and Smedt downriver in the boat to silence the researchers permanently. I am taking the helicopter to Georgetown to arrange the sale of the gold we have. The OMG office in Toronto can deal with the mess here once we're gone from this place."

The first sporadic drops of rain struck Gourde's shirt. He made no move for cover. "But—"

Billaud raised his hand dismissively. He'd made his decision. "Two hundred pounds of gold is too much to risk losing if Bakker and Smedt fail to carry out their orders. And you mustn't forget your share."

"I assure you, the problem will be resolved."

"If it is, we can reconsider our next move. Right now, I'm not willing to jeopardize five million dollars."

"And Escobedo Salazar is willing to pay?"

"He'll buy as much as we have to sell him."

Gourde motioned his hand toward the 300 series Sikorsky sitting idle. "Then let's load the gold now and leave this place."

"It's not that easy," Billaud explained, shaking his head back and forth. "It'll take time, maybe a couple of days. Besides, the helicopter would never get off the ground with you and me, the pilot, and all that gold aboard. So you'll stay here and keep an eye on the operation while I arrange the acquisition and set a time for delivery. "

"While you're gone," Gourde told him, "I'll have the crews working double time to dig as much gold from the ground as possible."

Billaud nodded at the promise of more riches. "I have waited for this moment for a long time."

"As have I."

"Then you will do what is necessary. And remember, no more foul-ups. We have too much to lose."

* * *

Karel Bakker stood next to Gregor Smedt inside the operations hut. The drizzle had turned to a heavy rain and began to pound the corrugated tin nailed to the pole rafters, funneling rivulets of water over the eaves and into muddy puddles on the ground. For the past five minutes, he had listened to Gourde explain what they were to do in the morning.

The knot twisting Bakker's gut tightened.

All his preparation—the risks he'd taken—were dangerously close to falling apart. The mine had spilled millions of liters of cyanide waste into the Mazaruni. Researchers were on the water assessing the situation. Traffic on the Mazaruni was dangerously close to being shut down.

And now Billaud was about to move the gold out.

Bakker felt he had no choice but to go forward with his plan. He'd made the arrangements. The people he dealt with were only interested in the gold. They did not concern themselves with the risks he took getting it to them.

112

Risks that could get him killed.

There had to be a way to get the gold out of camp without Billaud or Gourde becoming suspicious. And there was, he decided.

He and Smedt were being sent downriver to kill the scientists. He would follow orders and smuggle the gold out of camp under Gourde's watchful eyes. He'd never suspect that.

No one would.

CHAPTER 24

Jack let the.45 semi-automatic pistol in his hand lead the way. With his index finger on the trigger and his hand firm on the wood grip, he stepped into the darkness, not sure which direction he and Robert would run. Laughter coming from his left answered the question.

One-Eye, Scarface, and Driver were stumbling toward the hut totally unaware. Jack noticed they had their handguns stuffed in their belts. Obviously, they weren't expecting trouble. Then their gazes met his.

He had no choice.

Their hands went for the guns and he fired three quick shots, sending one man to the ground. The other two scrambled for cover behind the building.

Jack did not stop to see which man he hit. He and Robert ran in the opposite direction and ducked into the dense vegetation for cover as a spray of bullets tore into the bushes behind them.

Limbs snapped and plants swayed as they pounded deeper into the rainforest, moving as fast as they could in the dark. Jack could hear the men behind them curse. Two more shots shattered the quiet of night.

Then silence.

He kept going. Checking on the condition of their two cohorts would delay the thugs a minute. Time he and Robert could better use to put distance between them.

But in which direction were they headed?

Breathing heavily, Jack pushed himself to keep moving. In the dark and without the stars to guide him, he could only hope they weren't unintentionally circling back to the shack.

The jungle swallowed them.

Thankful for the thick cover, Jack found himself walking headfirst into low branches, stumbling over exposed roots, and slipping on mud. Twice he heard Robert cuss the gauntlet of vegetation that tore at their clothes and skin.

"You okay back there?" Jack asked. He stopped and looked at his friend who barely stood out in the gloom.

"I'd be better if I could see where I was going," he answered with a huff.

"If we can't see them; they can't see us."

Robert glanced behind him. "Think they're following us?"

"Not in the dark," Jack assured him. "They'd use the lantern; or flashlights if they have them."

"Then we should be able to see the glow of their light and I can't see a thing."

"I wouldn't count on it remaining that way for long. Gourde didn't strike me as a man who tolerates failure. Those assholes back there will be eager to make sure we don't get away."

"At least we've evened the odds."

"I'll feel better when we've put more distance behind us."

Jack continued to lead the way. Thirst and dehydration, along with the stifling humidity, sapped his energy with each step he took. Still, he kept moving. Around them, the jungle came alive with strange hoots, calls, and cries. His shirt was sweat soaked and torn in a dozen places.

The ground was, for the most part, flat. That made the walking less hazardous. But there were the exposed roots, stumps, and crawling vines to worry about.

All of them nearly invisible in the dark.

It was a vine that hooked Jack's ankle and sent him tumbling face-first into the muck on the forest floor.

"Shit." Picking himself up, he shook the mud from his hands.

"You hurt?' Robert asked as he approached.

"Just pissed. Let's keep going."

They walked for another hour before Jack stopped to rest. He had no idea where they were. But he did know they weren't chained inside that shack, which was enough.

They'd be dead by now if they were.

He sagged against the trunk of a Kapok tree. "We need to find someplace to wait for morning."

"Sounds like a plan to me." Robert leaned forward at the waist and rested with his hands on his knees. "I'm not fond of stumbling around out here in the dark. We've been lucky neither of us has ended up with a broken leg."

Jack glanced around. They were surrounded by thick vegetation. "This is as good a place as any."

They both sat on the ground where they were.

"I'm worried about Kazuko," Robert said after a minute. "That asshole Gourde just might go after them."

"I've been thinking the same thing," Jack answered. "Do you still have the keys to that plane?"

"In my pocket," Robert told him. "We never did get around to returning them."

"So technically we are still renting it."

"I did mention not knowing how long we would need it."

"There you go. Feel like doing some more flying?"

"Take the floatplane up river and pick her up?"

"And the others if they want to come."

"They most likely will when we tell them about Bjornson and Douglas."

Jack shook his head in disbelief. Justified or not, there had already been too much killing. "It's hard for me to believe they're dead."

"But you're not surprised?"

Robert's question was not difficult for Jack to answer. He wasn't surprised at all. Gourde would want them all dead.

"Not really," he said. "Hawk Nose and the other slimeballs probably still had the scientists' blood on their hands when they grabbed us."

"It only takes a minute to make a phone call," Robert pointed out.

Jack caught the glimmer of hope in his friend's voice. "Meaning Bjornson had time?"

"It's possible."

"We can hope he did. But we'll worry about that after we get the girls out of there."

CHAPTER 25

Bakker lay on his bunk in the corner of his work shed listening to the night sounds of the jungle, waiting for the morning sun to lighten the sky. It wasn't the heat and humidity of the tropical forest that kept him awake. The thought of smuggling forty pounds of gold out of the mining complex under Billaud's watchful eyes made it impossible for him to sleep. There was much to occupy his thoughts.

Death would surely be his punishment if he were caught. Gerard Gourde would be swift in his judgment.

But not if he doesn't catch me.

Gourde was only accompanying them as far as the boat he kept at the river. From there—Bakker reassured himself—it would only be him and Gregor Smedt in the boat. Smedt would not be so watchful. He would be more concerned with killing the scientists and hiding their bodies.

That's what they were being sent to Marshal Landing to do.

Bakker's only interest was the gold. That Smedt would be with him on the river was only a minor complication. Smedt was loyal to Billaud and Gourde only to the extent that he was paid for his work. Given the opportunity and the appropriate incentive, he was as greedy as Samsundar Balgobin had been.

For a moment, Bakker considered the possibility of killing Smedt and disposing of his body in the water. The Mazaruni was known to take lives. Corpses appeared often enough that one more would not arouse undo attention.

Even so, Bakker thought, why take the chance?

It might be wise to have Smedt along if he could be swayed by the lure of a small fortune in gold. There was always the chance Gourde's reputation for cruelty might be too much for the man to ignore. But that was unlikely, given what Smedt stood to gain out of the deal.

If he helps get the gold downriver.

Should Smedt prove troublesome, he could always be disposed of.

But none of that would happen until they arrived at the boat. And the gold remained undiscovered.

Bakker threw his legs over the side of his cot and lifted his leather backpack onto the sheet next to him. The bag sagged at the bottom in a way that betrayed the weight of the gold concealed inside.

The single bar of gold he would carry with him to the river.

He'd hoped to walk out of camp alone. Now he would have to carry the backpack with him without drawing attention to the prize inside. He lifted the forty-pound bar that gleamed even in the gloom of night. He couldn't help thinking he should have chosen a smaller ingot.

But if he had, the ruse might not have worked.

And the payday not near as gratifying.

Billaud had trusted him to smelt the gold wrestled from the gravel beds in the muddy pits and pour the heavy bars. The sight of all that gold, and the thought that none of it was his, drove him crazy with lust.

It was only right that he get his share.

And he was going to have it.

The gilded lead bar he'd molded to replace the one he held in his hands sat with the gold bars locked in the wire cage inside Billaud's hut. The moment Billaud moved the gold, the fake would likely be discovered. But not before it was too late. By then—Bakker assured himself—he would be far from this place.

And the gold would be his.

He set the bar aside and examined the pouch of his backpack.

An inside pocket offered a possible solution. It was sewn into the leather midline in the back of the pack. The bar would be noticeable to anyone who examined the bag, but its weight would not cause the bottom to sag once the pack was slung onto his back. His handgun and extra ammunition could be wrapped in a towel; and once the bundle was stuffed inside, no one would be the wiser.

And Gourde would be the fool, he thought, *not him.*

Outside, the sky was beginning to lighten. He left his pack sitting innocently on his cot and stepped to the open wall of his hut. Workers walked into the first blush of morning, stretching and yawning. Some urinated where they stood. Others wandered off in the direction of the privies.

It was time.

CHAPTER 26

The sky was beginning to lighten at Marshal Landing. The air was warm and heavy even at this hour of the morning. But the sun had yet to appear above the trees, saving them from the full heat of day. Kazuko helped Pillai carry two boxes of specimen jars down to the boat that was going to take them up the Mazaruni. The eighteen-foot wooden craft was the open style common to river travel. It was powered by a forty-horse outboard motor operated by a hand tiller.

They found their guide, Rodger Jagan, arranging gas cans in the stern of the boat that sat nosed onto shore. It appeared there were more bloated fish carcasses bobbing at the water's edge than there had been the day before. Pillai was disturbed by the sight.

The river was turning into a toxic soup.

"Make sure the people here keep their animals away from the water," she said to Jagan who turned at the sound of her voice. "And whatever you do, make sure they understand they can't use it for cooking or drinking either. They need to use the bottled water we brought until more can be ferried up from Bartica."

Jagan straightened and took the box from Pillai. "They have been told."

"I hope so," Pillai answered. "It could make them sick."

"You think the water is poison?"

"I know it is. And I believe we are going to find it even worse upriver."

121

Kazuko stepped next to Pillai and handed her box to Jagan. When he'd taken it from her hands, she turned to Pillai and asked, "Was Soukis ever able to reach Bjornson on the radio and make him aware of our findings?"

Pillai shook her head. "Unfortunately, not yet."

"But he'll keep trying?"

"Hopefully he'll have better luck today."

"I hope so," Kazuko said. She pointed at the dead fish. "It looks like the problem is getting worse."

Pillai eyed the carcasses. Mile for mile, she hadn't seen a deadly impact of this magnitude on aquatic life since the tidal wave of 2004, when thirty meter waves swept through the Indian Ocean.

She'd hoped to never witness that much death again.

"It does," she agreed. "And in a little while, we will find out just how bad the contamination is."

"Are you pretty ladies ready to get going?" Fletcher hollered down from the top of the river bank. He stood there holding an ice chest.

Kazuko rolled her eyes at Pillai.

Pillai pursed her lips, and said in a low voice, "I hoped he'd changed his mind."

Kazuko huffed. "We could be so lucky."

Pillai looked at Fletcher. "Are you certain you wouldn't rather stay here with Soukis? I'm sure he could use your help."

"And miss out on tagging along with two beautiful women? No way." He hurried down the bank and climbed into the bow of the boat. Quickly stowing the ice chest, he then turned and extended his hand in an obvious gesture to assist Pillai and Kazuko aboard. "May I?"

He was entirely too jolly considering the carnage littering the river. Pillai ignored his outstretched hand and climbed in without help. Kazuko followed. Taking seats in the center of the boat, they left Fletcher standing in the bow.

"We're ready," Pillai said.

A chuckle emanated from the stern.

Pillai didn't need to look to know Jagan was smiling. He'd obviously found the scene entertaining.

Fletcher shrugged, pushed off with a paddle, and sat down, as Jagan backed the boat away from shore. A few seconds later, they were planing over the surface of the river. Pillai scanned the water as the jungle-shrouded shoreline sped by. A serene view, had it not been for the multitude of dead fish floating on the surface.

Ten kilometers upriver they made their first stop. Pillai sucked in a breath of disgust as Jagan took them in close to shore. The number of carcasses pushed against the shoreline by the tide was staggering.

"My God," Fletcher said from up front. "The Geology and Mines Commission and the Guyanese Ministry of Health should be all over this."

Pillai was glad to see Fletcher finally taking the trip seriously.

"For whatever reason," she answered, "they're dragging their feet."

"'Why' is not important," Fletcher said. "I assure you they'll take action now."

She watched him snap half a dozen pictures. When he put his camera away, she said, "Let's collect our samples and get moving. I think it is safe to say the source of the cyanide that's killing these fish is farther upriver."

Kazuko glanced around. "Yeah, but how far?"

"Kaburi Rapids is another twenty or thirty kilometers. If we're still seeing dead fish, we'll collect another set of water samples there."

"And above the rapids?" Kazuko asked.

"A small village: Kaburi Landing. If we can make it that far."

"You're determined, aren't you?"

"I'm going to find the source of all this death. That's a promise."

CHAPTER 27

Jack and Robert stumbled out of the dense vegetation to the south and west of town. When the sky had finally lightened enough for them to see where they were stepping, negotiating the jungle's trip hazards had not been the challenge it'd been in the dark. Nor was the forest the foreboding world of bizarre hoots, calls, and cries that prey on a person's imagination.

"Let's think about this a moment," Jack said.

"What's to think about?" Robert asked. "We fly upriver and pick up Kazuko and get the hell out of this country."

"And that's what we'll do," Jack promised. "But you're forgetting something."

"What?" Robert furrowed his brow.

Jack raised his shackled wrists. "First we need to get these cuffs off."

Robert peered down at his own wrists as if he had forgotten they were shackled together. He sighed. "Too bad we didn't think to go through Hawk Nose's pockets for a key."

Jack scoffed. "And while we were at it, we could have stopped for a beer."

"I see your point."

"Face it; we were lucky we got out of there with our asses intact."

Robert scanned the residential buildings in front of them. "What we need is a good pair of bolt cutters."

Jack considered the possibility. He'd believed their kidnappers had driven them into the jungle west of town, so finding their way back had been relatively easy once the sun was up. Bartica sat at the confluence of the Mazaruni and Essequibo rivers. All they had to do was walk east. Finding bolt cutters in a community of strangers might not be so easy.

"We sure can't walk through town wearing these," he said.

"Too bad we can't go to the police."

"We're probably wanted men by now."

"We wouldn't be if you stopped killing people."

"I got us out of the shack, didn't I?"

"And I thank you for that," Robert said. "I'm sure we would have been dead by now if you hadn't."

"The girls, too. Remember that."

"How could I forget?"

Jack noticed Robert gaze unblinking at the town. That thousand-yard stare he got when he was lost in thought. It was obvious he was thinking about Kazuko and getting her to safety.

"She'll be okay," Jack said. "We'll make sure of it."

"I have to believe that." He eyeballed his handcuffs. "Do you really think the police know about the bodies back at the shack?"

"Doubtful. But we can't take the chance."

"Right." Robert held his wrists up in from of him. "And we can't just stand here talking about it. There has to be a tool shed or hardware store we can raid."

"Let's start looking."

They were in a rural area on the outskirts of town. The buildings were brightly-painted residential wood-sided structures of varying size and condition. Chickens wandered freely in the yards. Pigs and goats were penned behind fences of sticks and chicken wire. People were busy with their morning chores.

No one appeared to have noticed them.

Jack began the morning believing luck was once again on their side. That feeling didn't last long. Because the cuffs were in clear view of anyone taking an interest in Robert and him, they were forced to skirt the town where they had less chance of drawing attention. But even that plan turned dicey when a police car rolled by and they were forced to dive for cover behind some bushes.

"We're not getting anywhere like this," Robert said, clearly frustrated.

"Nope," Jack answered. "But our luck is changing."

"How's that?"

"See that tool shed over there?" Jack pointed at a residence across the road. "I bet we'll find what we need in there."

"Provided the owner isn't prone to shooting trespassers."

"It doesn't look like anyone's around the place for us to worry about."

Robert started walking. "There's no time like the present to find out."

Jack reached out and stopped him. "You stay here. This is my show."

"But—"

Jack did not give his friend time to argue. He handed him the .45 and took off at a fast walk across the road, hoping Robert didn't follow. There was no reason to chance both of them getting caught.

Or shot.

The shed turned out to be exactly what he thought it was. It contained shovels and hoes and rakes, plus an assortment of hand tools. There were no bolt cutters that he could see, but there was a rusted hacksaw. He dug a twenty-dollar bill out of his front pants pocket and tucked the edge of the crinkled Jackson under an oil can. Then he picked up the hacksaw and turned to leave.

"Is there something you want?" A man's voice asked from behind him.

Jack didn't want any misunderstandings that would get the police called. He slowly turned and faced the man. "Honest, Sir, I'm not here to cause trouble."

The guy was a couple of hundred years old with deep wrinkles and leathery skin. His back was straight and he held a menacing-looking machete. But there was a calm manner about the old guy that eased Jack's dread. Wisdom showed in the gent's dark eyes as he glanced from the handcuffs to the hacksaw to the twenty-dollar bill sitting on the workbench and back to the cuffs.

His gaze remained steady and clear as he eyed Jack up and

down.

Jack realized what he must look like after a night on the run in the jungle. His shirt and pants were snagged and torn in several places, and he was filthy. He waited, wondering if he should run and take his chances avoiding the police.

But then he saw a familiar look in the man's eyes.

At once he forgot about running.

He'd seen the same glint of understanding—like that of a caring father—in the blue eyes of Matapolu, the *Menehune* holy man who once saved him from certain death in the lava tubes beneath Kauai. Years had passed since their meeting, but not enough time for him to forget.

He'd never forget his friend.

And now—peering into this man's warm brown eyes—he found himself feeling something bordering on respect for the old guy, and a general sense of moral decency that would not let him run like a frightened thief in the night.

It seemed like an hour before the man spoke again. "I have something that will work better."

Jack felt a flood of relief. He'd judged the man's character correctly.

The old guy stepped to the bench, laid down the machete, and pawed through a large wooden box on the floor. It took a few seconds of digging, but he produced a pair of long-handled bolt cutters.

He held them up in front of him. "I think you were looking for these."

Jack did not hesitate. "You're a life saver."

He held his hands out in front of him and watched as the old guy cut the cuffs. They had ratcheted tight onto his wrist. It was a relief to have them off. But he still had Robert to worry about.

"My friend is across the street," he said, rubbing his wrists. "Mind if I borrow those?"

"I've got a better idea. Call him over here. If he looks anything like you, both of you can use a drink of water."

"I won't forget what you've done for us."

"A bad man would not have paid for what he was taking."

"We're not bad men," Jack explained. "But the men who did this to us are. They intended to kill us. Only we didn't give them the chance. And now our friends' lives are in danger."

Again, a glint of wisdom showed in the elderly guy's eyes that blazed with clarity and understanding. "And you do not want to go to the police?"

"I'm not sure they can be trusted."

"Call your friend."

Jack nodded, feeling comfortable with this man. *Trust*—he thought—is a valuable quality in a person. He wasn't going to waste it.

He turned and waved Robert over. Then he refocused his attention on the old man. "Please, sir, I'd like to know your name."

The old man arched a brow. "My name is not important."

"It is to me," Jack told him.

It took a moment, but he finally said, "Norman Varga."

"Jack Ferrell." Jack extended his hand.

Varga accepted Jack's offer of friendship. "Where do you go from here?"

Robert stepped into the shed, interrupting the exchange. He was as ragged and unkempt as Jack was. Still, there was an amiable nature about him that made people smile. Varga was no different.

Varga held the smile as long as it took him to look Robert up and down. He let it slip and said, "Aren't you a sight."

"Did I miss something?" Robert glanced back and forth at the two men.

Speaking to Varga, Jack said, "This is my friend Robert. We're trying to get to the marina across town. There's a floatplane there that we intend to fly upriver and pick up our friends."

"The friends whose lives are in danger?" clarified Varga.

"They're women scientists," Jack answered with a tone of urgency. "Part of an international team of researchers who are trying to find the source of the toxins killing the Mazaruni."

"One of the women is my wife," Robert added.

That got him a nod from Varga.

"I have seen the dead fish," he said. As if suddenly understanding the urgency of the situation, he hurriedly cut the cuffs from Robert's wrists. "I'll drive you there. It will be faster than walking."

"You should know," Jack added. "Two members of the research team were killed at their lab yesterday. The same people who kidnapped us murdered them. These are not nice men. I don't want you hurt."

"I will be okay." Varga's eyes narrowed into a look of resolve. "Help your friends before something terrible happens to them."

CHAPTER 28

Bakker lifted his backpack and slid the wide straps onto his shoulder, struggling to make the bag appear a fraction of its weight. He noticed the rain that fell an hour before had tapered off, giving way to clouds that hugged and probed the treetops with a ghostly mist high in the jungle canopy. And even though the mine and the tropical forest around it were shrouded in an eerie gloom, the stifling heat and humidity remained.

My last day in this place, he thought.

With the pack pulled tight against his body, he stepped out of his crude board hut ready to meet Gourde and Smedt who walked toward him from the center of the compound. Gourde carried his short-barreled, pump-action shotgun in his right hand. Smedt had his AK-47 and a stained canvas bag slung over one shoulder. His hand was clenched around the handle of a long, heavy-bladed bolo.

"Are you ready?" Gourde asked.

At that same moment, Billaud stepped from his cabin.

Bakker's hand dropped to the eight-inch hunting knife in the scabbard strapped to his side. The weapon was pitifully inadequate by comparison to Gourde's 12-gauge, but it was comforting just the same. He brought his hand up to his shoulder and hooked his thumb under the strap of his pack as he looked on.

Gourde always made him nervous. But he did not know which man to fear more: Raoul Billaud or Gerard Gourde. Different but the same: selfish, brutal men.

Of that, Bakker was sure.

Billaud stood looking at him from ten feet away. There was no mistaking the concern etched in Billaud's expression. But if he had suspicions, he was keeping them to himself.

Bakker pulled the bandana from around his neck and innocently mopped his sweaty brow with it. He did not want to appear nervous or in a hurry to leave camp. Nor did he want to draw either man's attention to his backpack.

He slid the bandanna back around his neck and calmly knotted it in place. "We should be going."

Gourde motioned a hand for Smedt to follow him and led the way into the jungle. Bakker remained a few steps in the rear so that neither Gourde nor Smedt had time to study the weight of his pack as he walked.

A precaution meant for the trail.

Bakker inched the straps higher on his back, willing the pack to not sag under the weight of the gold. There was little doubt in his mind Billaud paid close attention to the three of them as they stepped from view.

Bakker breathed a sigh of relief when he entered the cover of the jungle.

With his back out of sight of the two men walking in front of him, there was little for him to worry about until they reached the river. To calm his mind, he whistled a tune as they pushed hard through the tangle of undergrowth, moving quickly through the rainforest. It wasn't difficult for him to imagine Samsundar Balgobin fleeing in this same direction in his desperate attempt to reach the Mazaruni.

"Do not whistle too loud, my friend." Smedt pointed his machete at the treetops where several macaws took flight amid a flurry of loud squawks. "You frighten the birds."

Bakker chuckled. "I fear it is those big feet of yours that scare the birds. Not my whistling."

"And I fear you are wrong, my friend."

"And I fear the two of you will lose your tongues," Gourde interrupted, "if you do not cease this senseless chatter."

Bakker would not banter with Gourde, or test the man's eagerness to carry out his threat. They had sloshed through mud and pushed their way through tangles of vines and still they were close to a kilometer from the river. Much could happen.

But he tried not to let that possibility concern him. Neither Smedt nor Gourde had questioned what was in his backpack. Gold that would bring him a new life.

Or a swift death.

The flooding and the tangle of growth worsened when they neared the Mazaruni. Bakker was thankful the effort of sloshing through knee-deep muck and vines and over-exposed roots took the two men's minds off of him.

He was confident, now, that he would make it to the river.

And that the gold would remain undiscovered.

Even so, the question of whether or not he could convince Smedt to go along with the plan remained unanswered. And would remain that way until they were in the boat and on their way to Marshal Landing. Only then would he know the extent of the man's greed. Killing him was a most unpleasant option.

Something he would do without hesitation, but hoped to avoid.

More guarded than greedy, he still believed it was better to have someone with a gun to watch his back. Smedt—if he was willing—was the perfect person to have along.

Especially when there was killing to be done.

CHAPTER 29

Bakker felt a twinge of nervousness when they pushed through the last of the tangled forest growth. The eighteen-foot-long open boat—constructed of wood, painted red and turquoise and powered by a forty-horsepower Evinrude outboard motor—sat high up on the riverbank where it had been securely tied to a tree. There were three bench-type seats arranged crossways in the hull: one forward, one in the middle, and one in the stern for the man handling the motor. It had already been decided that Smedt—because of his experience operating the craft—would sit at the tiller.

That Smedt was handling the boat was for the best, Bakker reasoned. He would be too busy to concern himself with what was inside the knapsack.

He shrugged off his pack and wedged it under the bench seat in the bow, as far away from Smedt as possible. He was anxious to get downriver.

The quicker the better.

Without wasting a second, he began wrestling the boat toward the water. Gourde and Smedt helped. And with great effort, the three of them managed to work the craft into the river with the bow nosed up on shore.

He breathed a sigh of relief. Then he felt the vessel getting away from them and desperation gripped his chest. His hands slipped and he groped for a better grip as he imagined the boat, and the gold, disappearing downriver without him aboard.

That was not going to happen.

He planted his heels in the mud and held on. Gourde and Smedt did the same. Still the current threatened to tear the boat from their grasp.

Bakker was surprised by the power of the river. Determined, he held on—so did Gourde and Smedt. It took a minute for them to gain control, but working together they were able to keep the craft from drifting away.

"Keep in mind how swift this current is," Gourde cautioned. "You two have a job to do and I don't want you to take any unnecessary chances until those scientists are dead and their bodies disposed of."

"I can handle the river," Smedt answered. "Hold the boat while I get the engine started."

Even with the bow sitting on the muddy bank above the waterline, it took both Gourde and Bakker to hold the craft in place while Smedt climbed aboard. Bakker was thankful for Gourde's size and brute strength.

An asset under the circumstances.

But Bakker could not forget about the gold hidden in his backpack. He worried that Gourde would notice the unusual way the bag slumped under the weight of the heavy bar. The big man's eyes were constantly searching . . . for something . . . for nothing.

Always suspicious.

Bakker refocused his thoughts on what they were doing. Smedt had the fuel line attached and was tugging on the starter rope. The engine coughed, but didn't start.

Too long sitting idle, Bakker thought.

Smedt pulled on the rope again with the same result.

Bakker looked at Gourde and swallowed a nervous lump when he noticed the big man eyeballing the knapsack. It would only be a matter of time before his suspicious nature made him curious enough to search the pack's contents.

Smedt was still tugging on the rope without success.

The motor refused to start.

"Maybe you should give it a pull," Bakker suggested to Gourde to get the man's mind off of the bag.

"Good idea," he said. "Or we will be here all day."

Bakker struggled to hold the boat steady in the current. Without the aid of Gourde's powerful arms, the task was too much for one man to manage.

The stern swept sideways.

Bakker's feet slipped and he went down in the water. He gained his footing and managed to get control of the boat.

He feared he would lose the craft altogether if it happened again.

Gourde laughed, as though taking pleasure in the mishap. Bakker let him have his fun and breathed a sigh of relief when the big man pulled on the rope and the outboard motor sputtered to life amid a cloud of blue smoke.

Smedt kept the engine running, and Bakker sloshed onto the muddy bank and stomped his feet. He didn't like having any of the river water on him.

He knew what it had done to the fish.

Gourde followed him onto dry land and stomped his feet as well, shaking loose the water soaking his boots and pants legs. His indifferent expression made what he did appear to be more out of annoyance than concern.

"Glad that leak is downriver from here," he said. "I hate even the thought of swimming in that stuff."

Bakker didn't answer.

Apparently Gourde thought his comment was funny, because he grinned as though he'd told some great joke.

Not even close.

Bakker realized he had been holding his breath and released it. Relieved, somewhat, but he didn't dare take his eyes off Gourde. Anything could happen. Gourde was still smiling when he stepped past him.

A silent joke, possibly.

He frowned at Gourde's arrogance, but inside smiled in self-satisfaction.

The joke was on Gerard Gourde. The big man was the fool.

But for how long?

CHAPTER 30

Bakker stood motionless, held there by his thoughts. He felt the heat of the morning sun on his skin. The clouds blanketing the forest in mist had parted, and the intense fireball overhead burned into him like a laser beam.

He remained all too aware of the deadly wrath of hell that would fall upon him if the theft was discovered. The dice had been rolled. The gold was in the boat. The river was there beckoning to him.

He was ready to get moving, down the river, away from Gourde.

Far from his prying eyes.

In the next instant, a breath caught in Bakker's throat.

Gourde stood, furrowing his brow in the direction of the bow of the boat.

His expression hardened.

"You—" he said without finishing. His gaze turned on Bakker, but only for a second. It moved to the shotgun leaning against a tree ten feet away.

Bakker knew at once what happened.

The gold!

He glanced at his pack and saw the gold bar showing at the edge of the flap. The grip of his revolver showed there, too. Both had been jostled loose by the sudden shift of the boat when it had been caught in the current.

His plan was unraveling in front of him.

There was no trying to hide what was going on. Gourde had known at once the gold had been stolen. And he knew who took it.

Gourde lunged for his 12-gauge.

Bakker did not hesitate. He grabbed up his pistol and fired twice without aiming. Then he swung the gun on Smedt who sat stunned by the violent outburst.

Bakker did not give Smedt time to react. He lined up the sights and squeezed off two quick shots. Both .38 caliber bullets struck Smedt square in the chest and propelled him backward into the water.

His limp body was quickly swept away by the current.

A groan drew Bakker's attention back to Gourde. He was down on the ground, but getting up. There was a line of blood on his scalp above his left ear, but it was only a graze wound. It had been enough to knock the big man down, but not enough to keep him there.

Gourde got his feet under him. He charged.

Bakker swung the pistol and fired a desperate shot. At once he realized it had gone wide. Before he could pull the trigger again, Gourde's huge paw slapped the gun away as if it was nothing more than a boy's play toy.

That's all it took.

Bakker could not believe the man's quickness. The giant was on him, unleashing the brute force of an enraged grizzly bear.

He brought his arms up in defense, but was knocked backwards into the boat. His head slammed against the forward bench seat.

Stunned, he fought feebly to get free of Gourde's grasp. Only then did he fully realize the big man's tremendous strength. Gourde seemed intent on squeezing the life out of him. He fought to force back the darkness closing on the edge of his mind.

No use.

His consciousness dimmed further. Still he held onto life, hoping for a miracle.

In the next instant, the stern of the boat was swept downstream by the current, swinging the bow sharply around. The sudden movement was enough to cause Gourde to loosen his grip.

The opening Bakker needed.

He managed to work his right arm free of Gourde's vise-like

grip and hammer his fist into the big man's face.

The blow had little effect.

He hammered the big man's face a second and third and fourth time. Solid blows to the nose and cheekbones and chin. Punches that would put a normal man down and unconscious.

But the blows did little more than give Gourde a bloody nose.

Bakker shrank from the big man's murderous gaze. Death would not come easy. He groped for anything he could use for a weapon.

His hand found the bar of gold.

At once, Gourde was on his knees pounding with his fist. Bakker felt the bones in his face crunch under the beating.

A massive blow snapped his head back.

The gold bar slipped from his hand as he fell limp into the bottom of the boat.

His mind willed him to move, but he could only lie there. A numb empty shell of the person he'd been.

For what seemed like eternity, he could hear Gourde grunting above him from a thousand miles away. There was no pain from the savagery inflicted upon him, no way to make his body move.

Only his mind worked, short-circuited from the rest of him.

Blood from Gourde's flattened nose and the bullet wound in his scalp dripped warm, sticky wetness. It struck Bakker in the eyes. He couldn't look away. Through blurred vision, he saw a massive fist coming toward his face.

A final lethal blow.

He took one last breath. And then there was only blackness, as his consciousness dimmed completely.

CHAPTER 31

Gourde heaved Bakker's limp body overboard and watched it sweep away with no more feeling than he had for the dead fish down river. It was then that he noticed the current had carried the boat a hundred yards from where it had entered the water. Now he was downstream from the creek where the effluent had flowed unabated into the Mazaruni. The breach in the holding pond had been repaired and the tide of deadly leech water stopped. But the damage to the river system had been done. Here, scores of dead and bloating fish washed against the shoreline.

For a minute all he could do was stare.

The fight had left him both charged and exhausted. And he was bleeding from the scalp wound. He needed a minute to think. The initial plan was shot to hell. He had to improvise.

As he was swept farther downriver, he studied the shoreline of the Mazaruni. The Amerindian village of Kaburi Landing was coming up, maybe a quarter-mile away. He could go ashore there and care for his wound. And while he was resting, he could plan his next move.

There was no reason to go back to the mine. Nothing that required his attention waited for him back there. The scientists needed to be eliminated. He would see to it they were.

A lot depended on their deaths.

The forty-horsepower Evinrude was still idling smoothly. He

climbed over the center bench seat and took hold of the tiller. Applying power, he got the bow pointed downstream. Smedt wasn't the only one who knew how to operate the boat.

Gourde kept to the center of the river as he motored toward Kaburi Landing. The rage that only minutes before had fueled his determination to kill Karel Bakker was no longer there. It had drifted away along with the man's body. But he remained alert and on guard. When he spied a pair of dugout canoes pulled onto dry land, he knew he was nearing the village.

Death showed along the river's edge here, too. Not just bloated fish, but pigs and goats, as well. The toxic sludge had destroyed everything that had come in contact with the water.

But that was not his concern. He cared nothing about the dead fish or the animals. His thoughts were on tending to his head wound and moving on—to finish the job that was left to him.

He steered the boat toward shore, cut the engine at the last second, and nosed it onto the mud next to the dugouts. The air had a death-like stillness to it that added to the stench of rot in the water.

His stay here would be short.

Stepping over the bench seats, he picked up Smedt's AK-47, made his way to the bow, and hopped into two-inch deep muck that sucked at the soles of his boots. There was no time to waste. He quickly pulled the bow of the boat high on the bank to keep the craft from floating away, and turned to study the village.

Kaburi Landing had been little more than a half-dozen thatched huts, a few goats, pigs and chickens, and as many dugout canoes. What troubled him was lack of life anywhere—human or otherwise. The village was deserted. Not a dog, a goat, a pig, or a chicken . . . even the birds that lived high in the trees had strangely disappeared.

He slid the strap of the assault rifle over his shoulder. It was hard to not be taken aback by the eerie quiet of the village.

Drawn by the desire to explore further, he climbed the bank to the clearing where the village stood. It was then that he saw the bodies scattered about. Immediately, he realized the deadly toxin had done its killing here, too. But not everyone had died. Those who hadn't perished had fled into the safety of the jungle.

Back to where they came from.

He stepped into the clearing at the center of the village and peered at the body lying on the ground in front of him. There was something familiar about the man in the red shirt. It took a moment of staring at the bloated and darkened form, but he finally recognized the rotting remains.

Samsundar Balgobin.

Gourde smiled knowing Balgobin had died an ugly death here with the others of his kind. *A fitting end,* he thought, *for the man who dared defy me.*

But had Balgobin lost the gold in the process?

Using the end of the rifle barrel as a probe, Gourde examined the dead man's pants pockets and shirt. The barrel clanked against something metallic under the front of his shirt at his waistline.

So he had managed to hold onto his prize.

His death sentence.

Gourde detested the idea of having to touch the rotting corpse, but he had no choice. Not if he intended to have that gold.

He wasn't going to leave it for someone else to take.

Forcing aside his revulsion, he reached inside Balgobin's shirt and pulled the bar fee of the cloth binding holding it. He studied the ingot in the sunlight. It was twice as long as it was wide—the size of a small candy bar. No more than a few ounces. Perhaps ten thousand dollars' worth. A fortune in Guyana.

But a small price for a man to risk his life for. Balgobin had been a fool.

Gourde pocketed the gold bar without wasting another second thinking about Balgobin. Scanning the bodies scattered about and the abandoned-looking huts, he quickly concluded there was nothing for him here.

Even the water was poison.

The scientists were downriver. He had his knife and he had the gun. That's where he would go.

He walked back to the riverbank and stopped at the sound of an outboard motor. He listened. The high-pitched roar was getting louder.

Someone was coming.

He squinted into the mist. The boat was not yet in view, but it was getting closer. That much was for sure.

But who was in it? He wondered. And why were they coming to this place?

He glanced back at the bodies. The outside world was closing in on him. He only had a few minutes to prepare.

CHAPTER 32

Kazuko eagerly anticipated their arrival at Kaburi Landing. The ghastly scene appeared to worsen the farther they traveled upriver. The devastation here was as bad as anything they'd seen. Somewhere ahead of them lay the source of the toxins that decimated the aquatic life. The Mazaruni had become a killing ground.

It seemed nothing that came in contact with the water survived.

"Kaburi Landing is not far ahead," Jagan announced.

Kazuko was relieved to have made it this far. Kaburi Rapids had proved to be a formidable barrier. Had it not been for Jagan's skill at the tiller, they would have had to turn back. Or walk here through the jungle. Stopping now was something none of them wanted to do. Pillai most of all.

Kazuko heard the resolve in Pillai's voice when she talked about the toxins and destruction done to the river's ecosystem. Furthermore, she worked with the enthusiasm and intensity of a devoted professional dedicated to the cause confronting them. She was determined to find the source of all this death. And—Kazuko had to admit—so was she.

"I'm worried about the villagers," Pillai said, speaking loud enough to be heard above the roar of the outboard motor.

Kazuko motioned her hand at the dead fish along the bank. "You don't think the people know to avoid the river? Geez, look at it. I can't believe they wouldn't realize something is wrong with the water."

"They might, but then again, they pretty much depend on the Mazaruni for their survival."

Kazuko winced at the implication.

An entire village wiped out.

She stared at the carnage along the shore, unable to tear her gaze away from the sight of death no more than a dozen feet in front of her. The fervor she felt having finally arrived at the village was replaced with a feeling of dread.

"Those poor people," she said to Pillai. "I pray to God we're not too late."

By the look on Pillai's face, she had the same concern.

As they rounded the next bend in the river, Kaburi Landing eased into view. First the boats sitting on the bank, then Kazuko saw the rooftops of the huts nearest the water. All very normal looking, except no one moved about.

It was as if the village was asleep.

"I'm getting a bad feeling," Pillai said.

Kazuko didn't know what to say. There should have been at least a few people standing on the bank waiting to see who was coming up the river. She held her breath, hoping the scene was not as it seemed.

"I don't see any sign of life," Fletcher said. "Not even a goat or pig."

"Certainly looks dead," Kazuko admitted. Then she saw the animal carcasses floating among the rotting fish. She feared her concern had been realized.

Even the stench of death was worse here than downriver.

"We need to get ashore," Pillai said. She turned her gaze on Jagan and creased her brow as if to emphasize the urgency in her words. "I suggest you remain with the boat."

Jagan nudged the bow of their craft ashore next to the others perched on the muddy slope, and killed the engine. Kazuko imagined what was waiting for them. Hoping for the best, she pictured a sleepy village caught in the slumber of a warm day's siesta.

She hopped ashore and hurried up the bank ahead of Pillai and

Fletcher, eager to prove her worst fears wrong. Topping the rise, she stopped in her tracks.

It took a moment for the entirety of the scene to settle in.

Shock, then disbelief.

A light breeze shifted, bringing a strong stench of death to her nose. But that did not match the nightmare she looked at. In front of her lay several bodies in different stages of decomposition. Her first thought was that the water could not have done this to the villagers. They surely had fallen at the hands of a murderous band of killers. But that theory was quickly forced aside by reality.

The river had poisoned them.

Pillai stepped beside her and stopped as abruptly as Kazuko had. Undoubtedly gripped by the same nightmarish horror, she could only stare. When at last she could, she quietly spoke, "We're too late."

Fletcher appeared a second later. "You're right," he agreed, wrinkling his nose at the stench. "Nothing is going to help these poor people. I'm thinking we should grab some water samples and hightail it back to Marshal Landing and report this to the authorities."

Kazuko looked at Pillai for an answer. Fletcher was probably right about wanting to get out of there, but she respected her friend's opinion. It seemed wrong to just collect some water and leave without doing something more.

"What do you think?" she asked.

Pillai scanned the compound. Her gaze settled on a group of structures. "Let's check the huts. There could be someone inside who needs our help."

Fletcher stared at the two women. "You're serious?"

Pillai shot him a scathing glance and led the way.

He stood a moment, and then followed. "Okay, but we search together."

In spite of the horror around them, Kazuko had to chuckle. Fletcher obviously wasn't going to allow himself to be out-braved by a couple of mere women.

The first bodies they came to stopped Kazuko in her tracks. The victims' suffering showed in their tortured expressions. She reached and gripped Pillai's arm. Her friend turned and met her gaze.

For several seconds they looked at each other without saying anything.

Finally, Kazuko swallowed the acid that rose in her throat. She nodded at the dead. "These people did not die easily."

She and Pillai peered down at the tormented corpse of a shirtless Amerindian man, maybe thirty years old. Beside him was a bare-breasted Amerindian woman of about the same age. Both bodies lay twisted and bloated in a way that suggested they'd died writhing in severe pain. Their eyes and mouths were wide open; their protruding tongues blackened and swollen. The victims clutched their necks as if they'd struggled to breathe.

"Cyanide poisoning," Pillai pointed out. "Not a pretty sight."

Considering the concentration of deadly toxins downstream and what they must be here, the diagnosis was obvious. Still, it seemed to Kazuko no one had been eager to be the first person to point it out. Glancing around at the other bodies, she shuddered at the thought of what it must have been like in the village when people began to die with no way to help them.

Then she saw a mother clutching a baby to her breast. The picture of absolute innocence transformed into one of gruesome pain and death.

She wanted to scream.

"We can go anytime you're ready," Fletcher offered.

Kazuko wanted nothing more than to get out of there. She turned to Pillai for an answer. She saw the glassiness in her friend's eyes.

She let her own tears do her pleading.

"We have to be sure," Pillai said with a tone of understanding.

"Do we?" Kazuko asked. She couldn't bear the thought of having to look at that poor mother and her dead child a second time. Once had been enough. But in her heart she knew Pillai was right.

There was still a chance not everyone in the village had perished.

Pillai stood without answering. It seemed she looked inward. As though she were reliving her own nightmare—fighting to sort out her feelings.

Emotional scars slow to heal.

When at last she appeared to have gathered herself, she nodded almost imperceptibly. A silent acknowledgement directed at herself as much as to anyone else.

Kazuko offered a weak smile and nodded back.

Nothing needed to be said.

With that, Pillai turned and stepped toward the hut directly in front of them, stopping abruptly when the door to the cabin opened and a big man stepped out, holding an assault rifle pointed directly at them.

CHAPTER 33

Gourde stepped from the hut when the three people stopped and stared at the bodies of the dead man and woman. When he first saw the group approach—two women and a man, both women pretty, one of mixed Japanese descent—he recalled his conversation with Cheddi Norton and the man's description of the scientists at Marshal Landing. If it was indeed them, one man was missing from the team of researchers, but the woman of Japanese descent was distinctively beautiful. It was doubtful there were two such women on the Mazaruni. And the other exotic lovely with her, could be the woman scientist.

It seemed he wouldn't have to make the trip downriver after all. Was he so lucky? Nothing had gone right since leaving the mine early that morning. But then he did find the gold Balgobin had stolen. Surely that was a sign of good fortune.

My good fortune.

"You need not worry yourself over these poor devils," he said. "They are beyond help."

The scientists' gazes appeared to settle on the assault rifle.

At once their eyes widened. No one moved. No one said a word. They didn't even exchange glances.

They just stared.

Finally, with noticeable concern showing in her voice, Pillai asked, "You've checked the other huts?"

Gourde saw them staring at the gun in his hand. No doubt the AK-47 caused them alarm. They couldn't stop looking at it. His bloody scalp only added to their uneasiness.

Good, he thought.

There was little doubt in his mind that the three people in front of him were the troublesome scientists he believed they were. Still, he wanted to be sure. He'd kill them anyway, but at least he would know. There was no reason for him to waste time making a trip that wasn't necessary.

He asked, "You are the scientists from Marshal Landing?"

No one seemed willing to answer.

"Well," he demanded.

"We are," Fletcher answered. He squared his shoulders. "But how would you know that?"

Gourde smiled at the guy's boldness. He'd heard him talking. The young man had been the one who was anxious to leave—afraid of a few dead bodies. Now, he behaved as if he had suddenly grown balls.

A show for the women.

"That is unimportant," Gourde answered with casual indifference.

The pretty female scientists posed no particular threat to him that he could see. The man with the sudden urge to prove himself in front of the women might prove to be an annoyance—a problem easily rectified.

He leveled the AK-47 at the young man's head. The *Tat, Tat* of the automatic rifle shattered the stillness of the village, as Fletcher's skull exploded in a spray of gore.

Both women stood wide-eyed in stunned silence.

He let them stare at the twitching body of their friend on the ground, his head a wasted mess. A foot away sat his bush hat, soaked with blood and brain matter.

It was important they have a good long look.

He wanted the women to know fear.

"You are Pillai and Kazuko," he said coldly, recalling the names Cheddi Norton had given him. He brought the sights of his gun to bear on the two women, ready to squeeze the trigger.

The females huddled together in clear disbelief at what was happening. And like frightened animals, they glanced about as if looking for someplace to run.

He grinned, pleased that it had come to this.

CHAPTER 34

Jack drew in a slow, deep breath when Norman Varga steered his ancient pick-up truck into the parking lot at the marina. The Quonset hut where Philip Bjornson and Colton Douglas were murdered stood as still and lifeless as the two men who died there. The scientists had come to Guyana to help the people, not harm them. And they had died for it. Kazuko and Pillai were likely next, and the two men with them.

He and Robert planned to make sure that didn't happen. The women's safety was of the utmost importance. In his heart and his gut, he knew he and Robert were doing the right thing. Nothing would stop them.

Even so, he couldn't help but feel they could do more. They could go to the police and tell them about Gourde. And they could tell them about the men who had held Robert and him captive, and how he had killed one or possibly two of them to escape. But that would only delay them. By then, it might be too late.

It might be too late already.

Jack did not want to think about that.

Kazuko and Pillai were safe at Marshal Landing. They'd be there alive and well when he and Robert arrived to pick them up. Only then would he consider talking to the police.

The yellow and white De Havilland Beaver floatplane sat tied to the dock where Robert had parked it the day before. The aircraft

151

bobbed and tugged at its mooring lines, like an excited puppy straining at its leash, happy to see them return. Varga braked to a stop at the edge of the lot twenty-feet from the water. It was as close as he could get them to the plane.

He extended his hand. "This is as good as I can do, boys."

Jack gladly took the old guy's weathered hand in his, and pumped it. "I can't thank you enough for what you've done."

"That goes for me, too," Robert added.

Varga gave them a knowing nod. "Good luck."

Jack and Robert stood a moment watching him drive away. But that was all the time they wasted.

"You do still have the key to this thing," Jack asked, as he headed for the plane.

"Right here." Robert held the key up in front of him. It was connected to a braided nylon fob with a small plastic fishing float fastened to it.

Jack nodded on the move. "We have plenty of fuel, right?"

"More than enough, as long as you don't plan on going sightseeing."

"I think I've seen enough of Guyana."

"Then let's get this thing in the air," Robert said. "Hurry and cast off the lines. I'll start the engine."

Five minutes later, the plane lifted clear of the Mazaruni. Jack leaned toward his door and peered through the Plexiglas at the plane's shadow below. Water streamed from the rear of the pontoons and dropped to the river as the De Havilland Beaver gained altitude.

"Think they know?" Robert asked.

Jack turned from the window. "You're referring to Kazuko and Pillai, I assume?"

"I am. You think they got the news about Bjornson and Douglas?"

"We'll find out in about ten minutes."

Marshal Falls was already in view. Jack was eager to pick up Kazuko and Pillai, and the two scientists there with them. He wanted to be done with Guyana and gone from the country. The Ministry of Health and the Guyanese Mines Commission could deal with the cyanide problem. None of what was happening here was worth dying for. Too many were dead because of it, already. The mongrel vermin he killed were no loss to society. Bjornson and Douglas were. That bothered him.

At last, Marshal Landing appeared in front of them. Robert took the plane down low, and then he eased it onto the water and taxied toward shore. But the women they came for didn't come running to meet them.

Jack shot Robert a worried look and scanned the shoreline.

"I half-expected to see them standing down here by the river where we saw them yesterday," Robert said.

People from the village stood back watching while others wandered closer. Jack waited for Kazuko and Pillai to appear. They weren't among the onlookers. Surely the two women would have heard the plane and gotten curious. But the only scientist that showed himself was Soukis.

"I'll stay with the plane," Robert said. "See what Soukis has to say."

Jack already had the door open, ready to step onto the pontoon. He looked at Robert, sure he was every bit as concerned.

"Something is up," Robert said. "I can feel it."

Jack nodded. "We'll know in a minute."

"Make that thirty seconds," Robert said. He killed the engine and nudged the tips of the pontoons onto the mud.

"You got it." Jack rushed ashore.

Soukis stood waiting for him at the top of the riverbank. His hands rested on his hips. His expression showed he was surprised to see them there. But no more stunned than Jack was to find the women gone.

"Where's Kazuko and Pillai?" he asked, getting right to the point. He saw no reason to bother with pleasantries.

His question brought a furrowed brow from Soukis.

"They went upriver with Fletcher." He looked Jack up and down. "Can I ask what this is about?"

Jack peered down at himself. His clothes were filthy, his shirt snagged and torn from the night run through the jungle. And he had to stink.

He couldn't care less.

"Bjornson's dead," he answered coldly. "Douglas, too. They were murdered."

"Murdered?"

"At the lab," Jack said. "Yesterday, Robert and I found the source of the cyanide that's been poisoning the river. There's a massive breach in a tailings pond at a mine upriver near a village named Kaburi Landing. We told Bjornson and Douglas about the leak, and they were killed so they couldn't report it to the Ministry of Health. We're sure the man who ordered the murders wants you and your team dead, too."

"Are you're sure the mine's not far from Kaburi Landing?"

"Just upriver from there, according to the map in the plane." Jack narrowed his eyes in suspicion. "Why?"

"That's where Fletcher and the women were headed."

CHAPTER 35

Jack was close to exhaustion when he settled into his seat in the plane. But he wouldn't dare let himself doze. He exchanged looks with Robert and noted the weary resignation showing in the deep lines at the corners of his eyes.

He'd owe Robert big time.

Looking at the expanse of jungle spreading out before them, Jack took in the immensity of it. The thick sea of vegetation seemed to go on forever. The sight made him realize he had forgotten why he had been excited about accepting the bull shark research project in the first place. And why he had asked Robert and Kazuko to join him there.

"This hasn't exactly been the holiday you expected, has it?" he asked.

Robert cracked a tired smile. "I don't think you'll find it listed in any of the guide books, if that's what you mean."

"Kazuko's a big girl," Jack said, hoping to reassure his friend.

"And she's been in really tough situations before. We both know that," Robert admitted. "Pillai, too, from the way she talked. But they've stepped into the snake pit and don't know it. Being grown up doesn't have anything to do with it."

"Not exactly what I meant."

"I know what you were saying." Robert sighed. "She's street savvy. Both of them are. I don't know about the guy with them. He could be a total nerd. But even if he's some macho scientist, they are no match for Gourde."

"You've got that right," Jack agreed. "But we don't know if the sonofabitch—if it *is* him behind all this—even knows where to look for them."

Robert furrowed his brow. "Directly or indirectly Gourde's responsible for the murders of those other scientists. You know it, and I know it. Hell, he ordered us killed. As far as him or his thugs not knowing where to look for Kazuko and Pillai, I'm not going to bet on that."

Jack scanned the river ahead. He wouldn't make that bet any more than Robert would. Nor would he stake the women's lives on it.

There was no underestimating Gourde.

The bastard was capable of anything.

"So how long until we get there?" he asked.

"What's that?" Robert gave Jack a blank look.

"Kaburi Landing." Jack could tell his friend's mind had wandered. "That's where we're going, isn't it?"

Robert let the question hang in thought a few quiet seconds, then said, "You're probably right. There's no way Gourde or the scum working for him could know the women traveled to Kaburi Landing any more than we did. I'm just overreacting."

Overreacting. The possibility never entered Jack's mind, not even for a second. They were reacting exactly the way they should. They were getting the women the hell out of there.

He shook his head. "Not even a little bit."

Robert's gaze didn't waver. "So you haven't gone soft on me?"

Jack could see where this was headed. "You know me better than that."

Robert faced the windscreen. Jack watched his friend increase power, and then redirect his attention back on him.

There was more to be said.

Robert asked, "You were insinuating there was nothing to worry about, weren't you?"

Jack grinned. Now they were playing. "Was I doing that?"

"Of course you were," Robert said. "But I figured if you

considered the matter long enough, you'd come to your senses."

Jack was glad for the friendly banter. "Just took a little prodding."

Within minutes, Kaburi Rapids came into view, beyond that lay Kaburi Landing. Still some distance away, but they were getting close. He figured he didn't need to point out the white water. He saw Robert stiffen in his seat.

He knew what was coming up.

"Think there will be any argument?" Jack asked.

"From Kazuko," Robert shook his head, "no way. How about Pillai?"

"They already tried to kill her once. When she hears what happened to Bjornson and Douglas, I'm betting she'll be ready to get the hell out of there."

"Then we don't spend a minute more here than we have to," Robert said. "We load 'em up and fly out of this place."

"Home free, as they say."

Robert shot Jack a look. "I'll believe that when we're in the air."

"Five minutes—in and out," Jack assured him. "Nothing will go wrong."

CHAPTER 36

Gourde continued to smile as he tightened his finger on the trigger of the automatic rifle. Then he heard the familiar sound of helicopter rotor blades beating the air, and the smile slipped from his face. He peered into the sky and searched out the chopper. Not the Sikorsky Billaud used. It was a Bell 205 utilized by the government.

And it appeared to be making a pass over the OMG mine.

Gourde felt the gravity of the situation close in on him. He'd believed he was on the brink of gaining control of the problem and already it had fallen apart on him. In spite of his efforts to contain the threat, word had somehow reached Deputy Minister Paulette Sukhai's desk at the Ministry of Health.

There was only one answer. The scientist in Bartica had placed a call before his death.

The worst possible development.

"Drag these bodies under the bushes where they are out of sight," he ordered. He waved the barrel of the rifle toward the undergrowth to get the women moving in the right direction. "And be quick about it if you don't want to die like your big-mouthed friend."

Kazuko and Pillai exchanged worried glances.

"Let's do it," Pillai said.

"I don't know if I can."

Pillai sighed. "It's that or we die."

Kazuko leaned close and whispered, "What about our guide?"

"Jagan," Pillai kept her voice low, "I almost forgot about him."

"He was at the boat. Surely he heard the shots."

"Let's hope he has sense enough to hide."

Gourde grabbed Pillai and gave her a shove. "Move your ass, now!"

"Stop it," Kazuko said.

A backhand from Gourde knocked her to the ground.

Pillai helped Kazuko up. Without a word more, they went to work. The forest fringe was only a few yards away, making the job of pulling the bodies into the bushes less demanding. But even so, it obviously took all the willpower the two women could muster to manhandle the rotting corpses into the undergrowth.

"I can't touch her," Kazuko said to Pillai when at last only the dead mother and child remained.

Gourde had watched the helicopter circle the OMG mine. It was clear what they were doing. They'd likely make a pass over Kaburi Landing just to satisfy themselves that the villagers were safe.

"Them, too," he said, jabbing the barrel of his rifle at the mother and child. "And make it quick."

Kazuko glared at Gourde. "You're a monster."

"Perhaps," Gourde said. He leveled the AK-47. "And I can easily shoot you dead and be done with it."

Pillai grabbed hold of Kazuko's arm and tugged. Her eyes pleaded for Kazuko to do as they were told.

Kazuko huffed away her disgust. "Let's get this over with."

Gourde pulled a straw hat from a nail on the side of the shack and tugged it onto his head to hide the blood in his hair. Judging from the sound of the rotors beating the air, the government helicopter approached Kaburi Landing from upriver. He had not wanted to be standing out in the open when the chopper made its pass. But what choice did he have? The crew would surely land and investigate if they saw the village deserted. That's how it would look from the air.

This confrontation he wanted to avoid.

"Stand close to me and say nothing," he said to the women. Kazuko seemed to be the defiant one. He took hold of her arm and twisted it behind her. "Remember, I can kill them just as easily as I can kill you."

He kept Kazuko on her feet close enough to him so that no one standing in front of them could see her arm bent behind her. She seemed to realize it was useless to resist. He was relieved to see Pillai playing along as well. He didn't need any more trouble from these two.

Not that he wasn't ready for it.

He held the automatic rifle in his right hand with the safety off and his index finger close to the trigger guard.

He watched the Bell helicopter bearing the Guyanese government seal bank around the village and slowly settle onto its skids in the center of the complex. He'd hoped they wouldn't land. There was little he could do now but trust that the women were smart enough to not try anything foolish.

The co-pilot's door swung open and a man climbed out. He ducked to avoid the twirling blades. From the stressed look on his face, he was not happy to be there. Gourde let the man come to him.

Provided he didn't get too close.

"What's happened to everyone?" the official asked from a couple of yards away. His gaze fell on the gun but he did not appear to be disturbed by it.

"Moved into the forest," Gourde answered.

"My name is George Campbell," the official said, keeping his distance. "I'm with the Ministry of Health."

Gourde was glad he didn't have to shoot the man. He didn't need any more trouble. He had enough.

He said, "I've seen the dead fish."

Campbell glanced around curiously and pressed the back of his hand to his nose. "The smell's awful."

"It's the fish," Gourde offered. He knew the carcasses rotting in the water were only part of the stench, but he hoped to draw the official's curiosity away from the bodies in the brush. "Do you know what's killing them?"

Campbell motioned his hand toward the Mazaruni. "We're still looking into it. But apparently a mining operation on the other side of the river suffered a breach in its tailings pond. I'm afraid great quantities of cyanide leaked into the water. It's killing the fish and even some of the larger animals. We're warning people along the river not to drink the water or eat the aquatic life."

Gourde felt Kazuko stiffen and tightened his grip on her wrist. "Then we should be going before the danger worsens."

"That certainly would be advisable." Campbell's gaze shifted from Kazuko to Pillai. He smiled. "But only if you're traveling upstream. Until the danger can be fully assessed, river travel below this point is not recommended."

Gourde relaxed a little when he saw the official's lips curl up at the corners. It was the women. They'd proved to be a pleasant distraction.

And the reason for Campbell's death, should he step any closer.

Gourde kept Kazuko's arm twisted behind her. "Surely, you're not serious."

He saw the smile slip from Campbell's face.

"I assure you," Campbell said. "I am quite serious."

CHAPTER 37

Gourde tightened his grip on Kazuko's wrist and cast a warning glance at Pillai, as the high-pitched whine of the helicopter's turbine engine built into a deafening scream. He wasn't going to chance any last second heroics on the part of the women.

They would be dealt with, but only after the chopper was gone.

The whirling blades became a blur that beat the air into a vicious downdraft. The grass flattened; the nearby bushes and trees whipped about as if struck by the gale force of hurricane winds. He saw the skids relax as weight was taken off of them. Then all at once, the Bell 205 was airborne.

The government official was no longer a concern.

Letting go of Kazuko's arm, Gourde stood his ground and watched the helicopter bank and disappear from sight over the dense jungle canopy. One major annoyance had been dealt with. But there would surely be more.

Events were unraveling fast.

Once again, he found himself in a position of having to give careful thought to his next move. The unexpected appearance of the government official changed everything. The stakes had been raised. The mine would likely be shut down for a yet undetermined length of time while damage to the river system was assessed and extensive fines levied. The OMG main office in Toronto would become involved.

His and Billaud's plan was falling apart.

Billaud might yet slip away with the gold. The deal may still go through. Gourde wanted to believe he would get his share of the money. But then he knew there were no guarantees that would happen.

He had to think.

"On the ground," he ordered Kazuko and Pillai. "And sit on your hands."

Kazuko massaged her wrist and sat down next to Pillai. They exchanged worried looks.

"So what happens now?" asked Pillai, redirecting her attention to Gourde.

"You shut your mouth and do as you're told," he said.

He needed to not worry about the women for a moment. There were other things to consider. Like the forty pounds of gold in the pack in the boat, and the ingot he had stashed in his pocket.

A million dollars' worth.

He had to get the gold to Salazar on his yacht. Billaud was there now brokering a deal. Somehow Bakker had stolen forty pounds of that gold. Salazar would be expecting the entire amount.

He would be willing to pay.

And if Billaud failed to show, Gourde told himself, forty pounds was well worth any risk he would take getting it there.

He'd have his money even if Billaud didn't.

For a moment he eyeballed the women. He'd tired of the Amerindian whores at camp. If he had the time, he would strip the two women naked and satisfy his deepest, darkest carnal lusts. Sexual games that would arouse their inner beast; or leave them begging for mercy. Either way the game was the same for him. In the end, they would wish they were dead.

He noticed a coil of rope hanging on a nail hammered into the outside wall of the hut nearest to him. Lifting the thick cordage from the spike, he tossed it to Pillai. "Tie your friend's hands behind her back, and tie them tight."

She caught the rope and stared at it. Then she refocused her gaze on Gourde. Hatred showed in her eyes, so did a reluctance to do as she was told.

"I'll do no such thing," she said, letting her hand drop to her side. But she kept hold of the rope.

He was not going to give her time to think about what he'd said. Nor was he going to allow her to tell him what she would or wouldn't do. He stepped close and pointed the muzzle of his rifle at her head.

"That was not a request," he said. "It was an order."

Pillai looked down at the rope in her hand, and after a couple of seconds faced Kazuko. The expression on *her* face was just as disdainful. But what would further defiance on their part get them? Plainly, neither of them had a choice.

Kazuko quietly turned and held her hands behind her back.

"Sorry, but I'd better do as the prick says," Pillai told her. "I'll try not to make it too tight."

"You make it tight or I'll shoot you in the head and do it myself," grumbled Gourde.

"Do what you have to do," Kazuko said over her shoulder to Pillai.

Pillai took her time doing it, but she did as ordered. When she was done, she looked at Gourde. "What now?"

"Stand up and face me." He wasn't done with her.

Again, she did as she was told. Uncertainty showed in her eyes.

Gourde reconsidered his earlier thought. There was little time to waste on lustful indulgences, but he needed to teach these women a lesson. And he knew just how to do it. Humiliation was a good place to start. Make them feel less than human. He'd begin with Pillai and make Kazuko watch.

In one swift motion, he ripped the buttons from Pillai's blouse. The shirt fell open exposing her bra and the tops of her breasts. She was on the verge of being a few pounds overweight. It would add to her embarrassment.

Not that it mattered.

Pillai stiffened, but made no attempt to resist.

"You are wise to not disobey," he said. "You may, however, feel differently before I am done with you."

Again she did not move or respond.

Gourde pulled his knife from the scabbard on his belt and

slowly slid the blade between her breasts. "Believe me, you'll wish you were dead."

He saw her raise her chin in defiance.

A pathetic show of will.

He smiled. And with a flick of his wrist, cut the bra where it joined at the center. Her ample breasts spilled out. Her areolas stood out large and dark against her bronze skin.

A glimmer of lust sparkled in his eyes.

"You're a pig," Kazuko said through jaws tight with anger.

Gourde laughed. "Watch and learn."

Pillai stood firm. But she cringed when he started toward her with the knife a second time.

He held the blade for her to see it. He only intended to cut her a little. Make her bleed just enough.

But that's only to start.

The fear that had replaced her look of indignation brought a smile to his lips. She would be a long time forgetting Gerard Gourde.

If she lives.

The roar of a plane coming in low and fast swept the smile from his face.

He turned and looked toward the bend in the river downstream from the village.

Not there yet, but it was close. A minute, maybe two, no more.

"You," he motioned the rifle barrel at Kazuko, "inside the hut, now." He waited for Kazuko to do as ordered. Then he forced Pillai inside at gunpoint.

CHAPTER 38

Jack leaned toward the windscreen, studying the river ahead. He didn't want to miss the women if they had stopped to rest before challenging the rapids. On the periphery of his vision, he saw a helicopter coming toward them.

"We've got company," Robert said.

"I see it." Jack leaned back in his seat and studied the craft: a Bell, not the Sikorsky. "It's not Gourde unless he has moved up in the world."

Robert kept them on course. "We'll know soon enough."

The helicopter buzzed past them on the left side of the plane. He studied the chopper as it went by. "That was a government seal on the door of that eggbeater."

Jack brought his head back around and faced the windshield. He'd noticed the markings, too. There was only one explanation he could think of. "Bjornson must have gotten through to the Ministry of Health before he was murdered."

"Be my guess," Robert said.

"Which means Kazuko and Pillai are out of danger."

"We can hope."

Jack held onto the thought that the nightmare of the past few days was over. If government officials were aware of the culprit responsible for leaking millions of cubic meters of cyanide waste into the Mazaruni, there was no logical reason for Gourde to go after the research team.

Still, he couldn't help but wonder.

Gourde had done nothing to indicate he was anything close to logical.

Jack was sure Robert would agree. "We stick to our plan, right?"

"Nothing has changed," Robert assured him.

The next few minutes passed agonizingly slow. Finally, Jack saw the power boats pulled up on shore. One had boxes stacked in it; supplies for testing the water, brought there by Pillai, Kazuko and Fletcher. Then he saw the village.

Deserted.

Not what he had expected to see. At the very least Kazuko and Pillai should be collecting their water samples. Fletcher too, if he was around.

But no one was moving about.

"See 'em anywhere," Robert asked.

"They must be inside one of the huts." Jack wanted to remain optimistic.

"Hope you're right."

Robert set the plane down with practiced skill and taxied it toward shore next to the boats.

Jack *did* hope he was right. But after all he and Robert had been through with Gourde and his band of cutthroats, he wasn't as sure as he'd liked to be. The unexpected had turned into the expected.

He pulled back the slide on the .45 semi-automatic to assure himself there was a round in the chamber. There was. He released the clip into his hand and saw three more. Four shots . . . it was all he had left.

He prayed that was enough.

When they were close to shore, Robert shut down the engine and let the plane coast onto the muddy riverbank. The pontoons hit the muck with a jolt and remained there.

"Are you waiting here?" Jack asked as he opened the door to the cockpit. He figured Robert would want to go with him.

"No way," Robert said, unbuckling his seat belt.

"Will the plane stay put?"

"I wedged her pontoons high enough on the mud to hold her.

It should be good enough for as long as we're going to be here."

"Let's make it fast," Jack urged.

"You start with the huts on that side and I'll check the ones on this side," Robert suggested. "We'll meet in the middle."

"Sounds like a plan."

Together they raced to the clearing at the top of the slope. With little more than a quick glance around by each of them, Robert went left and Jack went right. He carried the Colt .45 semi-automatic he had taken off Hawk Nose. A necessary precaution given what they had been through. There was only one thought on his mind: finding Kazuko and Pillai and getting out of there alive.

What worried him was what had happened to the women.

They should have shown themselves by now.

CHAPTER 39

Gourde pushed the plank door closed and peered through a gap in the boards. He had a view of the clearing leading to the river and the brown water of the Mazaruni beyond. A perfect vantage point to see who was coming.

He turned and faced the two women. First there was the government helicopter. Now this. The world was closing in on him. But there was no going back.

Not now.

Again he pressed his eye to the crack in the door. The engine roar was loud now. The plane was close. A second later he saw a floatplane come into view and settle onto the surface of the river. The same yellow and white floatplane that passed him in the helicopter the day before. The plane Robert and Jack flew. There weren't two alike in the territory.

But how could that be?

Somehow the two men had escaped from the cabin. They were handcuffed and chained to a stove. And yet they broke free. There was no way that should have been possible.

Alive when they should be dead.

He cursed Cheddi Norton.

And now they had flown here to warn the research team. *The women . . . .* Why else would they have come to Kaburi Landing?

He fumed, ready to burst from the hut and shoot them down.

His face flushed warm. No one did this to him and lived.

No one!

But then . . .

Almost as quickly as he'd become incensed by the situation, he swallowed his anger as rage gave way to reason.

River travel was no longer an option. This was his way out.

He watched the plane. After all the things that had gone wrong, this could very well be the stroke of luck he needed. Or was it providence?

All he had to do was play his cards right.

He turned and looked at the woman with her hands bound behind her. And the woman standing next to her, Pillai—she would be of no use. Kazuko was the ace in the hole.

When he saw Jack and Robert step ashore, he stiffened, ready to make his move. Out the door, hold the gun to the woman's head, and force Robert to fly him and the forty pounds of gold to Salazar's boat.

Robert and his troublesome woman could be done away with then, after they had served their usefulness. The other two could be dealt with now.

Off to his side, Kazuko and Pillai took a step backward. He noticed the women move. It was enough to remind him they could still cause him trouble. Not that it would change what was going to happen.

"On the floor," he muttered. "Do as you're told and you might live a little longer."

Kazuko narrowed her eyes. "What are you going to do with us?"

"That depends on your boyfriend."

"Robert?" Kazuko stiffened.

Gourde curled his lips into a sick smirk. "He's going to fly me to Georgetown. You'll be coming along."

"But—"

"Enough talk. On the floor . . . and keep your mouths shut."

Kazuko's hands were tied behind her. Pillai's shirt hung open. Her arm was pressed flat against her breasts. A modest gesture. They were in no position to argue.

"Now," he said.

That would hold them until he was ready. When they did as they were told, he returned his eye to the crack in the door. Jack and Robert were already at the top of the riverbank. Both of them moved fast.

And careless.

Gourde continued to watch the two men. The pieces were falling into place. It would only be a minute now. They were making it easy for him. And then he saw Jack head toward the huts on the opposite side of the village.

Dammit.

He hadn't counted on the men splitting up. He focused his attention on Robert who continued to walk directly toward him. He'd wait until he was closer. But not too close.

Then he would spring his trap.

He remained confident in his plan. Robert would have no choice but to do as he was told or die. Jack, too. Neither of them would let anything happen to Kazuko and Pillai.

The women would give him the time he needed.

"You," he said to Kazuko. "Stand here." He pointed to the floor beside him. "And you," he looked at Pillai, "stand next to her."

They moved, but not fast enough.

"Hurry," he said. "And keep quiet."

Pillai hastily knotted her blouse at the waist and helped Kazuko to her feet.

Gourde returned his eye to the crack. The moment Kazuko stood next to him, he stepped back, jerked open the door, and shoved her out ahead of him.

CHAPTER 40

Jack walked fast in a low crouch with the semi-automatic pistol in his hand. He heard commotion on the opposite side of the compound, looked, and saw Kazuko stumble sideways onto the ground. Her hands were behind her. *Tied.* She hadn't reached out to break her fall.

He spun with the bore of the .45 pointed in that direction.

Robert was stopped in his tracks. A fraction of a second later, Jack saw why. He held his shot.

It was Gourde. And he was dragging Pillai along with him.

Her hands were free, but she was in no position to resist. Gourde wore a khaki shirt with sleeves rolled to the elbows and bush pants. The same clothes he had on the day before. Only now he carried an AK-47 assault rifle with the muzzle pointed at Robert.

Thirty yards, Jack thought, too far for a pistol shot with Pillai in the line of fire. *Run*, he told himself. And do it now. You have no choice but to find another way to help them.

Instead, he hesitated.

Mistake.

Gourde let go of Pillai, turned, and fired a short burst from the hip. A bullet seared the skin on Jack's left arm. The others went wild.

Jack turned to the jungle and ran.

When he was well within the cover of the foliage, he crouched and looked back at the compound. Gourde had been more confident

172

in the rifle than in his being a good shot. *Spray and pray* as it was called.

That was his mistake.

Peering through gaps in the plants, Jack could see his friends and Gourde in front of the shack. Gourde had the gun pointed at Robert. Kazuko was sitting on the ground. Pillai was on her knees, but she had managed to edge backward a few steps. Gourde did not appear overly concerned about her.

And he hadn't shot any of them yet. That meant he was keeping them alive for a reason.

The plane.

It had to be. That's why—Jack reasoned—Gourde hadn't killed them on sight, and why the big man hadn't chased after him.

Gourde needed a pilot.

Robert.

Jack knew all too well there was nothing he could do at the moment but wait and hope none of them were executed before an opportunity to save them presented itself. He had the .45 and he had four rounds. Enough to do what he needed to do, but not at this range. He had to move closer without getting shot in the process.

He'd be no good to anyone, dead.

He'd give the situation a second or two to play out before he made his move. Just to be sure.

Gourde's vicious scheme became clear when he jerked Kazuko to her feet and used the barrel of the gun to move Robert toward the plane. Exactly what Jack figured would happen. But where were they flying to?

And what about Pillai? She obviously did not figure into the plan.

He tensed his muscles, ready to run. There was a lot of ground between him and Gourde to cover. But he couldn't let the big man kill her.

She deserved every chance.

Jack considered his options: Try to sneak around the village and flank him; or run straight at the man and hope for the best. One course of action would take time he didn't have. The other was suicide.

His decision was made for him when a dark-skinned, machete-wielding man ran from the jungle fringe near Gourde.

A desperate act bent on surprise.

But Gourde was quick to react. He shot the man dead.

Robert made a move. The muzzle of the rifle stopped him. He straightened and pulled Kazuko close.

Pillai ran for the forest.

Like Jack, she had no choice but to flee.

She'd be next to die.

But she never gave Gourde the chance. Jack saw the big man's expression harden in desperation as he kept the gun trained on Robert.

The stranger had died, but his death allowed Pillai to escape.

Now there was only Robert and Kazuko to worry about.

"Get going," Jack heard Gourde say.

He was definitely not spending any more time there. He let Pillai go without giving chase and marched Robert and Kazuko toward the plane.

Jack watched them walk in a tight group. He was hoping for a clear shot. But the opportunity wouldn't present itself as long as Gourde kept Kazuko close to him.

Which is exactly what he did.

The trio walked to the plane without stopping. Gourde swept the compound with his gaze but kept the rifle pointed at Robert.

Jack could sense his friend's helplessness.

He moved sideways in the undergrowth, staying hidden while at the same time keeping them in sight. He still hoped for a clear shot. It wasn't happening. And then the three of them descended the riverbank, making it even more unlikely he would get a chance to take the big man out.

A second later, he heard two cracks of Gourde's rifle.

Not at Robert or Kazuko; something else.

What?

Resolve settled in when Jack watched them push the plane off the mud and climb aboard. Gourde—with a backpack in hand—followed Kazuko onto the rear passenger seats. Robert sat in front doing the flying.

Jack couldn't stop what was happening to his friends. All he was able to do was watch.

He bit back his frustration.

Crouched low amid the branches of the bushes, he saw the propeller spin to life with the roar of the engine. A minute later, the twin pontoons skimmed the surface of the Mazaruni. And all at once the plane was airborne, heading east.

That's all he knew.

That, and the glaring fact that the situation could not end well.

CHAPTER 41

Jack broke cover and sprinted across the compound to check on the man Gourde had gunned down. The sight drew him up a few feet short. There was no reason to check for a pulse. The guy was obviously dead—shot in the head. Half of his skull was missing. Most of his brain with it.

The man on the ground was beyond help, but Pillai was in the jungle, hiding.

For good reason.

Jack scanned the forest fringe. He didn't see her, but he did notice the stench of death was strong on this side of the village. There was no doubt in his mind, more than this one poor soul died here. Several, judging by the smell.

And then he saw the bodies tucked in under the foliage.

More of Gourde's bloody handiwork. Or perhaps the river had killed them. It didn't matter which. The end result was the same.

"Jack." It was Pillai's voice.

He looked and saw her step from the bushes and walk tentatively toward him. He could see now what Gourde had done to her, or intended to do. The tails of her shirt were tied together at the waist, but there was no mistaking the blouse had been ripped open. And her bra was cut in the middle.

Jack didn't need to see her tattered clothes and the fear widening her eyes to want to kill the guy. But it made him swear an oath.

Gourde was a dead man.

He tucked the .45 into his waistband and reached out to her. "Are you okay?"

She took his hand in hers and stepped closer. "He didn't hurt me, if that's what you mean."

He picked up on the desperation in her voice. He felt the same. "Do you have any idea where that asshole was making Robert take him?"

"He mentioned Georgetown."

Jack glanced around. His gaze swept over the bodies lying in the brush. "It's just you and me here, I take it?"

Her eyes searched his and held. He waited.

"That monster shot Fletcher," she managed.

Jack heard her voice catch in her throat as she said it. Without question, she was upset by the murder of her friend. She was a strong-willed lady struggling with her feelings, keeping her emotions in check. But barely.

Hearing Fletcher's name made him aware that he had forgotten about the other member of the team.

Kazuko and Pillai had gone upriver with Fletcher, he'd been told.

"That man there, who was he?" Jack nodded at the corpse, the machete lying nearby.

"Our guide, Rodger Jagan," she answered with a sigh.

"And the others?"

"I can't be sure," she said. "I think they died from cyanide poisoning."

He studied the position of the corpses. If the villagers had been poisoned by the water in the river, they hadn't died where the bodies lay. They'd been moved. "Did Gourde drag the bodies there?"

She peered at the ground. "He made me and Kazuko do it."

Jack did not see a need to press further. He eased Pillai close and took her into his arms. She didn't resist.

And he held her.

She wrapped her arms around his waist and settled her cheek onto his shoulder. His mind swirled with a myriad of thoughts. She felt good in his arms: warm, soft, all-woman flesh nestled tight against him. *Quite inviting and easy to become lost in.* But the desire stirring inside him would have to wait. Robert and Kazuko were speeding toward Georgetown or God knew where else, leaving Jack no time to spend languishing in a beautiful woman's embrace.

Still, it seemed a hug was exactly what Pillai needed. And now he realized, so did he.

"There's nothing for us to do here," he said after a moment. "We have to find Robert and Kazuko."

She pulled away, sniffing back a tear, and peered toward the river as though she'd arrived at the same conclusion. "There's the boat we came in."

He'd already considered that option. He wasn't excited about running the rapids he'd seen from the plane, but it seemed that was their only choice. He sure didn't want to try to hike all the way to Marshal Landing.

"If you're good to go," he said. "We'd better get a move on."

"There's nothing keeping me here," she answered.

That was all he needed to hear. He led her straight to the boat with the boxes of supplies stacked in it. The growl in his stomach reminded him he hadn't had anything to eat or drink since leaving Norman Varga's house. Food could wait. Not their thirst. Grabbing a couple of plastic bottles of water, he handed one to Pillai.

"We won't be good to anyone if we keel over from dehydration," he said.

She offered a weak smile and unscrewed the cap, but she didn't raise the bottle to her mouth and take a drink. He waited. She had to be as thirsty as he was.

Suddenly, her hands began to shake.

He didn't blame her. She'd been forced to endure a lot. She'd go through more before the ordeal was over.

They still had to make it downstream for help.

"You're okay," he said in reassurance. "We'll get through this. So will Robert and Kazuko."

Her doe eyes met his. They were glassy with tears.

"Martin, Rodger, those other people that died here," she said, nodding toward the village, "they didn't deserve to die like that."

"No, they didn't," he agreed.

"What makes men like Gourde do such awful things?"

"Some people are just born evil."

"He can't be allowed to get away with this."

"He won't."

Jack emptied his bottle in three long gulps and tossed the empty into the bottom of the boat. Still operating on adrenalin, he climbed over the food, water, and analysis equipment and took a grip on the tiller to the outboard motor. Only then did he realize the reason for the shots he heard. Gourde put a bullet through the center of the engine cowling and into the motor.

But there had been two shots.

He dreaded what that meant. "The motor's ruined," he said as he scrambled ashore. "I'll check the other one."

Pillai hurried along with him. She stood on the bank while he climbed aboard to make a check of the outboard.

"Well?" she asked.

He looked at her, wishing he had better news. "Same as the other one. A bullet through the heart."

"What do we do now?"

He studied the dugout canoes. He had no desire to end up in the water. And they no doubt would if they tried shooting the rapids in one of those. But they could use the paddles.

"We row."

CHAPTER 42

Jack gathered two of the sturdiest paddles he could find and a couple extra for good measure. Maneuvering an eighteen-foot wooden boat with paddles more suited for a canoe was not going to be easy. But at least they were traveling with the current. They'd let the river carry them to Marshal Landing. And with a little skill and a lot of luck they would be able to keep the boat off the rocks.

He counted on both.

Handing a paddle to Pillai, he shoved off and hopped aboard. And when he dug the wooden blade of the paddle into the water to straighten the boat out in the current, he realized just how difficult a task they were up against. It was like trying to maneuver a fallen redwood.

The first minute felt impossible. A calamity of rowing errors on both their parts.

Neither of them spoke.

They dug their hand-carved, short-handled oars into the water in a furious effort to control the craft. But the current grabbed hold of the stern and spun the bow around so that it pointed upstream.

Jack huffed his frustration. If they continued downstream sideways or even stern first their chances of making it through the raging cataract alive were slim.

"You forward paddle," he said, finally. "I'll back paddle."

She rested her pitifully inadequate oar on the gunwale and

gasped for breath. "I thought that's what we *were* doing."

"We were," he admitted with a tone of disappointment, "first one direction, then the other. But we weren't working together. We need to get this thing pointed downstream bow first or we'll never make it through the rapids."

"What we need is a motor, or at least a rudder of some sort."

"Right," he said. "And that gives me an idea."

"What idea is that? Surely you're not telling me you can fix the outboard?"

"No, but I might be able to fashion a rudder of sorts."

There was no time to waste talking. He removed the line securing the supplies and grabbed up one of the extra paddles. The current was carrying them downriver surprisingly fast. If he was going to get it done, he needed to do it now.

Before it was too late.

Working as fast as he could, he tilted the Evinrude, raising the prop out of the water, and locked the motor in place. Then he went to work lashing the paddle to the propeller shaft housing. He had to lie partly on the transom and partly on the engine cowling to complete the process. Even then it was shaky, but he got it done. And when he had the line wrapped and tied as tight as he could manage, he lowered the makeshift rudder into the water.

"That should do the trick," he said. "At least it should help. But we still need to straighten this thing out."

"Let's do it then." She put her paddle in the water and started rowing.

Jack threw his legs over the rear seat and joined in. Working in concert and with great effort, they managed to straighten the boat. And none too soon.

The white water of Kaburi Rapids came into view fifty yards ahead.

"Hold on," Jack yelled and manned the tiller.

He had to place his trust in the makeshift rudder. They were at the river's mercy now.

The raging current grabbed hold of the boat and swept it forward as if the motor had suddenly kicked in. But it was the river narrowing, forcing millions of gallons of water through the boulder studded shoot as if blasted through a fireman's nozzle, that supplied the power.

If they survived, it would have everything to do with luck.

He saw Pillai working her paddle, doing her best to keep the boat straight. But it was difficult for her to row and hold on at the same time. It was like a theme park ride where anything could happen. Most of which were not good.

And one outcome, unthinkable.

He sure didn't want them to end up in the river with a mouth full of cyanide water.

"Forget about trying to paddle," he yelled above the roar of the rapids. "Just hold on and try to not get wet."

She didn't answer, but he saw her drop the paddle into the bottom of the boat and grip the forward edge of her bench seat with both hands. He hoped she could hang on. When she glanced over her shoulder at him he saw a look that betrayed unmistakable determination. She would never allow herself to be thrown overboard by the waves. The boat would have to sink first.

With a smile of renewed perseverance, she refocused her attention on the danger looming in the rapids ahead. There was little about this woman he didn't admire and respect.

She was a fighter.

Without power from the outboard to speed the boat along at a velocity beyond that of the current, he found it was difficult to keep the craft on course. Had it not been for the makeshift rudder, the wooden hull would surely have been swept sideways and dashed to pieces on the boulders. But at times, even the extra steerage was not enough. He repeatedly fought the tiller, working it from side to side, like a steering oar on a raft to bring the bow back in line.

A desperate act destined for failure. It was like being sucked into a funnel. Still, he fought the current with one thought on his mind: make it through the rapids and it was clear sailing all the way to Marshal Landing.

They had to make it.

And then he saw the rocks parting the water directly in front of them.

CHAPTER 43

Jack heaved on the tiller, desperate to maneuver the boat into the center of the channel. It was no use. He was helpless to stop what was happening. The river was in control of the fragile craft.

And the bow was headed straight for a boulder.

All he could do was hold on and hope Pillai did, too.

"We're going to hit," he yelled.

"Jack—" was all she could manage in reply.

A second later, he felt a hard thump that jarred him in his seat and threatened to rip the tiller from his grasp. Wood cracked, but held together. Water sloshed over the side. He managed to hold on and watched Pillai being tossed sideways onto the stack of supplies, as boxes spilled their contents into the bottom of the hull. An instant later, he felt the bow ride the pressure wave up and over the edge of the monstrous rock and slide sideways into the roiling water beyond.

The boat tipped.

He was sure they were going over, but somehow the vessel righted itself and stayed in one piece. But they were caught in a swirling eddy, like a rubber duck being sucked down a drain. For what seemed like forever, they were held there. Then all at once, the craft broke free of the whirlpool and they were thrust back into the rapids.

He frantically fought the turbulence to put the boat on a straight course. It seemed he was powerless in the grasp of the Mazaruni. The river would take them where it wanted them to go.

And there was nothing he could do to keep that from happening.

He peered ahead hoping to see calmer water. What he saw instead, were great waves kicked up like rooster tails, and menacing monoliths.

The worst was yet to come.

With great effort on his part and a lot of luck, the bow finally came around, taking the tumultuous hell head on. He fought to keep it there and was relieved not to be going downriver sideways or even stern first. But he couldn't help wonder if the wooden hull would stay in one piece if it took another hit. The shattered skeletons of less fortunate craft littered the riverbank on both sides.

Kaburi Rapids held its own boneyard. And there was room for yet another victim. More lives lost.

He prayed they weren't the next two.

Pillai had moved back to her seat. And by the way she held on, he knew she was determined to not let herself be knocked around by a river that seemed intent on killing them both.

She peered wide-eyed over her shoulder at him as if she wanted to say something, but held her thoughts. The look in her eyes was enough. There was nothing he could tell her that would relieve the fear he saw there. Even if he could be heard above the unremitting roar of the raging torrent.

All he could do was pray.

The vessel continued through the rapids. The fragile hull bobbed and bounced over submerged rocks as it was sucked through one watery shoot after another. With the passing of each obstacle, he was more and more certain they would make it through alive.

Then a car-sized boulder appeared in the water ahead.

The optimism he had just a moment before was replaced with certainty that their boat would be smashed to pieces.

He held his breath.

A loud thump and a violent jolt spelled doom. But the wooden hull sideswiped the unyielding stone without splintering apart. And once again, they were caught in the suction of a swirling eddy.

He let himself breathe, unable to believe their luck.

Like before, they were eventually kicked free of the whirlpool and tossed back into the turbulence. He wanted to believe they were through the worst of it, and held onto the hope it could only get better from this point on. Which at the moment didn't appear to him to be possible.

The vessel dug into the wall of waves and took water over the bow. The hull spun sideways and slammed into a rock. He heard wood crack. The craft regained an even keel and continued on in the relentless current.

The soaking they were getting was enough to wet their clothes, but not enough to drown them. A wild ride, but nothing like the one he'd taken on the island of Kauai when the incoming tide sucked him through a submerged lava tube and spit him out in a grotto deep beneath the Na Pali coast.

A smile of reassurance from Pillai brought him back from his thoughts of that day on Kauai. After a moment he understood what she was grinning about. The roar of the rapids was diminishing. The surface was smoother. He studied the channel ahead. And even though there were no boulders churning up the water, the river was moving them along unbelievably fast.

Suddenly, he saw Pillai stiffen and glance back at him. Then he heard it, too. A great rumble of water.

The relief he felt turned to a vision of a final monstrous rapid. White water more terrifying than any they had gone through. He wondered how Pillai's guide had gotten them past such a seemingly formidable barrier. That became obvious when he saw calmer water on the opposite side of the river.

But without a motor they were a victim of the current. They had no choice but to ride it out.

The boat was moving along at a good twenty knots and appeared to be funneling into a narrow trough between two large boulders. As they approached the concentrated surge, the rumble of cascading water became deafening.

He didn't need to tell Pillai to hold on. She was already doing that. There was nothing more they could do. The nightmare held them firm in its grasp. They were going over.

All intelligent thought evaporated from his mind as the boat shot though the gap bow first. The craft came terrifyingly close to smashing against the gigantic boulders, but skirted by. And then it dug into the turbulence below, sending up a wave of water that flooded over the hull. Instinctively, he clamped his mouth shut and held his breath. Only when he was sure the vessel had somehow remained afloat did he let himself breathe.

He was afraid he had lost Pillai, but she was sitting on her bench, soaking wet and swearing at the world.

Very much alive.

The boat had a foot of water filling it to the bottom of the seats, but the hull was intact. They had taken on the worst the river had thrown at them and won. But his relief was short-lived.

In the next instant, a massive boulder concealed inches below the surface of the water splintered the port side of the hull a few feet ahead of Pillai. She screamed. Next, the shaft of the outboard hit something hard and unyielding.

At once, the motor ripped loose from the transom, taking wood with it. More water flooded in through the split hull.

He had no choice. With so much water flooding in, he had to move forward and take a seat next to Pillai. She moved about as if she didn't know if she should stand up or remain sitting. He pondered that same question himself.

He laid a calming hand on her shoulder. "Don't abandon ship yet."

Her eyes opened wide. "But we're sinking."

"Not entirely."

The boat had a little more to give. Had it not been made of wood, the craft would have sunk. But the partially submerged vessel moved sluggishly through another short spill of rapids and then they were clear of the whitewater. The hull was a ruined mess, but the boat stayed afloat.

"You all right?" he asked.

Pillai sighed. "Alive."

He nodded. "You didn't swallow any water, I hope."

"I kept my mouth closed. You?"

"Hard to do in all the excitement, but I managed." He searched around for their paddles and found one. "I'll row us ashore."

Pillai pointed, "There's a creek over there. Aim for that."
He hoped for the best.

CHAPTER 44

Two of Salazar's armed security personnel escorted Billaud up the steps to the top rear deck of the drug lord's hundred foot yacht. The private launch that had brought Billaud from the harbor at Georgetown, remained to return him to shore when his business aboard was concluded. He tolerated the inconvenience of meeting on the ship and followed along with his weasel-faced escorts and their automatic weapons. He was anxious to negotiate the sale of the gold and thought about asking them to hurry, but opted for discretion. The past day's events prompted him to act fast.

But careful.

Having gazed upon the yacht's ostensible opulence beyond the mere size of the gleaming white vessel, he couldn't help thinking Salazar had more money than he knew what to do with. He could more than afford any deal they struck.

The price would be to both their advantages.

Billaud welcomed the shade of the awning stretched taut over the rear deck. He'd begun to perspire . . . for two reasons.

He couldn't calm his nervousness. Not until he was off the ship and on his way back to the mine. Only then would he relax.

The canopy, at least, would block the sun.

"I want to thank you for meeting with me on such short notice," he said to the dark-haired, middle-aged man he recognized from their meeting a month earlier.

That's when the ball was put into motion. It was time to consummate the deal. The price of gold had hit a record high.

Salazar appeared to consider his words. Dressed in a black silk shirt unbuttoned to the middle of his bare chest, he sat alone at a table set with a midmorning breakfast of scrambled eggs, fruit, toast, and coffee. Armed men stood beside and behind him. The chair opposite him was empty. He wore a heavy gold chain around his neck and massive gold rings on several of his manicured fingers. Sunglasses hid his eyes.

The man had obviously watched way too many American movies.

"I did not expect to hear from you for another month." He did not get up from his seat or extend his hand in greeting. He slowly returned his fine China coffee cup to its matching saucer with casual indifference. "Something has changed?"

"It has," Billaud said.

"Well?" Salazar forked up a bit of melon, and chewed.

Billaud noticed he hadn't been asked to sit. Nor had he been offered coffee or something to eat. Not that he was hungry. He considered sliding a chair away from the table and taking a seat anyway. He humbled himself to no one. Not even the Canadian mining corporation he worked for.

But that would gain him nothing.

He'd make Salazar the exception.

In explanation, he said, "There have been certain inconveniences that have arisen which make it necessary for me to negotiate the sale of gold now rather than later."

Salazar laid his fork next to the food on his plate and stared directly at Billaud. "These inconveniences you speak of, they will not cause problems for me?"

Billaud understood Salazar's concern. The man was a drug supplier of immense wealth and power. On the surface, people and governments believed he was a rich businessman and philanthropist operating well within the law. He did not want that image to change.

But that was Salazar's problem, not his.

"Your involvement is only the purchase of the gold," Billaud assured him. "The problems I speak of will be Toronto's issues to resolve once I have my money and am gone from this place."

Salazar's gaze did not waver. "The Guyanese government will not be happy when they discover they did not receive their five percent."

"The government is not my concern."

"Nor mine." Salazar smiled. "As long as the business we conduct here remains between you and me."

Billaud glanced nervously at the automatic weapons held by Salazar's security personnel: Heckler & Koch MP5 9mm submachine guns. German design—one of the most widely used submachine guns in the world—favored by military, law enforcement, intelligence, and security organizations.

And Escobedo Salazar.

"Gerard Gourde and I are the only two who know," Billaud said. "No one else has any knowledge of this transaction."

"How can you be sure of that?" Salazar's tone was calm but sharp edged.

"What are you suggesting?"

"I'm suggesting nothing. I'm telling you that I intend to conduct further business in Guyana and I do not want to become the project of some overzealous bureaucrat out to make a name for himself."

Billaud did not completely buy Salazar's concern. The man was wealthy beyond imagination, and powerful in ways that immense sums of money can buy. So what was this game he was playing? Was it his way to drive down the price? Or was it merely an exercise of intimidation and control?

His way of doing business.

Billaud asked, "Why would a man like you fear an underpaid official in a pissant country like Guyana?"

Salazar's expression remained impassive behind his dark glasses. "Politicians and governmental bureaucrats can be bought, or dealt with in more severe ways if necessary," he said. His tone turned cynical. "But even a lowly official in a pissant country—as you put it—can open the watchful eyes of international drug enforcement agencies. It is my neck that is on the line here, not yours. If the deal you seek with me has designs beyond making you rich, it would be wise of you to remember this: you will most certainly die first."

Billaud ignored the drug supplier's jackal shrewdness. There was no mystery in what was going on here. He and Salazar were entering into a short-term relationship of minimal trust built on respect for Salazar's power and cold, efficient willingness to kill anyone standing in his way.

Not unlike himself, thought Billaud.

"The events I spoke of spun out of control quickly in spite of my efforts to prevent that from happening," he offered, hoping to dispel Salazar's concern. "But as I already said, they have no connection to you. So there is no need to threaten me. And do not concern yourself over Gourde. He has as much to lose as I do if word of this transaction were to find its way to the wrong ears."

Salazar's expression reflected doubt. "Pray that it doesn't."

More intimidation . . .

Billaud studied the unmistakable look of uncertainty etched on Salazar's face. The man did not trust easily. No doubt he suspected everyone. The price he paid for dealing drugs.

Much the same as stealing gold, thought Billaud.

He was weary of the drug dealer's threats.

"I came here to conduct business," he said. "Can we discuss the gold now?"

CHAPTER 45

Billaud stepped aboard the launch, eager for the quick shuttle back to shore. He was less than satisfied with the deal he had struck with Salazar. The gold should have gotten him more than the three and a half million they agreed upon. But the man had proven to be more difficult than anticipated. It appeared the drug dealer's desire for gold was slightly less than his obsession for people to fear him.

The thought made Billaud chuckle inwardly. One man the jackal and one the fox.

Two men the same.

They were both getting what they wanted.

And now he had to move fast. Salazar had proven to be unpredictable and prone to violence. There was the possibility he would insist on renegotiating the transaction regardless of his initial offer.

Billaud couldn't chance that happening. Not now. Not with so much on the line.

And it wasn't only money at stake. If the deal fell through, there was the cyanide contamination in the river to consider. And even more serious than that, the scientists' murders loomed over his head.

Jail might be the least of his worries.

It came as a relief when he saw Gedeon McLean waiting for him at the dock. The helicopter pilot had proven his worth. All it would take to spoil the entire plan was one word from him to the wrong person. The small payoff he'd get to insure that didn't happen was money well spent.

"The bird is fueled and ready to go," McLean volunteered.

"Good," Billaud told him. "We leave for the mine, immediately."

"I have a cab waiting."

Billaud followed McLean to the taxi and slid onto the back seat. McLean climbed in on the front passenger's side. Before he had the door pulled closed, he said to the driver, "The airport, and make it fast."

"As you wish." The driver started the tiny sedan and chirped its tires when he mashed on the gas pedal and sped the car away from the harbor without delay.

Not fast enough.

Billaud settled into his seat for the short drive to the waiting helicopter. But he couldn't shake an increased sense of urgency with each passing minute.

Time was running out.

* * *

Billaud nervously scanned the cloudy sky during the hour-and-a-half return flight to the mine. Below him the Mazaruni flowed dark and untamed. There was much for him to be anxious about. His first thought when Gourde delivered the news that Jack Ferrell and his friend Robert had been dealt with, was that there was time to move forward with the plan in a cautious manner.

Now he wasn't so sure. Much could have happened during the few hours he was gone from the mine.

Anything was possible.

He could only hope Gourde had managed to contain the problem. Bakker and Smedt may have already silenced the research team at Marshal Landing. All trace of their bodies erased. Only then would he be able to relax.

In the distance, he saw the yellow and white floatplane flying east and dismissed it. Jack Ferrell and Robert were dead. So were the scientists at Bartica. The loose ends that threatened to unravel his plan had been eliminated.

Or had they? He suddenly feared things had gone badly.

The worst of which were realized when he dialed in the governmental channel on the chopper's radio and heard a flurry of chatter between pilot and base about the leak at the mine. Officials were talking about shutting down the entire operation until a full assessment of damages could be made.

He felt his face flush hot with anger. The research team at Marshal Landing must still be alive. Bakker and Smedt had failed.

They had been warned.

He had tolerated Salazar's threats because he had no choice. He'd made his own against the men who worked for him. And he was just as intent on carrying them out.

But the blame did not rest solely on their shoulders.

Gourde had traveled here with him years earlier to oversee the operation of the mine. And when prices skyrocketed on the world market, they conspired to take the gold for themselves.

A perfect plan.

And Gourde failed to see his orders carried out. That simply should not have happened.

The mine came into view and he cooled some. Not toward Gourde; or Bakker; or Smedt. He would deal with them decisively. But first he'd have the gold loaded aboard the helicopter without delay and consummate the transaction with Salazar.

Nothing would prevent him from getting that money.

All of it!

He convinced himself he would eliminate Gourde for his failure. There was no room for a partner who betrayed his loyalty—even someone who considered himself a friend. Bakker and Smedt would never receive a penny for their part in the theft. That had been a foregone conclusion from the beginning. But Gourde's incompetence had come as a surprise. The man never failed to do what was needed.

Till now.

He studied the compound as the helicopter neared the ground. The men toiled in the pits the way they always had. For the time being, they were still pulling gold out of the gravel beds. But where was Gourde?

The chopper's skids settled onto the ground. He continued to glance about. Gourde should have been there to meet him.

What more can go wrong?

CHAPTER 46

Jack dug the blade of the paddle deep into the water and heaved back on it. The muscles in his arms and shoulders bunched under the effort. The water-logged craft moved with the current and reluctantly toward shore. Like rowing a fallen tree.

And all too slow.

He'd begun to itch in the toxic soup that soaked his clothes and flooded the boat. What he didn't know was if the itchiness was from his mind tricking him or if cyanide was actually burning through his skin.

They needed to get to that stream.

Pillai clawed at her arms and vigorously rubbed each one. She shot him a look over her shoulder and said, "Let's hurry and wash this contaminated water off our skin."

She was thinking the same thing he was.

With so much water in the boat, he couldn't beach it high on dry ground. A minor problem since they were already soaked. He managed to wedge it on the muddy bottom close enough so they only had to wade a few feet to reach the stream.

He followed her out of the boat. "Go," he said. "I'm right behind you."

She glanced behind her and kept going.

The clean water beckoned them both.

They waded into a deeper section of the stream together. There was no needless discussion, no nervous chatter. Only urgency on both their parts to get the cyanide rinsed from their clothes and skin.

He stripped off his shirt and pants and boxers and rinsed the toxic sludge from them while he stretched out in the flowing water. The relief was immediate. He noticed Pillai turn her back to him and do the same. Her bra had been discarded at the village, but she still wore white cotton bikini panties suitable for work in the jungle. Other than the modesty of turning her back while she washed, it didn't seem to bother her to strip in front of him.

She was as eager as he was to scrub away the chemicals threatening to poison them.

He tossed his clothes into a pile onto the stream-bank and made an effort not to look at her, but caught himself staring as he languished in the refreshing coolness of the water. Their attraction to each other the first day they met had been immediate and undeniable. Looking at her now, he felt that sensual lure even more. She was a smart, wonderful, brave lady.

And she was beautiful . . . all of her.

He wanted to take her in his arms and kiss her long and passionately. To give in to a need brought on by their brush with death. Satisfy the desire burning in his loins.

It was impossible for him to look away, but he tried. Then he saw her stand and turn her big dark eyes on him. He wondered if she struggled with her feelings the way he was battling his own.

Two denied lovers caught in an impossible situation.

For an eternity they stared at each other. He could practically feel her gaze sweep the length of his body . . . as his gaze did her. It wasn't enough.

Not for him, or her.

He rose out of the water at the same time she started wading toward him.

It seemed corny to want to run to her like a character in an old movie, but he did. He took a step and she sloshed to him.

No inhibition. No childish embarrassment.

Warm woman flesh pressed against his. A jolt of excitement shot through his body like an electric shock. And they were entwined in each other's arms, lips pressed together in a passionate kiss. Reassurance. Comfort as much as desire.

For a long moment they just held each other. His hands slid to her waist and he pulled her to her toes. They clung to a kiss for an eternity before separating.

And when their bodies were apart, the jungle around them came alive with bird sounds he hadn't noticed until now. It was as if nothing mattered. Nothing was wrong in the world. Then he was abruptly pulled back to reality by the telltale *whop, whop, whop* of a helicopter larger than the two-passenger bug Gourde flew in. Still a ways off, but getting louder.

Someone was coming.

Their way out.

Robert and Kazuko had never been far from his thoughts—even on the river when fighting the rapids. But he'd allowed himself to become caught up in the tender moment with Pillai. Undeniably, the mutual attraction was there. It seemed inevitable they would wind up in each other's arms.

No expectations, no regrets.

He gripped her shoulders, eased her close to him, and kissed her once more on the lips—quick and without the passion that'd fueled the earlier embrace. The brief interlude of intimacy they had shared was not lost. But any further explorations would have to wait.

"Break's over," he said. "Time to get dressed."

She returned his peck on the lips and hurried to where her soggy clothes lay in a pile next to the stream. Pulling on her pants, she said, "Saving lives doesn't leave much time for romance, does it?"

He had to laugh. There was something about her that made him feel warm inside and very much alive. Just looking at her took his breath away.

"Just because I let you have your way with me," he kidded, "doesn't make me an easy mark for all wanton girls looking for a good time."

She tied the tails of her blouse together at the waist and shook out her long dark hair. And then she was smiling. "Who are you trying to kid? You are most definitely easy."

He shrugged and tugged his pants up around his waist. "Maybe

I just have a thing for exotic, young, shapely women stranded in the jungle."

She started walking toward the river bank. Glancing back at him, she asked, "Brings the animal out in you?"

"You have no idea."

"Oh, I think I do."

He finished dressing, tucked the .45 into his rear waistband, and let the shirttail cover it. Hurrying, he caught up to her and took her hand in his. She stopped walking and looked at him in a way that made his knees go weak. He wanted to wrap her in his arms and kiss her and not let go. He wanted to forget the dangers they'd faced, and those that lay ahead. And he wanted to forget that Robert and Kazuko were being held at the mercy of Gourde.

But he could never abandon his friends.

They needed him.

He gazed into Pillai's dark eyes and made a promise, "Next time I take you in my arms it will be in a king-sized bed, with a bottle of expensive champagne chilling in an ice bucket on the table beside us."

There was a quiet moment. Nothing was said by either of them. It was as if just the thought of such a wonderful time together was enough to make everything right.

All at once she rose on her tiptoes and kissed him. Pulling back, her smile returned. "The caring, the kiss we shared, you were wonderful."

He chuckled softly. "Lady, you haven't seen anything yet."

CHAPTER 47

Jack waved his arms above his head, and out of the corner of his eye he saw Pillai doing the same. Given the roar of the bird's engine, it was useless for them to shout in order to draw attention. The helicopter had come in low over the river: a Bell 205 with a government seal pasted on the door. He figured it was the same one he and Robert saw earlier. It made sense. There couldn't be that many like it flying around.

They yelled anyway—just in case.

They didn't want the crew to fly by and miss seeing them.

The chopper made a wide looping turn, swung in close to shore, and hovered there. The violent downdraft beat the water flat and kicked up a cloud of debris from the bank. Jack recognized the passenger peering through the side window in the rear door.

Alec Soukis.

He raised his palms in front of his face to shield his eyes from the blast and saw the researcher point. He guessed Soukis had come looking for Pillai and the rest of the team. A valiant effort to take them to safety, but too late to do Robert and Kazuko any good—or Fletcher. But not too late to fly Pillai and him out of there.

He had to get to Georgetown and find Robert.

But first the helicopter needed to land. He scanned the riverbank. The only place where there was enough room for the chopper to set down was the small clearing where he and Pillai stood. Even

200

then, the pilot would only be able to set one of the skids on dry ground. And he'd have to keep it there long enough for them to climb aboard. A dangerous maneuver—he knew—but it was their only choice.

If the pilot knew what he was doing he could pull it off.

Turning to Pillai, who was standing directly beside him, Jack pointed over his shoulder at the jungle fringe. He maintained confidence in the rotorhead's flying ability. He had to. Otherwise they weren't going to make it. But the pilot needed them to back off if he was going to have enough clearance to attempt the maneuver.

He hoped the guy understood what they were doing.

"Give them room to set down." He yelled loud enough for her to hear him.

Pillai nodded and the two of them hurried back to the tree line. And when Jack stopped and faced the river, he saw the pilot position the craft close to shore and settle the passenger side skid onto the mud.

Just as he hoped, the pilot was amazingly skilled.

"Let's go," he yelled.

Taking Pillai by the hand, he ducked under the spinning blades and led her to the rear cabin door. He opened it and helped her aboard. She climbed inside, and he entered right behind her.

They plopped onto seats next to Soukis, and Jack reached for the door. Almost before he had it closed and latched, the chopper was airborne. He buckled himself in and slid on a pair of headphones that were hanging on the bulkhead. At once, Soukis was asking if they were all right and what happened.

Pillai had slid on the other pair of headphones. Her voice—reflecting excitement and bewilderment—cut in, "What are you doing here? How did you know?"

"Mr. Campbell"—Soukis nodded at the man looking back at them from the seat next to the pilot—"stopped at Marshal Falls to warn the villagers not to drink the water. Jack and Robert had stopped by earlier looking for you and Kazuko. They told me about Philip and Douglas. When I told Mr. Campbell our team was researching the problem and that you had gone upriver, he told me he'd possibly seen you at Kaburi Landing. We were both concerned, so we flew up here to make sure everything was all right and to tell you to return to Marshal Landing. I hadn't expected to find you stranded on the river with Jack. What happened to Martin and the others?"

The pilot continued upriver. Jack realized where they were headed.

"We need to turn this thing around," he interrupted. "There's no one alive at Kaburi Landing. But Robert and Kazuko are, and they need my help."

"What are you saying?" asked Soukis.

"Martin's dead," Pillai said. "He was shot. So was our guide."

Jack explained, "A man named Gourde—he's connected to the mine responsible for poisoning the river—shot them both and took Kazuko hostage at gunpoint so Robert would fly him to Georgetown."

"Philip and Colton . . . now Martin—" Soukis shook his head, sadly. Leaning toward Campbell, he said, "Ask the pilot to fly us back to Bartica. We can talk to the police there."

Jack grew more frustrated as the chopper banked into a wide turn. He wondered if Soukis understood the seriousness of what he'd been told. Enough time had already been lost. Every hour counted.

Robert and Kazuko needed help, *now.*

"I need to get to Georgetown," he demanded. "My friends need my help."

"Pillai and I have to get back to the lab," said Soukis. "Our equipment, all our work is there. Arrangements have to be made."

Jack sat a moment in tense contemplation. Soukis wasn't getting it, or he placed too much faith in the local police.

Faith Jack didn't have.

And there was another problem he'd thought of. Gourde's thugs were there. They'd be out for blood.

His blood. Maybe theirs, too.

"I'm not sure that is a good idea, not yet." He had to make Soukis understand. "It might not be safe for you."

"I appreciate your concern. We'll notify the authorities."

"And what then?"

"They'll look after your friends."

"I'm not so sure."

"I can have the pilot drop them off in Bartica," offered Campbell. He'd obviously been listening in. "And take you on to Georgetown with me."

Jack scanned the anxious faces of the people seated next to him. Soukis looked determined, but no more than he was. "Just so I get there," he said. "And we don't waste any more time than we have to."

"I'm going with you," said Pillai.

Jack hadn't expected her to insist on going along. The idea of leaving her in Bartica with Gourde's killers on the loose didn't exactly sit well with him. But the nasty business ahead would likely turn very ugly, very fast—given what he had in mind. And no matter how much he enjoyed being with her, he didn't want her caught up in what he planned to do to Gourde, or anywhere nearby when it went bad.

"As much as I would like to have you with me," he said, "I think it would be best if I do this alone."

"And if I don't see you again?" Her tone reflected concern.

Jack knew what she was getting at. She was worried about him, and for good reason. Still, he had every intention of coming out of the situation alive . . . along with Robert and Kazuko.

He couldn't imagine it any other way.

"We have a date, remember?" He gripped her hand. "I'm not going back on my promise. You just give me your word you'll stay safe."

She gripped his hand. "You're the one who needs to be careful."

CHAPTER 48

Robert set the floatplane down on the surface of the ocean, thankful for smooth water. A rough sea could have spelled disaster for all of them. This way they had a chance. Now there was nothing he could do but follow orders. The gun muzzle pointed at Kazuko's head made sure of that.

"Okay, I got you here," he said. "I don't suppose you'd consider swimming the rest of the way?"

Gourde grabbed a handful of Kazuko's hair and jerked her head back. Her eyes pinched tight in pain. But she didn't cry out.

The big man's lips curled into a smirk. "How about I just shoot her?"

Robert winced.

"Not so funny, huh?" Gourde said when he didn't get an answer. He pointed with the gun. "Take us in close to the yacht."

Robert taxied the plane in that direction—doing what he was told. He'd held onto the belief he and Kazuko could come out of the situation alive if they went along with Gourde's demands. A sinking feeling in his gut said otherwise.

The situation was getting worse, not better. Still, he had to play along—for the time being—and hope he was wrong.

"What then?" He had to ask.

"Depends." Gourde's tone reflected uncertainty.

Robert wondered if Gourde was playing by ear—grasping at

straws.

The actions of a desperate man.

Robert didn't know who he should be more afraid of, Gourde or the man on the boat. He doubted either of them could be reasoned with, but Gourde had the most to lose. The man on the boat could simply send them away and that still left Gourde with the problem of what to do with his hostages.

Caught between a rock and a hard place.

Robert didn't like the odds.

"You've got your gold," Kazuko said, massaging her scalp. "Take it and go. You don't need us."

"I want you to keep your mouth shut," Gourde snapped.

"She's right," Robert pointed out. "It's obvious the gold in that bag is the only thing that matters to you. Take it and take your country. We're out of this place the moment you let us go."

"This is not my country," Gourde grumbled. "And you'd be wise to keep your mouth shut as well."

"If you don't like this place any more than we do, think about it." Robert still hoped to be able to reason with the guy. "We're out of here; you're out of here. We'll never see each other again."

"You're half right, anyway." Gourde answered.

Robert didn't need to be told which half he was right about. But he was not ready to accept death as being inevitable. Not while there was still fight left in him. Also, Jack was out there. He would not run out on them. There was always a chance the cavalry would arrive in time to save the day.

With that thought in mind, he motored to within thirty-feet of the yacht and shut down the engine. He wasn't surprised to see armed men waiting for them; their automatic weapons pointed in their direction.

"This is as close as I can get," he said. "It's your show."

Gourde did not answer. He opened the door to the cockpit, and hollered, "Tell Mister Salazar that Gerard Gourde is here to do business with him. He'll know who I am."

Robert watched one of the armed men lower his gun and walk in the direction of the rear deck. Hopefully the owner was a reasonable man, and not the killer Gourde was.

Almost as soon as the plane floated to a stop, it began to slowly drift away from the anchored yacht. There was minimal pitch and roll in the calm sea. Nothing had changed. Still, the tide and the onshore breeze made it impossible for the plane to hold its position.

The gap widened.

"Keep us up close," Gourde protested.

"I'll have to start the engine to do that," Robert answered. "And then we need to tie off to that ship or we'll just drift away again."

"Do it," Gourde demanded.

Robert taxied the plane up close to the yacht a second time and shut down the engine. He could only imagine what Gourde had in store for them. He'd keep them alive as long as he needed someone to fly the plane. And to make him do that, Gourde needed Kazuko. That meant they'd both stay alive a little longer.

Perhaps long enough, Robert thought. He still wasn't counting Jack out.

To Gourde he said, "Holler up and tell them to throw down a rope. We're already starting to drift."

"You do it," Gourde said. He shoved the rifle muzzle under Kazuko's chin.

Robert wasn't about to argue. He'd do anything that would buy Kazuko and him another few minutes of life.

"Throw down a line," he hollered from the open cockpit door.

The gunman who'd walked aft was almost back to his post. As he approached the other men, he motioned with a wave of his hand to the man nearest him. Robert couldn't hear what was being said, but a second later a nylon rope was tossed down. He climbed from the cockpit and secured the end of the line to a strut supporting the pontoon he stood on.

From the deck of the ship, the gunman yelled, "Mr. Salazar says you can come aboard. Wait where you are and we will send a boat to pick you up."

Robert hoped this was the end of it.

He opened his cockpit door to relay the information to Gourde and saw he had his door open. He was in the process of dragging Kazuko out of the cabin by her arm, rougher than he needed to.

"You pig," she screamed, as he hauled her out the door. "You're hurting me."

Robert cringed. There was no limit to the man's cruelty. He wanted to climb through the cabin and wrap his hands around the big man's throat and squeeze the life out of him.

A taste of the hurt he so eagerly dished out.

But Robert knew that if he tried he would only succeed in getting her killed—him, too, most likely.

"You're here," he said, "let us go."

Gourde manhandled Kazuko onto the pontoon. She stood massaging her wrist where he had grabbed it. He pointed the muzzle of the AK-47 at Robert. "I'm not done with either of you yet. Cause problems and I'll put a bullet in your little lady friend's pretty face."

Robert squeezed his eyes shut at the grisly vision. He had to back off. Pulled from the thought by the roar of an outboard, he opened his eyes and saw the fifteen-foot Zodiac speeding toward them.

He'd take his chances with Salazar.

CHAPTER 49

Robert stumbled on the gangway and almost fell. He resented being pushed along by his armed escort. There was no reason for it. Nor was there a reason for the armed man in front of him to drag Kazuko along by her arm.

Salazar's men were no better than the asshole Gourde.

A rifle butt prodded Robert another step aft. He didn't bother to look behind him. He was more worried about Kazuko's safety.

They only wanted to be away from there.

Far away . . .

They had no interest in the owner of the boat or what he was doing in Guyana. Any deal he struck with Gourde was between the two of them.

Salazar had to know that.

Robert wanted to say as much. Still, he kept his mouth shut. That was the smart thing to do. He could see no future in provoking the armed men. They were only paid thugs. But Kazuko struggled with every step. She was having a harder time tolerating their barbaric treatment.

"Let go of me," she groused, and tried to wrench her arm free.

The grip on her wrist tightened. Kazuko's expression screwed into a knot of pain. Robert bit back his rising anger.

"You're hurting me," Kazuko said between clenched teeth.

"Move, puta," The man holding her arm shoved her onto a

stairway leading to an upper rear deck.

Robert clenched his jaw. There was nothing else he could do.

But it didn't make him less irritated. He and Kazuko had to play along and hope for the best. Even though it seemed like they were being marched deeper into hell.

He followed Kazuko up the steps, doing his best to stay close to her. Maybe they would leave her alone if he did. A not-too-gentle prod in the back by a rifle barrel made sure he stayed in step.

It wasn't necessary.

A half minute later, he stood on the aft deck looking at a dark-haired, middle-aged man dressed in a black silk shirt unbuttoned to the middle of his bare chest. *Salazar.* The man sat alone at a table. Armed men stood to the side and behind him. He wore a heavy gold chain around his neck and massive gold rings on his fingers. Sunglasses hid his eyes. He sipped from a coffee cup.

One look at Salazar told Robert the man was a drug dealer.

Not what he'd hoped for.

But he welcomed the shade of the awning stretched taut overhead. He gave Kazuko a reassuring smile. He was as scared as he had ever been; she had to be as well. At least they weren't forced to stand in the direct heat of the mid-day sun.

But that did not change the fact that they were prisoners.

He scanned the deck. Salazar's goons stood with automatic rifles trained on him and Kazuko. He noticed the guns were equipped with noise suppressors. No one on shore would hear the shots if they were fired. That was evident. No doubt he wanted people who came aboard to know that.

It had a psychological effect.

Even Gourde glanced around as though he were nervous with all the firepower focused on them.

Serves you right, asshole.

The bastard hadn't been shoved along the gangway getting here, Robert thought, but at least the sonofabitch stared down the same bores Kazuko and he had to deal with.

A small measure of satisfaction.

He paid close attention when Gourde stepped to the table. The backpack had been stripped from his hands. A man armed with a submachine gun slung from a black nylon strap stepped forward and laid it on the table.

"Mr. Salazar," Gourde began.

Salazar raised a hand, stopping Gourde. To Robert, Salazar said in an accent unmistakably Spanish, "I can't say I am happy to see you here."

"I assure you we don't want to be here." Robert fought his nervousness, doing his best to act calm. He glanced at Kazuko. "Since none of this concerns us, we'll be on our way."

"Perhaps you do not understand the seriousness of the situation."

"I think I do understand. This man forced me to fly him here. Your goons have gone out of their way to be especially unpleasant." Robert glared at Gourde, hoping to focus the blame on him and away from Salazar. "That can be overlooked. Just let us go."

"It's unfortunate Mr. Gourde saw fit to involve you. But he did, and that cannot be undone."

Robert straightened. Salazar was not proving to be an understanding man. But at least he hadn't killed anyone . . . yet. There was still a chance he could reason with the man. He obviously enjoyed money.

That was evident by his lifestyle.

Robert waved at the opulence of the boat. "I'm sure we can arrive at some sort of deal that would make it worth your while to let us go on our way."

There was a moment of silence and he hoped he'd hit a soft spot. He held his breath.

"I am not interested in bargaining with you," Salazar said with total indifference. "You have nothing I want or need."

"Surely there must be something," Kazuko implored.

Robert was surprised she stayed quiet as long as she had. When her temper did not get in the way, she had a disarming manner that people warmed to. Maybe she could work her charms on the man.

They had nothing to lose.

Salazar smiled. "A provocative proposition. But my only concern at the moment is what to do with the two of you."

Robert felt the situation slip another notch.

She wasn't offering her body.

Kazuko's expectant expression slipped, and Robert quickly added, "How does a million U.S. dollars sound? Take us to shore and I'll have it wired to any account you wish."

"We do not have to go ashore to do that. I have a computer here."

"You might have a computer. But part of the deal is you let us go. I cannot be sure you'll hold up your end of the bargain if we stay here."

"Do not listen to this man any further," Gourde interrupted.

Robert saw Salazar's expression harden. There was no doubt he was a man of power who was not accustomed to having someone tell him what he could or couldn't do.

He gives the orders.

Stupid on Gourde's part, Robert thought. Maybe that could work in their favor.

"Who are you to tell me what to do?" Salazar's expression held the steel edge of a threat.

"I meant no offense," Gourde answered. "My interest lies in the gold I want to sell you. What you do with these two after we make a deal is up to you."

Salazar flattened his palms on the table and straightened in his chair. Robert took that as a sign Salazar was irritated.

They were no better off than before.

"Mr. Billaud has already been here," Salazar said. "If there is more to discuss, we will do that when he returns."

"But—" Gourde took a half-step forward.

At once a strong hand gripped his arm, stopping him in his tracks. Guns shifted in capable hands. Looks were exchanged.

Robert sidestepped his body in front of Kazuko.

"Do not provoke me," Salazar said, with a dismissive wave of his hand. "I see by the dried blood in your scalp, it is only by good fortune that you are here. It would be most unfortunate for you to press your luck further."

Gourde fingered the wound on his head and glanced around as though studying the armed men.

Robert held his breath and pressed closer to Kazuko. He didn't want them to be caught in crossfire. It was Gourde's predicament.

He kept his mouth shut.

"As for you"—Salazar turned his gaze on Robert—"the question remains as to what I am going to do with you."

"What about the million dollars? Do we have a deal?"

"Nice try. But I do not believe you have the money." Salazar motioned his hand toward two of his men. "Jesus, Gato, take the woman below."

Robert watched the two men drag Kazuko kicking and yelling into the salon. It was clear what was going to happen. His anger drove him to within a fraction of an inch of making a grab for Salazar's throat. The submachine guns at the ready in the hands of the drug dealer's security force made that impossible.

He prayed she would be safe.

Taking a deep breath, he silently swore Salazar would pay . . . with his life.

Still, he couldn't stand there and watch her dragged away.

"Keep your hands off of her," he said, fighting the urge to lunge at the man. But he couldn't stand not doing anything. He took a step and stopped at the sound of the guard's guns coming to bear. It tore at his gut not to rush after Kazuko. But he'd do her no good dead.

"You are in no position to make demands." Salazar's voice was void of concern.

It was easy to tell he had no qualms about what he was doing.

Robert held onto his resolve to see Salazar dead. Still, he realized the futility in making threats with no way to carry them out. Words meant nothing to a drug-dealing monster like him.

He narrowed his eyes and asked, "What do you intend to do with me?"

Silence . . .

He waited for an answer. It seemed like forever.

After a long moment, Salazar faced his men. "Sink the plane and toss this man overboard. Make it look like an accident."

Salazar's answer hit like a thunderclap.

Robert knew he had no choice. He glanced at the starboard railing. A couple of seconds was all he needed. A scream from Kazuko provided it.

He steeled himself to not be distracted by what caused her to cry out. He inhaled and held it. The guard's heads turned in the direction of the salon.

His chance.

He didn't hesitate, and reached the railing in two long strides. The instant he leaped, he heard a muffled 'pop' and felt the burn of a bullet crease his scalp.

CHAPTER 50

Robert hit the surface of the ocean stroking hard. His head throbbed as if it had been hit with a hammer, and the wound burned from the saltwater, but that meant nothing. All he could think about was getting away from the barrage of bullets ripping into the sea around him.

He arched his body and dove toward the bottom.

At ten feet, he leveled off and kept kicking—working his arms to the side to help propel him away from the deadly onslaught coming from above. The zipper sound of bullets streaking through the water ceased. The ocean was warm; visibility was forty-feet or more. Clear enough for the gunmen above to make out his silhouette. He hoped the surface chop prevented them from seeing him.

It was his only hope.

He angled for the shadow that marked the bottom of the ship's hull, and prayed all eyes were focused on the water astern where he had gone overboard. His oxygen was nearly expelled. He had no choice but to swim for the bow and a breath of air.

An impossible distance.

At last the anchor chain appeared in the gloom. But still a dozen yards to go. It wasn't going to be easy.

He swam steadily toward the bow, willing himself to make it. Fuzziness closed in on the edges of his vision. His heart beat a loud *thump, thump* in his ears. He dry swallowed to buy himself an extra few seconds. That he was risking exposure was without question.

There was little choice—do that or die.

He broke surface under the curvature of the bow on the port side. He sucked in several breaths of air while orienting himself. For the moment he was in the clear, but doubted he'd stay that way for long. Salazar would insist on seeing a body. And the man was not going to leave the floatplane tethered to the ship where it could be used to make an escape.

The order had already been given to sink it.

A crescendo of muted automatic weapons' fire signaled the end of the yellow and white De Havilland Beaver. Robert skirted the bow and watched the aircraft go under: engine first, then the tail—a nosedive for the bottom.

His hopes sunk with the plane.

Still, he had to stay alive. He was Kazuko's only hope.

For a moment he considered climbing the anchor chain up to the deck and going after her. But that would only get him killed. He'd be no use to her then.

He considered his choices. There was only one that wouldn't result in certain death.

His death.

He'd have to make it ashore and get help from the authorities. A half-mile was not too far for him to swim.

Providing he could avoid the watchful eyes of Salazar's men. Surely they would be watching the water waiting for him to show his head.

His fears were realized when he heard the scuffing of shoe soles on the teak above, joined with sporadic gunfire. They were roving the deck, shooting at any splash or shadow that vaguely resembled a man in the water.

He could hear talk, but it was in Spanish. Then he heard Salazar. "See any sign of him?"

"Not that we know of for sure," a man answered.

A second man spoke up in a deep-toned Spanish accent, "There is much blood on the railing where he jumped overboard. He moved fast but I was faster. He was dead when he went into the water."

"Then we should see his body," answered Salazar.

"Perhaps a shark ate him," the man with the deep voice said. "Or maybe the current swept the body away."

"Perhaps," Salazar said. "Keep looking."

Robert listened to footsteps fade away. At least two men had walked aft: Salazar and another man, possibly the third. He couldn't be sure. One of the men could have remained to keep watch. He could be up top right now looking down at the water, ready to shoot.

There was no way to know.

Robert felt the apprehension tighten his chest. He couldn't hold onto the bow forever. Help was on shore, which was a half-mile swim through open water—if he didn't drown. And if a shark didn't get him.

A real possibility.

Salazar had made the choice for him. He pulled off his shoes, tied the laces together, and draped them around his neck. Then he took several deep breaths, inhaled, and ducked under the water. He was an accomplished swimmer. He was sure he could put some distance between him and the ship before he would have to surface for a breath.

Stroking hard, he swam perpendicular to the boat. That Kazuko's fate rested in his making it to shore, pushed him well beyond his normal endurance. Another twenty feet.

And another.

His chest burned . . . his heart thudded in his ears.

He had to breathe.

He forced himself to swim a half-dozen strokes more.

When he surfaced, he resisted the urge to raise his head high out of the water and thrash about gasping for air. Instead, he broke it lightly and leaned his head back, taking in the badly needed oxygen with his face and mouth only inches above the water. A breeze ruffled the surface chop.

He was glad for that.

Even so, he could only hope a guard's eyes weren't looking in his direction at that exact moment. He wanted their eyes focused on something else . . . or nothing.

He didn't pause to look behind him.

It would gain him nothing.

He ducked under the surface, putting more distance between him and the drug dealer's yacht. It appeared to be working. He was still alive.

During his third trip to the surface, he did hazard a look back at the boat.

Close to a hundred yards separated them. Salazar's armed security force still roamed the decks, but their guns weren't aimed at him.

A speck on the ocean at that distance.

It was time he swam hard for shore.

Hopefully, the local authorities weren't on Salazar's payroll.

CHAPTER 51

Kazuko stood a few feet inside the narrow companionway at the far end of the ship's salon and glared at Salazar's man—the tall one with a spider web tattoo on the side of his neck. Gato, Jesus . . . she didn't know which one he was. She had only heard the men's names called out as she was dragged inside against her will.

And then she had heard gunfire. A sickening sound that she knew could only mean one thing.

Robert . . .

But she kept her hopes up that he was alive.

"I told you to keep your hands off of me," she swore, looking from one man to the other.

The guard facing her smiled. *Spiderweb*. His lips spread wide showing a mouth full of perfect white teeth.

Much too white.

She didn't like the look he was giving her.

"It's not our hands you should worry about," he said in an unbelievably cruel tone. "Before Salazar finishes with you there will have been many men's hands all over your body."

The implication was clear. She felt like she would throw up. A sour taste lodged in her throat. She swallowed the bile that had silenced her.

"He can't do this."

"He can do whatever he wants," the bearded man behind her

said.

She felt his breath hot on her neck. They pressed in on her, twisting her gut into a knot of panic. She turned so that her sides were to the men.

She wouldn't let them—

The door to the salon was there; she could see it.

Maybe . . .

She made a dash for the door. She had to get topside…get to Robert.

Spiderweb's strong arms stopped her. He shoved her backwards into the grasp of his partner. She felt the guard's beard on her bare neck.

She screamed.

Beard's hand clamped over her mouth.

She clawed at his cheek and tried to bite his fingers.

"Bitch," he grumbled, pulling his hand away.

Before she could orient herself, Spiderweb slapped her. The passage way dimmed in an explosion of stars.

She brought her head up and blinked away a tear.

Spiderweb's expression hardened. "You'll wish you had not done that to Gato. He has claws of his own."

Parallel scratches on Gato's cheek oozed red. Now she knew who was who. She drew satisfaction knowing she'd drawn blood. And figured she'd pay for it. But so would they.

She wasn't done fighting.

Both men seized an arm and hauled her down the companionway, forcing her deeper into the bowels of the ship.

"You can't do this." She kicked and struggled to pull free.

Their grips only tightened. She didn't give up.

One level down, Gato and Jesus shoved her into a small cabin. She stumbled forward and scanned the room for somewhere to run. Spartan furnishings and a single porthole window. Small wardrobe closet.

No other exit.

She faced Gato and Jesus. Their names weren't important now. "Please," she said. "Don't do this."

All she got were lecherous grins in return.

She knew the kind of filth that clogged their minds and steeled herself for what would come next. There was still some fight left in her.

Before she could react, Jesus shoved her onto the narrow bed.

Her stomach sank into a swirl of queasiness. But that didn't stop her. She bounded off of the mattress and swung at Jesus's face.

He caught her hand and punched her in the belly.

She doubled over, choking and gasping for breath. And at the same time, she sank to her knees. She could hardly lift her head.

"No. Please." The small, weak plea was all she could manage.

Jesus stood her up by her hair and ripped her blouse down the front. Gato was right there, reaching. He grabbed her from behind and pinned her against him. She had no fight left in her. It took all her will to stand.

That didn't seem to bother the two men.

Jesus did not stop with the shirt. He tore at the waist of her pants and jerked them to her ankles. A gleam showed in his one good eye when he stared at her smooth cinnamon skin. It was obvious the sight of her naked body aroused him.

His lips drew back in a sneer of animal lust.

The strength to resist gone from her body, she worked up a mouthful of saliva and spit in his face.

"So there *is* some fight left in you after all," he said.

She glared back at him as he wiped the spittle from his face with his hand. Then his rough fingers and palms were all over her breasts.

She slumped in Gato's arms, plunging into humiliation and terror.

This can't be happening.

She screamed. The outburst got her another backhand across the mouth. She tasted blood.

Jesus liked to hit.

At once both men's hands were all over her. Pinching her nipples and laughing. Groping, probing sensitive flesh—a suffocating nightmare of degradation that stripped her will away. She cringed.

And then they threw her onto the bed.

"We'll finish this later," Jesus said. "It would be wise to mind your manners when Mr. Salazar comes to see you."

"You're all pigs," she said, gathering her strength.

The insult did not seem to bother either man. They both turned and left the cabin. The sound of the lock being set in place sent a chill coursing through her body.

They would be back.

What then?

CHAPTER 52

Kazuko pulled on her torn clothes and tied the tails of her shirt in front. She stepped to the door and gripped the handle. She heard more gunfire from automatic weapons. A sporadic series of muffled pops, nothing more—but she recognized them for what they were.

A good sign, she thought. If Salazar's bodyguards were shooting, Robert could still be alive.

What else would they be shooting at?

She'd heard the latch close, but tugged on the door anyway. It was bolted tight.

The porthole?

She looked. It was too small for her to fit through. But she could see the ocean on that side of the ship. Maybe catch a glimpse of Robert swimming away. He was an excellent swimmer. He could make it to shore.

When she pressed her face to the glass, there was no sign of him, only a broad expanse of water.

Her shoulders sunk as despair crept in on her.

Robert was out there somewhere—she held onto that belief. Jack and Pillai were alive, but stranded in the jungle.

There was nothing for her to do but take a seat on the bed and wait.

Salazar would show up soon enough.

Jesus and Gato, too.

And then what?

She didn't want to think about that. She only wanted to believe that she would somehow come out of the ordeal in one piece.

Someone would come to rescue her.

As long as she was alive, there was a chance.

I'll find a way to persevere.

Convincing herself she could stay strong no matter what had been easy when she stood alone in the cabin. But that no longer seemed possible when the door opened and Salazar stepped inside.

When Gato and Jesus walked in behind him, she lost all hope.

They had returned to finish what they had started.

She stood by the bed and stiffened her back. The soreness in her stomach threatened to double her over. If defiance meant anything, she was showing all she had left.

"You have no right to keep me here," she said.

Salazar made no move toward her. He stood in the middle of the cabin, confidence showing on his face. "I do what I please," he said.

"That includes kidnapping?"

"If it pleases me."

"You think you are above the law. Think again."

He smiled. "No one who cares about you knows you are here. No one alive, that is. And when I am done with you, there will not be enough left of your body to find."

"Do you enjoy threatening women?"

"My dear, you have no idea what I enjoy. But you will soon."

A cold, eerie feeling snaked through her gut. Mad and terrified, not a good combination for holding one's tongue. She was both.

"If you're going to kill me"—she raised her chin in defiance—"do it."

"Soon enough," Salazar promised. "Unfortunately, I have business to attend to and do not have time for the prolonged sex games I have in mind."

She narrowed her eyes in disgust. "You bastard."

"I am many things, but I am not a bastard. My father trained me well. Some of what he taught me you might even enjoy. And after I'm done with you, you will pleasure my men; all of them."

She saw the gleam in Jesus and Gato's eyes. She already knew their barbaric cruelty. It wasn't hard to imagine how far their perverted pleasures would go.

Filthy pigs.

Anger swept aside fear. Tears welled as her body smoldered with fiery rage. She lunged like an enraged panther in the night and slapped Salazar's face. Not with enough force to knock him down, but hard enough to back him up a half step.

The swiftness of her attack surprised even her. It felt good to see him flinch under the sting of her palm.

Even if it wasn't enough to stop what was going to happen to her.

Just as quickly as he had been staggered back by the blow, he straightened. His eyes flared, and he shoved her onto the bed.

Jesus and Gato stepped toward her.

She could see the gleam in their eyes. They had undoubtedly waited for this moment. A raised hand from Salazar stopped them.

He rubbed his cheek. "You'll regret that."

His threat changed nothing. She wouldn't give him or his men the pleasure of backing down.

Not now, not ever.

"Go screw yourself," she said as she regained her feet. "Robert is going to come back here and kill you all. You might have your fun with me, but you'll die for it. That, I promise."

Salazar laughed.

She hardened her gaze. "You think that's funny?"

"This Robert guy you are talking about, you're referring to the pathetic excuse for a man you came here with. He is no concern to me. My men shot him and dumped his body overboard."

She sucked in a breath of disbelief.

Lying bastard.

Salazar would say anything to demoralize her.

She regained her composure. "All that shooting I heard . . ."

"The plane." His lips curled into a cruel smile. "I couldn't leave it floating out there for some nosy official to find."

His words silenced her. Fearing the worst, she hadn't considered that possibility when she heard them shooting.

Now she had to admit to herself that what he said was true.

But could she possibly believe Robert was dead?

Her shoulders slumped in despair. "He can't be . . ."

"Believe me," he said. "No one is coming to save you."

CHAPTER 53

Robert raised his head and chanced a glance at the yacht. The boat now sat well over a hundred yards away. He no longer worried about his head showing above the water, unless the gunmen used binoculars, they wouldn't be able to see him. But the swim to shore was taking longer than anticipated.

A lot longer.

And he wasn't out of danger yet.

Aware that there was still the possibility he could be spotted by the gunmen on the yacht, he chose his strokes carefully, mindful to make as little splash as possible. Soon, he began to chill. The adrenaline that had powered him on the boat and in the water minutes after leaping overboard quickly seeped away. And with it, the events of the past day and a half sapped the strength from his body. The relatively easy half-mile swim was turning into a grueling test of fortitude and will.

But the thought of Kazuko on that boat in the hands of Salazar and Gourde kept him swimming.

Nothing will keep me from going back for her.

Ten minutes into the grueling ordeal of reaching land, his arms felt like they had twenty-pound weights strapped to them. His legs had lost much of their kick and his pants were beginning to drag him down.

He couldn't let that happen.

Drawing on a Navy trick he'd learned from his grandfather who had served on the USS Enterprise in WWII, he stripped off his wet khaki bush pants. The concept was quite simple, really. He tied a knot in the ankles and swung them over his head to catch air, creating a reasonable float.

The makeshift life preserver provided relief—he no longer felt like he would sink into the sea and fade into oblivion, deep in its briny depths—but he wasn't content to just bob like a cork and let the surge carry him ashore.

Even if that were possible, he'd have to wait for the tide to change.

When that would be, he didn't know. Since hitting the water the current had continually threatened to carry him out to sea. And it was much stronger than he anticipated.

There was a chance he might never make it to shore.

* * *

It was midafternoon when Robert felt his feet scrape against sand. For the first time since entering the water, he no longer worried about sharks. A half minute later, he staggered out of the water and onto a beach a mile south of Georgetown. Exhaustion consumed him, and he collapsed with his cheek flat against the sand. The urgency to save Kazuko remained. But he couldn't will himself to move. His muscles protested with even the slightest effort.

He had to rest.

When his eyelids popped open, a sinking feeling swept over him. The sun was lower in the sky. How much lower? He had no idea how long he had been asleep—if indeed he had slept. Nor did he have any idea what time it was. Closing his eyes was the last thing he remembered.

All at once it dawned on him.

Salazar . . . the yacht.

Kazuko.

He peered across the water and was relieved to see the gleaming white vessel hadn't moved.

He checked his Rolex. The crystal was shattered.

Slowly at first, the final events aboard the boat came back to him. He fingered the wound above his left ear, remembering. His leap overboard; the rail passing under him as he dove headfirst into the ocean; gunfire; the burn of a bullet creasing his scalp; a tug on his left wrist. A bullet had nicked the bezel of his watch. That was the only explanation that fit.

Better the watch than the hand.

He sighed. That he had left Kazuko in the hands of Salazar and his cutthroats continued to gnaw at his gut. He could only imagine what they'd done to her.

And what he imagined wasn't good.

Dammit!

He stared at the yacht—silently cursing Salazar—and tugged on his sodden pants and shoes. The boat hadn't moved. But how long would it remain there?

He started jogging toward Georgetown. Every minute counted. Somehow he had to find the strength to keep going.

Kazuko's life depended on it.

The heat and humidity had been bearable by the water. Less so when he reached the dirt road slicing through the jungle foliage rimming the beach. A minute more into his run he was pouring sweat. His head throbbed; and he felt the first longing for a cool drink. When he licked his lips, all he tasted was salt from his swim in the ocean.

Any other time he would have slowed to a walk and conserved the little strength he had left. Thinking about what Kazuko was being forced to endure aboard that boat kept him running. He'd drop before he gave up.

That would never happen.

Now that he was on a road he hoped to catch a ride into town. And if he didn't, he'd run the entire way. And then he'd find a policeman and make him understand what had happened. Kazuko would be freed from her nightmare before the sun set. Salazar would be made to pay. And Gourde would get what was coming to him. So would the other men involved in the murders of the scientists.

Nothing would bring back the dead. The country would be as

it always was.

But there would be a few less bad people in the world.

And he and Kazuko and Jack could have a peaceful drink, or three, together and count their good fortune.

But that would be a long way away from Guyana.

In time.

First he had to save Kazuko. He prayed it wasn't already too late.

CHAPTER 54

It was late in the day when the pilot set down at the airfield in Bartica just long enough for Pillai and Soukis to disembark. Jack got off too, but only to hug and kiss Pillai. He shook Soukis's hand and couldn't resist smiling at the look of shock on his face. The man was obviously surprised by his co-worker's display of affection.

Perhaps he had approached Pillai romantically at one time and been rebuffed.

"Thanks for coming to the rescue," Jack said to Soukis. "Take care of this lovely lady for me."

"I hope you find your friends and that they are all right," answered Soukis.

Jack nodded. "I guarantee it."

With that, he was back aboard the chopper. He gave a twirling motion with his index finger and they were off.

"We'll go straight to the police station," Campbell said when they were airborne. "You're sure about this man Gourde?"

"I'm sure he killed at least two men himself and ordered the death of Bjornson and Douglas here in Bartica. And I'm convinced the murders were done to hide what was happening at the mine."

"The mining operation will be shut down," Campbell promised. "And if what you say about Gourde is true, the police will take care of him. And anyone else responsible for intentionally dumping cyanide into the Mazaruni River will be hunted down and imprisoned. They won't get away with this."

Jack hoped that was true, even believed it. He wanted to, anyway. But he also knew he couldn't totally rely on the authorities to do what needed to be done.

Not with Robert and Kazuko's lives on the line.

His mind focused on how he would save his friends. The only plan he could come up with at the moment was one shot full of holes. Still, it was a plan. He'd fly into Georgetown, tell the police what happened, find Robert and Kazuko wherever they were being held captive, and set them free. Then the three of them would get the hell out of the country as quickly as possible.

He leaned his head back and closed his eyes as weariness settled in. The only thing keeping him going was the mental image of Robert and Kazuko and how happy they would be to see him. And how happy he'd be to see them.

He'd rest when everyone was safe.

And they would be, he promised himself.

A white car with a government seal on the door was waiting on the tarmac when they touched down at the airport on the outskirts of Georgetown. George Campbell had radioed his supervisor at the Ministry of Health and arranged for the rendezvous. The wiry, little, middle-aged man that Jack had come to like led the way, and he followed close behind. Everyone in the guy's department seemed quite excited by the news of what was going on.

But no more thrilled than he was to finally be there.

Time—he feared—was running out for Robert and Kazuko. He might already have arrived too late to save them. But he didn't want to think that.

His friends were very much alive. He felt it.

What he didn't know was for how long. Gourde did not strike him as a forgiving man. He was a cold-blooded murderer.

And he'd kill Robert and Kazuko the instant they no longer served a purpose.

Jack kept that in mind as he hurried to the car.

He had to find them.

Their driver held open the rear door and Jack climbed in. He settled onto the seat as Campbell slid in next to him, formal and business like. When the car sped away en route to the police station, he felt a bit like a captured fugitive.

For good reason, he mused. He'd killed at least two people. The police just didn't know it.

Or maybe they did.

That would complicate matters immensely. He'd considered the possibility more than once and hadn't allowed himself to be swayed by whatever consequences that would bring him. It simply did not matter. His friend's lives were at stake.

He faced the side window.

Pedestrians' heads turned as the car sped past them—and turned away just as quickly. No one that he could see appeared overly impressed with the official seal on the door. Poor people making a living any way they can; too busy surviving to care about what some government bureaucrat was up to.

The driver pulled up to the main entrance to the police station and let Campbell and Jack out at the curb. Jack stretched and looked at the front of the building. White plaster over some sort of brick, probably. Old two-story construction—it wasn't at all impressive to look at.

He turned to Campbell and said, "I hope they know what they're doing."

Campbell let the comment slide. "We'll be talking with Captain Arjoon. He's waiting for us."

"Then let's get to it."

Jack wanted to believe talking to the police wasn't a wasted effort on his part. It was something he had to do, but he wasn't holding his breath. He'd know soon enough. But would it be timely enough to save his friends?

He couldn't give up hope.

With that in mind, he followed Campbell through the entrance doors, up a flight of stairs, and into an office on the second floor. A man dressed in crisp white uniform with a badge and something pinned to the collar, was sitting behind a cluttered desk when they walked inside. He stood and introduced himself as Captain Stephen Arjoon, in charge of criminal investigations.

Jack extended his hand. That was the extent of his pleasantries.

Time was of the essence. He asked, "You've been briefed on what's happened?"

Arjoon shook Jack's hand and motioned to the two empty chairs in front of his desk. "Some," he answered. "Have a seat and tell me everything you know about what happened."

Jack wasn't sure how much to tell the officer. The man appeared confident—if looks were any indication—but was it wise to admit to killing two men and possibly a third? Every last detail would likely come out in the end, but he could see no sense in bringing that up until there was reason to.

It would only get him mired down in an investigation that would likely land him in a jail cell—even if only for the night—and do little or nothing to help find Robert and Kazuko.

More hours lost.

He'd stick to the details of the two cold blooded murders at Kaburi Landing and the kidnapping of Robert and Kazuko. Gourde was the killer they needed to be looking for. And, of course, Captain Arjoon would have to be told about Pillai. Besides, he may already know about her. By now, she would have given her statement to the police in Bartica.

Which might even speed things up.

Anything to get things moving.

He was anxious to find Robert and Kazuko.

Before it was too late.

CHAPTER 55

Jack took a seat in the closest empty chair and shifted his weight back and forth trying to get comfortable. It was difficult for him to sit still when he should be outside looking for his friends. He did not intend to spend a lot of time in the chair.

Without delay, he relayed the events of the day as he remembered them, being careful not to deviate from what he'd planned to tell Captain Arjoon. Thankfully, there were not a bunch of questions he couldn't answer. Having George Campbell there with him helped. So did his appearance.

". . . and then we flew here," Jack finished.

Captain Arjoon gave Jack a long investigatory look. It was as if he searched for the truth in the determination etched in his expression.

Jack stared back. He hadn't lied.

But he hadn't exactly told him everything, either.

After a long moment, Arjoon turned his gaze on Campbell. "Is there anything you can add that he hasn't already told me?"

"Nothing, sir."

Jack watched the police captain lay his pen down on the pad in front of him. He seemed satisfied with what he'd been told.

Or that was how he wanted it to appear.

Jack detected an air of suspicion lingering behind the man's eyes.

At last, Captain Arjoon rolled his chair back and stood up

behind his desk. "I'll put my men to work on this immediately and let you know what we find."

Jack could see he and Campbell were being dismissed. He was relieved to be done, at least for now. There would be a lot more to talk about later.

He stood and offered his hand to the Captain. "If the plane is here," he said, "it should be easy to spot."

Arjoon gave Jack's hand a quick shake and nodded politely at Campbell. "We'll let you know."

"I'll be at the Princess Hotel," Jack told him. "Just as soon as I get a room."

"Good choice."

With that, Jack turned and walked out of the room. Campbell followed and caught up with him. He seemed anxious to get back to work.

He asked, "Can I drop you at the hotel?"

Evening was not that far off. Jack had no intention of spending the daylight he had left sitting in a room. But he needed to check in. He'd been fighting exhaustion, and at some point would collapse. Besides, the hotel was where Arjoon would contact him with information. Until then he would do what he could on his own.

He had to hurry and find Robert and Kazuko. Having seen Gourde's handiwork, they likely would not live out the day.

And the day was quickly coming to an end.

"You bet," he said. "The sooner the better."

When he walked out of the building, he noticed a man staring in his direction—white, American, possibly English, or even Canadian—with three days growth of dark beard stubble. The guy wore a khaki shirt with sleeves rolled to the elbows and tan bush pants. He looked like he had just stepped out of a jungle movie. The same man stepped into the lot behind them when they walked to where Campbell's driver had parked the car. Jack's gut reaction was he was being followed.

But by whom?

He was glad he hadn't been searched. The handgun remained concealed under his shirt, but he wasn't about to draw it. Not unless he had to.

He'd wait and see.

When they drove out of the lot, he peered through the rear window to see if the man was still there. He was. And he was standing in the lot in the same spot he had been when they drove off. That was confusing.

He'd expected the man to follow.

Even more disconcerting, he couldn't believe his gut instinct had failed him. But that was the way it looked. He was rarely wrong in matters of self-preservation.

Perhaps it was just a spooked imagination.

A lot had happened already.

Still, he might be right. He'd know for sure if he saw the man again.

They arrived at the hotel a few minutes later. The Princess was where he had stayed his first night in Guyana. That seemed like a lifetime ago.

Campbell got out of the car at the portico and pumped Jack's hand. "I hope you find your friends."

"I'm sure I will," Jack said. "Thanks for your help."

Campbell climbed back into the front passenger seat and the driver sped away without delay. Jack watched them go. Then he scanned the people and grounds around him half expecting to see the stranger from in front of the police station standing there. Failing to notice anything or anyone suspicious, he stepped inside the hotel lobby and registered.

Ten minutes later he was in his room. A shower first to wake up, and a quick bite to eat to keep going, then he would comb the docks for the yellow and white De Havilland Beaver. The floatplane had to be there somewhere. Find that, and he would find Robert and Kazuko.

They would surely be close by.

The hot water breathed life into his body, and offered some relief to his sore muscles. If there had been more time he would have washed his clothes. There wasn't. He stood at the foot of the bed staring at the filthy clothing wishing he didn't have to put them back on. At least they'd been rinsed in the stream. A small consolation, but one he'd have to live with.

He was buttoning his pants when he heard a knock.

Lost in thought, the rap on the door startled him. He glanced that direction then his gaze shot to the pistol.

The .45 semi-automatic lay next to his shirt on the bed in front of him.

He might need it.

Cautious of who was outside his room, he grabbed the handgun and held it behind him. He only had a couple of bullets left in the magazine. He hoped he didn't have to use them.

But he was ready.

"Who's there?" he asked before unlocking the deadbolt.

"I'm here to help," said a male voice.

"You got a name?"

"My name is unimportant. What you need to know is that I know what's going on, and I can help you find your friends."

Jack considered the situation and who in Georgetown would know about Robert and Kazuko besides Gourde. George Campbell, his driver, and Captain Arjoon did for sure, and they were the only ones who knew where he was staying. That meant word had to have come from one of them.

Or had it?

He decided he'd take a chance. But stay ready for anything. Just in case.

He turned the deadbolt and stepped back three paces, moving to the side out of direct line with the doorway. Then he said, "Open the door, but don't come in. Not until I have a look at who I'm talking to."

The knob turned and Jack tensed.

At once he had the .45 up in front of him and aimed.

The door swung open and Jack swallowed. He was face to face with the stranger he'd seen watching him outside the police station.

CHAPTER 56

Jack was tired of surprises. For a split second he contemplated shooting the man, just in case. But then the guy wasn't armed—no weapon in his hand, anyway. Still, that didn't mean he wasn't trouble.

There seemed to be no shortage of that.

Jack kept the .45 pointed. "You said you could help—talk."

"Do you mind lowering that gun?" the man asked. "Makes me nervous."

"Who are you?" Jack couldn't care less if the guy was uneasy staring into the muzzle of a gun.

"Let's just say we're on the same side."

"What's this 'same-side' crap? This is about me and my friends."

"Partly, yes," the man conceded. "But there's more going on here than you and your friends' involvement."

"You didn't answer my question." Jack was tiring of playing twenty questions.

"Are you aware there is a file on you that makes for interesting reading?"

"You ran a check . . . you're with the government?"

The man nodded. "The United States government—I'm DEA."

"Why didn't you just say so?"

"Cautious, I guess. Can we talk now?"

"I thought that's what we were doing?"

"I mean about your friends."

Jack gave the man a good, long look and lowered the semi-automatic pistol. If the agent could help, he was listening. Anything that would save Robert and Kazuko.

"In here," he gestured. "Or do you want to talk somewhere else?"

"The bar by the pool. I want to show you something."

"Picture's worth a thousand words?"

"Something like that."

Jack studied the DEA agent. "You still haven't told me your name."

"William Ryan," the agent replied.

"Is that your real name or just what I'm supposed to call you?"

Ryan smiled.

"Okay, Ryan, after you."

Jack waited for the man to walk ahead. He wanted the guy in front of him before he tucked the .45 into the waistband at the small of his back. Warming to the guy was not going to be easy. He'd trust him for now, but only so far. Knowing there would be witnesses around when they talked eased some of the tension.

Ryan walked off in the direction of the stairs leading to the pool. Jack leaned his head into the hallway and glanced in both directions before fully crossing the threshold, committing himself to whoever might be waiting for him outside his room. When he was sure they were alone, he pulled the door closed and followed a few steps behind the agent. Time was slipping by. He didn't like the delay.

Or the games.

A minute later, he walked onto the pool deck. Half a dozen guests lounged in the warmth of the afternoon sun. Not as many as he would have liked, but enough to make it an unlikely spot for a double-cross.

"Okay," he said, "we're here. Now, what's this about?"

"See that boat out there?" Ryan asked. He led Jack to an empty table that offered them a view of the gleaming white yacht sitting a half mile offshore.

"I see it," Jack said, taking a seat.

"The *Margarete* is owned by a man named Ramon Salazar.

Among other things, he deals in drugs and stolen antiquities. A real bad ass, you can be sure of that. But he's also ingratiated himself with high-ranking Mexican and South American government officials. Without going into detail, his political contributions have pretty much allowed him to conduct business without interference."

"By contributions, you're talking bribes?"

"Money, drugs, smartphones—whatever it takes."

"Okay, so what does he have to do with my two friends?"

"Gold."

"What do you mean?"

"Large quantities of gold and diamonds are being dug from the Amazon basin. A big part of it by illegal mining enterprises operating without permits. In countries like Guyana, revenue generated from taxes on the production of gold accounts for a large portion of the government's operating budget. Drug dealers are constantly seeking ways to legitimize their illicit profits. The recent trend is to buy gold from these black market miners—effectively robbing the government of their share—and then sell it on the world market for a substantial profit."

"You're not telling me anything I don't already know," Jack said. He felt a surge of impatience. "Get to the point."

Ryan held Jack in his gaze, and after a moment peered across the water in the direction of the yacht. Its shiny white hull and tinted glass gleamed bright in the sun. Innocent opulence to the unassuming eye.

He nodded. "I believe your friends are on the *Margarete*."

Jack looked. "But the plane . . . ?"

"It was there earlier this afternoon. I watched it land and taxi in close. Then it sat there."

"But it's not out there now."

"Sunk."

What? Jack locked gazes with Ryan. "You're saying it sank?"

"Not at first; and not without help."

"But they're alive?"

"I believe your friends are, yes. How long they will stay that way, I can't say."

"You were talking about the plane, what happened?"

Ryan turned his gaze on the yacht. "I wanted a closer look at what was going on so I went to my room to get my binoculars. When I returned a few minutes later the plane was going down, nose first. My guess is Salazar's goons shot the pontoons full of holes. His men are known to carry silenced MP5s so the gunshots wouldn't have been heard by anyone on shore."

Jack felt his hope for Robert and Kazuko's safety sink with a vision of the yellow and white De Havilland Beaver disappearing beneath the waves.

He took a deep breath and let it out. "Why would Salazar do that?"

"To keep your friends from leaving—eliminate witnesses—your guess is as good as mine."

Jack didn't care what happened to Gourde—the worse the better. But he refused to believe Robert and Kazuko had gone down with the plane. And from the way Ryan was talking, he didn't either. He'd said he thought they were on the *Margarete*.

They have to be.

It took every ounce of willpower Jack could muster to remain calm. He was barely holding it together. Even the slightest bit of reassurance would help.

"You think my friends are still on board."

"The woman, anyway." Ryan's expression hardened. "Salazar's not above keeping her around for entertainment."

Jack stared at the yacht. That was not the reassurance he needed. But if she was there, he'd save her. No matter what it took to secure her release, he'd do it.

"We need to get out there."

Ryan didn't hesitate. "Now that I know what happened, we will."

Jack rose from his chair and flattened his palms on the table. "What about the police? Can we count on them?"

"Salazar is connected. They'll be slow to take action."

"But you informed Captain Arjoon what was going on?"

"Until you briefed him, I didn't know what was going on."

"Then afterwards—you told him about the plane landing out there, right? Surely he has no choice but to move on Salazar."

"He hasn't called you, has he?"

"I've been out of my room."

"Trust me, he hasn't. And he likely won't. He knew about the plane before you checked into the hotel. I told him about it five minutes after you left. If he was going to call, he'd have called."

Jack feared the police couldn't be trusted. It seemed he was right. "Okay, the DEA then—your guys?"

Ryan shook his head sadly. "No can do . . . not in time, anyway."

Hushed understanding settled on the table and for a moment neither of them spoke.

Jack dropped into his seat. "Then it's just us—"

Before he finished what he was saying, a man's shouting abruptly jerked him from his thought.

Frowning, he searched out the source of the disturbance.

It only took a second.

On the street, half a block away, a man was yelling at a uniformed police officer and jabbing a finger toward the water. The officer stood shrugging his shoulders and waving his arms as if he didn't understand what the infuriated man was saying, or trying to get him to do.

Jack wasn't interested in other people's problems. The man looked homeless. Perhaps he was drunk or mad from too much sun. It didn't matter which. The guy was of no concern to him.

Then he took notice of the man's blond hair and familiar face. *Robert!*

"He's still alive," he heard himself say as he thought it. "That's my friend down there, the one I was telling you about."

"What?" Ryan asked.

"Robert's alive."

"Where?"

Jack pushed out of his chair and took off running.

CHAPTER 57

Jack reached Robert a few seconds ahead of Ryan. He edged past the policeman and threw his arms around his friend.

Robert's eyes widened, and for a moment he looked like someone who had just been greeted by a group of friends yelling 'surprise' on his birthday.

Jack couldn't contain his smile. "Damn, I'm glad to see you."

Robert pushed away. The smile was contagious. His lips curled into a broad grin.

He held it, and then let it slip just a little. "Not as happy as I am to see you."

"You know this man?" the policeman asked Jack.

"I certainly do," he answered, happily.

"Then I think it would be wise for you to get him off the street. I believe he has had too much to drink."

"He's not—"

"We'll take care of him," Ryan answered for Jack before he could protest further. "I'll make sure of it."

Jack and Robert quietly stood by.

Ryan's promise seemed to appease the policeman. He nodded. "See that you do, or I will be forced to arrest him."

"Arrest—" Robert straightened. His expression hardened with indignation.

Jack feared what would happen next. He knew his friend better than anyone. He also knew he'd been pushed to his limit. It wouldn't take much more to put him over the edge, especially with Kazuko's life in danger. He took Robert by the arm and quickly led him toward the hotel.

"That won't be necessary," Ryan said to the officer, and rushed to catch up with Jack and Robert. The policeman refrained from further comment.

Robert glanced back as Jack led him along. The fire that showed in his eyes was enough to know he was still angry.

"Asshole," he muttered.

Jack frowned at his friend and looked to see if the officer was following them. He was standing where they had left him.

Good thing.

Jack turned to Robert and asked in a hushed tone, "What happened to you guys? Where is Kazuko?"

Desperation showed in Robert's eyes. There was no misunderstanding the intensity burning there. Jack had seen the look before.

More than once.

"She's on that boat out there," Robert said. "Bastard tried to shoot me. And he would have if I hadn't jumped overboard." Robert nodded in the direction of the yacht sitting offshore. "I was trying to explain it to that jackass cop when you showed up. The stupid sonofabitch didn't appear at all concerned."

"Don't worry about him. Tell me what happened."

Robert looked at Ryan and back at Jack. "Who's your friend?"

"William Ryan; he's DEA."

"I can speak for myself," Ryan said. He extended his hand. "I'm here to help you get your girl back."

"Good." Robert pointed toward the water. "Call in a SWAT team. Hell, call in the Marines. We have to get Kazuko off that boat."

Jack felt as though he was letting his friend down. A major disappointment. But then he was doing everything he could do. Nobody—other than Robert—wanted Kazuko off that boat more than he did.

"I only wish we could," he said. "But even if it were possible, they wouldn't get here in time. I'm afraid it's just us."

"How about the police? You've talked to them, I'm sure."

"Doesn't look like they'll be much help, if any at all."

"Okay, us then." Robert was definitely anxious to get busy rescuing Kazuko. "You have a plan?"

"Ryan and I were coming to that when I saw you." Jack clapped his friend on the back. "Let's get you up to my room where we can talk. We'll figure out a way to go out there and get Kazuko off that boat."

The three of them faced the ocean and watched a power boat speed toward the yacht. It was impossible to see the faces of the men with their backs turned. *More* armed men? Unsavory guests, perhaps. Neither prospect was good. The game was changing by the minute.

He exchanged a nervous glance with Ryan. Concern showed in the DEA agent's expression.

"Let's get a move on," Jack said to Robert, who wore the same worried look.

Robert didn't resist. He quietly followed Jack up the stairs and along the hallway leading to his room. Ryan was right there with them.

They all had a lot to think about.

At the doorway to the room, Robert turned to Jack and said, "I know you understand how much Kazuko means to me. I can't spend a lot of time talking. You saw that boat and the men inside. We need to come up with a plan, and fast. Gourde's on the yacht with her, so are a bunch of men with machine guns. And I didn't like the look in the eyes of the guy who owns that overpriced tub."

"Kazuko means the world to me, too." Jack inserted the key card and opened the door. "We'll only take as much time as we need to make sure we all come out of this thing alive."

Jack stepped into the room. Robert and Ryan followed him in, and Ryan closed the door and locked it.

"Take a shower," Jack said to Robert. "I'll order up some food. Sorry I can't help you out with a clean set of clothes."

"I don't need a shower and I don't need to eat," answered Robert. "And I sure don't need clean clothes. You know all I want is to get back out to that boat and get Kazuko."

"I do." Jack's gaze did not waver. "I also know you well enough to recognize you're running on fumes. You won't do any of us a bit of good if you fall over in the process. Now take a shower. You'll think better with a clear head. I'll have burgers brought up."

"Jack's right," Ryan agreed. "Another five minutes won't change a thing."

Robert exchanged glances. Jack could see his friend struggle to contain his frustration. Worry ate at him like a cancer.

He wasn't alone.

"Tell the cook to make it fast," Robert said, as he stepped into the bathroom.

Ten minutes later, Robert emerged with wet hair and two day's growth of beard. Evidently, he hadn't bothered to shave. Jack and Ryan sat at the small round table in the corner of the room. The food wasn't there yet.

"Better?" Jack asked.

"Better."

"Good, now tell us what happened."

Robert took a seat on the edge of the bed. He relayed in detail what happened aboard the yacht. When he was done, the questions came.

"So it's all about black market gold and money laundering," Ryan commented.

"To them," Robert groused. "I only care about Kazuko."

"I agree," Jack said without hesitation. "To hell with the gold, and to hell with Salazar's dirty money. They're Guyana's problem."

"The gold, yes," answered Ryan. "But I've made Salazar my problem. We'll rescue your girl first. But I am not letting that drug-dealing bastard slip through my fingers again."

Jack noted Ryan's resolve.

Everybody wins.

Was that even possible?

He felt a cold chill of anticipation creep up his spine. No matter what plan the three of them came up with, there was the unremitting possibility something would go terribly wrong.

CHAPTER 58

Kazuko paced the cabin holding on to the belief Robert was alive—that Salazar had lied to make her lose hope. Anything to demoralize and destroy her. She wouldn't let him get to her. She had plenty of fight left to endure whatever disgusting humiliation Salazar subjected her to.

More than mere will to survive.

Her thoughts returned to Robert. He was the key to her freedom. Jack, too. He was still out there searching.

Of that she was sure.

Neither Robert nor Jack would abandon her.

For the hundredth time, she searched the cabin for anything that could aid in her escape. The room's bare furnishings, the locked door and the small porthole, left her little hope of getting out of there on her own. Even if she could break the glass she could never fit through the opening. Help would have to come to her.

When it did, she'd be ready.

She pressed her face to the glass and peered at the water. There was nothing for her to do but wait.

She was still staring out the porthole when she heard the click of the lock on the door. Her breath caught in her throat. Her stomach twisted into a knot. She swallowed a sour taste.

Salazar. . .

She jerked her head around.

For a long, tense moment she watched the door slowly swing open. She didn't move, or make any attempt to run. To try and flee was useless. She tightened her hands into fists and waited.

Her eyes widened in surprise.

She took a deep breath, and muttered, "I didn't expect a woman to be part of Salazar's filthy little game."

The woman held her response and cautiously entered the room. Long black hair hanging loose down her back, brown skin, two-piece white bathing suit with a sheer sarong tied around her waist—Hispanic. She glanced over her shoulder and looked back and forth nervously, as if checking to see if someone watched from the companionway. In her left hand she held a plastic bottle of water and something wrapped in a linen napkin. Food, perhaps.

Kazuko felt the knot in her stomach relax.

"My name is Annett," the woman said in a low tone. "Here's food. Take it. You will need to keep up your strength."

"Salazar sent you?" Kazuko took the offering, realizing just how hungry she was.

"No one knows I'm here," replied Annett. "They mustn't find out."

"But you're a guest aboard the boat, are you not?"

"I was in your place once: a year ago. I know what they are capable of. Salazar's hospitality only extends as far as the degree I pleasure him. Should he become angry or unsatisfied with my actions, he would take great satisfaction in making it quite painful for me."

Kazuko touched a finger to her busted lip. She still tasted blood.

"I see you have felt the sting of his anger already," said Annett, pointing at the bruised flesh. "That is only a fraction of what he is capable of."

"If you know what he plans to do to me then why not help me escape?"

"That would only get us both killed."

"Maybe—I say it's worth a try."

"You do not know this man . . . what he'd do."

"Leave the door unlocked. There's no way he could know it was you. Besides, I can bring the authorities here. You'd be free of this perverted freak."

"And if I left the door open, where could you go? Armed men patrol the decks."

In her mind Kazuko could still hear the gunshots released from the legion of automatic weapons. No way could she forget about the blood-thirsty guards, especially Jesus and Gato. They were the worst of the bunch. At least the others hadn't put their hands on her. *Yet.*

"I might be able to sneak past them and jump overboard, maybe I wouldn't. But I would have a chance. That's more than I have locked inside this tiny cabin."

"And when they catch you, it will be worse than if you had remained here."

"Then I won't let them catch me. I'll dive into the ocean and lose them in the waves. I'm a good swimmer."

"Like your dead friend?"

Kazuko sucked in a breath. "You don't know he's dead."

"He's dead. Shot. Just like you'll be if you try something. And me, too, if I'm caught helping you escape."

Kazuko looked at Annett for a long moment. If the consequences were so great, it made no sense for her to chance bringing the food. Unless she was there for some other reason. Perhaps Salazar had sent her after all.

Another of his games.

"Why are you really here?" Kazuko asked. "Did you come to frighten me more than I am? Don't bother; I am scared . . . terrified, more like it. But I also have plenty of fight left in me. If that pig Salazar or Jesus or Gato or any of his other men try to force themselves on me, they will find out just how tough I am. If you came here because you were concerned about me, leave the door unlocked and I'll take care of myself."

The two women exchanged worried looks.

"I came to bring you food and water," Annett said. "Not scare you. If you leave this room, you will surely die . . . or worse. Sorry, you ask too much of me."

"You know what they have planned, right?"

"Sadly, I do. These men have no scruples and even less

conscience."

"And yet you think it is best for me to become their plaything?"

"I think it is best to live."

"And become someone like you?" Kazuko winced at her own words, but made no attempt to conceal the derision showing through in her voice.

Annett's gaze dropped to the floor.

Annett was ashamed of who she was; Kazuko could easily see that. There was no reason to condemn the woman further.

"It is not my place to judge you for the choice you made," she said. "But it's up to me to decide whether or not I risk my life trying to escape."

"It is," agreed Annett. "But I will not be part of it."

Kazuko quietly watched her chance to escape step from the cabin and pull the door closed behind her. The lock clicked shut.

CHAPTER 59

Billaud stood on the deck of the twenty-foot power boat and gripped the corner of the seatback in front of him, bracing himself as the launch coasted to a stop next to the yacht. The day was quickly winding down. He remained anxious to be done with his business aboard *Margarete*. He had a plane to catch.

And he intended to be on it.

But first he had to get the money the gold inside the bag would bring him. His sixty percent of the agreed upon three and a half million dollars would more than provide him with the life he wanted. And if he didn't have to split the take with Gourde, all the better. Even if the man showed up for his cut, he could be eliminated. A simple matter of putting a bullet in his skull.

The temptation was too great to ignore. They had been friends for a long time, but no friendship was more important than money.

Nothing was.

He held onto the thought as Salazar's armed bodyguards ushered him along the companionway leading aft. The barrels of their automatic rifles remained leveled. At the front of the procession, two burly men carried the gold. The bigger of the two hefted the bag with three bars inside of it. The other man carried a bag containing two bars.

There was no talking. Billaud glanced over his shoulder at the guards with the guns. He eyed the big men in front of him. There was obviously a lack of trust, even now.

No honor among thieves, he thought. The cliché fit.

He stepped onto the rear deck and stiffened. His gaze locked on Gourde. The man looked surprised. As well he should. He wasn't supposed to be there.

Billaud contained his own astonishment and considered the situation.

Something had gone wrong at the river.

The only answer that fit. But what did it matter now? The fate of the scientists was of no consequence at this point. All that was important was getting his money and getting out of there.

Still, he wanted to know what happened.

The two muscular men carrying the gold set the bags on the deck next to Salazar. The forty-pound bars clanked together as they settled on the teak. The men stepped back, standing with their arms crossed.

Billaud felt everyone's eyes focus on him.

Gourde stood from his deck chair. His bemused expression cracked when the corners of his lips curled up. Billaud did not share the feeling. He'd hoped to never see the man again.

"So, you're here," he said.

Gourde's smile slipped. "A change in plans that could not be avoided."

"Bakker and Smedt?"

"There was trouble on the river. They're dead."

"And the research team, I trust they are dead as well?"

"They are no longer a problem."

Billaud was not sure what that meant. Did it even matter now?

"Join us," Salazar said from his seat next to the table. With a casual wave of his hand, he motioned to a deck chair beside Gourde.

Billaud noticed an edge to the man's voice. He scanned the armed men with their sub-machine guns held at the ready. He didn't have a choice.

Frustration tightened the muscles in his jaw. He stepped to the chair and took a seat. He still had questions for Gerard Gourde.

They'd have to wait.

"Mr. Gourde and I have been talking," Salazar began. "He

explained your little problem with the Ministry of Health."

"Screw Deputy Minister Sukhai." Billaud focused on Salazar.

Salazar smiled.

Billaud did not see the humor in his statement. "The Ministry of Health would not have been a concern if Gourde had not bungled the handling of the scientists investigating the contamination to the Mazaruni. But what's done is done. The mine and its owners in Toronto are no longer my concern."

Salazar placed his elbows on the tabletop and casually tented his hands. Behind his fingers, he continued to smile, as though entertained by the turn of events. But at who's expense?

Billaud found his behavior disconcerting.

"I find what you say quite interesting," Salazar said after a moment. "It seems Mr. Gourde makes a habit of being troublesome. He has presented me with a most unfortunate situation as well."

"I had little choice in the matter," Gourde spoke up.

"And I have taken care of the situation." Salazar's expression hardened. He dropped his hands to the table. "I suggest you be thankful for that."

Gourde showed no sign of backing down. "The woman will amuse you and your men, I'm sure."

Billaud shifted in his seat. His brow shot up. "You brought one of the scientists here . . . a woman? You told me they were dead."

Gourde glared at Billaud. "I told you they were no longer a problem. I assure you they aren't."

"Apparently, that's not the case."

"But it is."

Gourde's expression softened. "You and I have known each other far too long to let this spoil our trust. The gold is here. Let's finish our deal with Mr. Salazar and be done with this country."

"Ah, the deal." Salazar's voice drew Billaud and Gourde's attention.

Billaud did not like the tone.

"I'd like to conclude our transaction and go," he said, in a hurry to be done.

Salazar's smile returned.

"Are you referring to the one you and I struck earlier?" He raised his hand and snapped his fingers. "Or the one Mr. Gourde and I were just about to make?"

CHAPTER 60

Billaud was taken aback by the question. But then it made sense. Gourde had proven his lack of loyalty by trying to cut his own deal with Salazar.

The man should never have been trusted.

He had known Gerard Gourde to be a big mean-tempered bastard capable of anything at any given moment. Big and brutal, he enjoyed hurting people. Double-crossing a partner would certainly be on the list.

Why wouldn't it be?

Now he wanted to reconsider his earlier decision to keep his part of the deal and make the sixty/forty split as originally agreed upon.

Put a bullet in the man's brain and be done with him.

The big guard with a thick chest and heavily muscled arms stepped forward and set the two gold bars Gourde had brought, on the tabletop. The smaller bar made a dull metallic sound when it clanked against the larger one.

Billaud narrowed his eyes at Gourde. "You have an explanation for this?"

Gourde didn't flinch at the accusation. "That scum Bakker stole it from under our noses. When I discovered what the little shitpile had done, I killed the worthless ass and tossed his body in the river like the rest of the garbage. I had no choice but to bring the gold here."

"Smedt?"

"Bakker shot him before I knew what was going on." Gourde pointed. "That small bar there is the gold Balgobin ran off with the other day. I took it off his body at Kaburi Landing."

"You killed him?"

"I would have, but someone or something got to him ahead of me. It didn't really matter. But there was still the research team to worry about. With Bakker and Smedt dead, I intended to take care of them myself."

Billaud eyed the forty pound gold bar suspiciously. That Gourde had recovered it and brought it to Salazar was dubious enough. He'd no doubt intended to cut his own deal and keep the money for himself. A bigger question remained.

One that needed answering.

He turned his gaze on Gourde. "How can it be that Bakker had that bar on him when the bars at the mine where all accounted for when I had them loaded onto the helicopter?"

"That's impossible." Gourde started to stand.

"Sit," commanded Salazar. He snapped his fingers and pointed at the bags Billaud brought with him.

Again, the burley bodyguard stepped forward. Without a word, he effortlessly lifted each of the five bars from the bags and set them on the table.

Each one matched the others next to it. Gold in color, about the size and shape of a common brick, layers showing from having been poured into a mold—exactly the way a person would expect a solid gold bar to look.

Salazar waved him back. "So now I wonder who is playing who for a fool."

Billaud spoke up, "I assure you no one is playing *you* for a fool."

"We shall see."

Billaud watched Salazar carefully examine the bars, lifting each one and turning it over in his hands before returning it to the table. When he was done with the first scan, he picked up one that he'd already examined. He scratched it with his fingernail and held it close to his face for a careful inspection.

Then, he looked at Billaud. "You brought this one with the others," he said.

"All five—two hundred pounds worth—exactly as I promised."

Out of the corner of his eye, Billaud saw Gourde paying close attention to what was going on. If he was nervous, he didn't show it.

Salazar sighed. "So, Mr. Billaud, you thought you could cheat me?"

"I'm sure I do not know what you are talking about."

"This bar"—Salazar pointed—"is lead, though it has been gilded to appear as if it is solid gold."

Billaud rose to his feet. "That is not possible."

Salazar motioned him back into his chair. "But a fact, just the same. Now I have to ask myself what to believe."

Taken aback by the accusation, Billaud took his seat. There was only one person who might be able to shed light on how this could have happened. He looked to Gourde for an explanation.

"Balgobin worked in the smelter," Gourde offered.

Billaud understood the implication. He nodded at Gourde and faced Salazar. "That must be how he managed to steal the gold bar he took from the mine without us noticing the theft."

Salazar stared back as if he expected to hear more.

Billaud and Gourde looked at each other. Billaud could not think of any other way the switch could have been made.

He waited, not sure what more to say.

The quiet was deafening.

"And now you attempt to steal from me," Salazar said after a moment. He turned to the burley bodyguard standing at his side. "Albert, tell the captain to raise anchor. We depart immediately."

CHAPTER 61

Jack stepped onto the tiled corridor fronting his room and walked toward the railing overlooking the ocean. Robert and Ryan followed. So far no viable plan had been arrived at. He knew they had, at best, a few minutes to come up with something they could agree on. The day was winding down with only a few hours of sunlight left for them to work with. Another look at the yacht might help.

"Maybe we're over thinking this," Robert said as they walked.

Jack shot him a sideways glance. "Caution is the better part of valor."

"You have an answer for everything."

Jack could hear the stress in his friend's voice. He couldn't let it cloud his thinking.

"When it fits," he said. "And right now we can't run off half-cocked."

"I'll have my gun fully cocked when we go out there."

"You don't have a gun."

"You do."

"And four bullets."

Robert held out his hand. "Give the gun to me. I'll put those four bullets to good use."

"That's not enough to mount an assault on a boatload of armed men."

"Ryan must have a gun or two." Robert turned to Ryan. "What

258

do you think?"

Ryan stopped walking and looked at Robert and Jack. "You're serious?"

"I am," Robert said over his shoulder. He turned and kept walking.

Ryan caught up with them. "I've got a gun, but not the kind of firepower you need."

"Face it," Jack said. "We're outgunned and outmanned. I'd just as soon not charge in with guns blazing."

"He's right," Ryan said to Robert. "We'll only get ourselves killed."

Robert looked from Ryan to Jack. "Well then?"

Jack shrugged. "Obviously, we need to come up with a more peaceable solution. One that doesn't involve a lot of shooting, if that's possible."

"Peaceable." Robert shook his head. "It's for certain we can't stroll up to Salazar and talk him into letting Kazuko go. He gets one look at me and he'll start shooting. He thought his men killed me going overboard or I wouldn't be here. I don't think the sorry bastard will hesitate for a second to finish the job."

Jack made it to the railing. He turned to Robert. "Talking didn't exactly figure into my way of thinking."

"Nor mine," agreed Ryan.

"We're in agreement then," Robert said. "Let's hurry and think of something. Knowing Kazuko is out there on that boat with that lousy sleaze-bucket is driving me nuts."

"You're not alone," Jack told him. He understood Robert's concern. He was sick with worry, himself. But they couldn't charge out there and ride in a circle, shooting arrows at Salazar like a tribe of angry Indians in an old-west movie.

Still, they had to do something, and fast. He'd hoped the DEA agent would have been more help. Something didn't feel right. The agency should have been behind him. He should have been eager to call on them for assistance.

He wasn't.

A thought occurred to Jack. One he'd toyed with earlier. He looked Ryan in the eyes. "Your agency isn't sanctioning this vendetta of yours, are they?"

It took a moment. Finally Ryan answered, "At first, but not now. I'm here on my own. That's why I can't bring them in . . . even if there *was* time."

Jack scoffed. "Something we're in short supply of." He narrowed his eyes at the yacht and went rigid.

Sonofabitch.

"We could call in the Guyanese army for all the good it would do us." He jabbed his index finger at the yacht. "We're out of time."

"Shit," Ryan said. "Salazar's on the move."

"There." Robert pointed toward two red and white jet skis sitting on wheeled dollies just above the tide line. A nearby plywood sign read, *For Rent*. A dark-skinned man in a big hat stood there ready to take customers' money.

Jack was already moving.

"Go," shouted Ryan. "I'll commandeer a boat and catch up."

Robert passed Jack on the stairs and ran onto the sand two steps ahead of him. Robert definitely wasn't waiting.

Neither was Jack.

He dug into his pocket on the run and tossed a damp wad of cash at the man standing by the sign and ran straight to the Kawasaki jet ski sitting poised and ready in front of him. Robert was already rolling his into the surf.

Jack got his going at the same time Robert did. They buried the throttles and sped through the waves after *Margarete*.

The tide wasn't helping, but Jack didn't back off.

At first, his jet ski rode up and over the swells in a rollercoaster motion that raised his stomach and dropped it just as quickly. Then, as the craft gained speed, he and the machine were propelled into the air with each wave as it rolled under him. And each time it went airborne, the jet ski slammed into the water with enough force to jar his teeth. But somehow he managed to hold on, as skill and sheer determination kept him from being tossed from his seat.

He chanced a glance to his right. Twenty yards away, Robert straddled his machine with the engine screaming. By the looks of it, he was having just as tough a time.

And was no less determined.

Jack motioned with his hand for to Robert to press the pursuit—more out of encouragement than necessity.

Riders to the rescue.

Jack took a wave head on and came down hard. The craft fishtailed under him and he got control of it.

The swells showed no sign of letting up.

With so much of his concentration focused on keeping control of his jet ski, it was difficult for him to put his mind to work on anything other than catching up with the yacht. Even so, he couldn't help thinking that boarding a boat the size of *Margarete* while the monstrosity was sitting still was one thing, boarding that same boat while it was moving would be quite another.

Not to mention taking on a half-dozen men armed with submachine guns.

Some rescue.

He kept the throttle buried to its stop.

He still had no idea what he and Robert would do when they reached *Margarete* and doubted Robert did either. Jumping on the jet skis and going in pursuit of the yacht had been reactionary on both their parts with one goal in mind: catch up to the boat before Salazar sailed away with Kazuko onboard.

That was still the plan, and they were narrowing the gap.

He would have to come up with something clever, and quick.

Then he noticed the distance between him and the yacht widen. *Margarete* had picked up speed and turned north along the coast. He jammed on the throttle, but it was as far as it would go.

The machine had nothing more to give.

Kazuko was at the mercy of Salazar.

CHAPTER 62

Salazar motioned to his men to lower the barrels of their automatic rifles. He no longer believed he needed them pointed at Billaud and Gourde to keep them in their seats. He would be rid of them soon.

"What is the meaning of this," protested Billaud.

Salazar walked to the port bulwark and peered over the side at the coastline a mile away. Green and lush. He'd been inconvenienced enough by their clumsiness. That was coming to an end.

Now.

He turned and put his back to the gunnel. "Your inept actions have caused me to rethink my plans. I will keep the gold at half the price. The two of you, and the woman Mr. Gourde so clumsily brought onboard, will be getting off here."

Billaud shot to his feet and pointed his finger. His eyes flared. "But we had a deal. You can't go back on your word."

"Can and will." Salazar snapped his fingers.

Albert gripped Billaud by the shoulders and forced him into his chair. Gourde looked on, making no attempt to get up or protest.

Salazar was mildly surprised at the man's inaction.

"You have a choice," he continued. "Take the deal, or not. But either way I keep the gold. Remember, I can just as easily kill each of you and have my man Albert toss your bodies to the sharks."

Billaud did not look happy. "This is crazy," he yelled.

"Your choice."

Billaud exchanged glances with Gourde. Nothing was said.

Salazar felt increasingly pleased with his decision, and did not intend to spend any more time debating the issue with Billaud or Gourde. By themselves these guys were nothing. But he had no idea what misfortune might befall him if they turned up dead. He intended to conduct further business in Guyana and did not need governmental hassles getting in the way of his plans. It was easier to pay the men off at a fraction of what it would have cost him and be rid of them. They and their problems had already brought enough trouble. Even the smell of their sweat was nauseating.

It was time to be done here.

He faced Albert. "Tell the captain to stop the boat. Our guests are leaving."

"Billaud is right," Gourde spoke up from his seat. "You can't dump us overboard and expect us to swim to shore."

"So you have balls after all," said Salazar. He smiled.

Gourde nodded. "Big balls; a dick, too. And I intend to keep them."

"So you let Mr. Billaud do your talking for you?"

"There is not much I can do to change what's happening when your men have their guns aimed at our heads."

"And if they weren't?"

Gourde stood and pointed at Albert. "I'd tear Big-Boy there a new asshole. Then I would start in on the rest of your men, and then you. When that was done, I'd finish off by showing that half-breed Japanese bitch in the cabin below just how big my balls and what goes with them, are."

"An interesting proposition," Salazar said. He was mildly amused by Gourde's bravado. "And a stupid one."

"Not so stupid if you're about to be dumped overboard."

"I see your point." Salazar noticed Albert eyeing him with the predatory look reserved for moments like this. He shook his head, registering the disappointment in the big man's eyes. "But I'm afraid it is needless boasting. You'll be leaving in the Zodiac along with Mr. Billaud and the woman."

"And if she goes to the police?"

A risk Salazar was willing to take. "She's your problem. What you do with her when you are off this boat is your business. I strongly suggest you not give her the chance."

Gourde's eyes narrowed into angry slits.

Salazar could guess what he was thinking.

"The money?" Billaud asked, rising to his feet next to Gourde.

"Take it with you . . . throw it in the sea. I do not care. And you can keep the Zodiac. Call it a good-faith gift."

Billaud glanced at Gourde and nodded. Undoubtedly, he'd decided half was better than the alternative, even after the split. Gourde's gaze met his with the same resolve. Gourde nodded back.

"One more thing," Salazar said. "I never want to see either of you again."

"Let's get this done," Billaud said.

Salazar motioned to Albert. "Lower the Zodiac."

"The woman?" he asked.

For a moment Salazar reconsidered his decision to be rid of her along with the two men. Keeping her onboard for a few days could prove to be quite entertaining. But then she wasn't worth the additional trouble she could invoke upon him.

He turned to Jesus and Gato. "Bring her."

CHAPTER 63

Kazuko stopped pacing and faced the door to the cabin. The familiar clank of anchor chain was all she needed to know the boat was preparing to get underway. With that came a sinking feeling more desperate than any she'd felt before.

Help's not coming.

She rushed to the porthole and stared at the open sea, hoping she was wrong.

No police boats. No military gunboats.

In the distance two jet-skiers raced on the waves, kicking up a shower of spray behind their personal water craft. Simple, harmless fun in the waning hours of the day. Vacationers oblivious to the depravity in play so close to them.

There would be no rescue.

Still—

She pressed her face to the glass and strained to see astern. Perhaps help was coming and she just couldn't see them. Hope strengthened her resolve. Robert can't be dead. And nothing will keep Jack away.

They'll come for me. I know they will.

The deck under her feet vibrated as the massive engines powered up and gained RPMs. She felt the boat move and watched the sea slip by. Slow at first, then faster. She kept her eyes pressed tight to the glass, holding on to the last shred of hope. And when she felt the boat turn, tears welled in the corners of her eyes.

She would never see Robert or Jack again.

Hopelessness threatened to drag her into the deepest darkest corner of despair. She straightened and wiped the tears of fear and defeat away.

"I won't give in," she swore aloud. "Not without a fight."

She pinched her eyes shut, forcing back the moisture blurring her sight. And in a moment of reflection came the vision of Jesus's hands on her, groping, probing—a vileness forever seared into her memory. His dark eyes wide open with sadistic lust.

She clutched at her tattered blouse.

If only . . . I could have killed him.

Her single focus at that moment—survival. Nothing had changed. Not her will. Not the anger simmering inside her. She would survive.

I will.

Lost in thought, she hadn't noticed the engines slow—their RPMs dropping to an idle. All at once she realized the boat was stopping.

Perhaps . . .

She listened, but didn't hear the fall of the anchor. No clatter of chain. There was only the quieting drone of the diesel engines.

Again, she pressed her face to the glass.

Nothing.

A momentary stop. There could be a number of explanations. Some good, some bad—it would only be a guess. One thought lingered.

For how long?

There had to be some way . . . ?

Annett. If only she had . . .

Kazuko reflected on their meeting. She recalled hearing the click of the latch, but she hadn't tried the knob. Was it possible it had been a ruse and that Annett had only pretended to lock the bolt?

Her only chance.

She knew she would have to somehow sneak past Salazar's armed security team to reach the upper deck, and be ready to jump overboard when the yacht got underway. With the boat moving, they may not even notice an unusual shift in the pitch of the hull when she made her leap, or hear her splash. By the time they discovered her missing, there would be no turning back to search for her. They'd never find her in all that water.

Steeling herself, she stepped to the door and gently twisted the knob.

Click.

The knob turned, releasing the catch.

Unlocked . . .

She wasn't off the boat yet. But at least she had a chance.

My only chance.

To the left lay the salon, the door opening onto the upper deck, Salazar, and his group of thugs. To the right lay the unknown.

She eased the door open a crack.

There was but one thought on her mind: step quietly into the companionway and run as quickly and softly as she could. Into the unknown.

Muscles tensed to make her escape, she stepped back and swung the door inward.

CHAPTER 64

The sight of Jesus standing in the doorway with his hand outstretched and Gato directly behind him, made Kazuko go rigid. For a second she couldn't move or speak. Then, she found herself backing up. Almost stumbling.

Disgust and fear rose sour in her throat.

She got control of herself and stood firm. She did not intend to give them the satisfaction of watching her cower in the corner like a frightened child. Especially Jesus. The man had put his hands on her. He'd pay if he tried it again.

They both would.

"Stay away from me you one-eyed creep," she demanded.

"You're not happy to see me?" Jesus asked.

"I said stay away." She drew on every ounce of strength she had. They took a step closer.

"I warn you, don't come near me. That other pig, either."

"Why do you speak to me that way?" Jesus took another step. His lips curled into a sick, sadistic smirk that betrayed the sordid desire smoldering in the recesses of his twisted mind. It was obvious he did not intend to do as she asked. He lifted his hands in a questioning gesture. "Didn't we have fun last time we were together?"

"I'm warning you." She held her ground.

"My sweet puta." He stepped closer, his hand extended. "You do not need to be afraid of me."

"Or me," Gato joined in. He smiled and ran his fingers down the scratch marks on his cheek as if they were a badge of honor.

She didn't answer.

"Come to me." With his fingers, Jesus motioned her to him.

She didn't move.

"Be a good puta and do as you are told." Jesus took another step.

She knew he would. She'd counted on it. At once, she lashed out hard and fast. In a finely-timed move, she brought her right foot up between his legs and solidly into his crotch. She didn't miss.

Jesus grabbed his balls and crumpled to a heap on the floor, emitting a loud groan. He managed to curl into a fetal position and lie there. He continued to groan, but the fire of lust in his good eye was gone.

She backed up a step and stood ready to deal another debilitating blow, this time to Gato.

"I warned him," she said. "Now I'm warning you. Keep your hands off of me."

"You do not understand." Gato stayed where he was. His lips curled up slightly at the corners, possibly at the expense of Jesus's condition. "We came here to bring you to Mr. Salazar. You are going ashore."

"He's letting me go?" She relaxed a bit, but remained ready.

"The boat is waiting for you now."

Kazuko did not trust Gato or Salazar. But if it got her topside and off the boat she'd play their game. "Step away from the door and don't touch me. I know the way to the salon."

"As you wish." He shrugged indifference. "But I will be right behind you. And be thankful I follow orders. You would not be so happy otherwise."

She didn't need an explanation.

"And if Jesus hadn't been such a pig," she said, "he wouldn't be on the floor."

Gato's gaze dropped to Jesus. "You best do as you are told before he can stand. He will want a piece of you for what you have done to him."

Gato moved to the side, away from the door. She watched him to make sure it wasn't a trick to try and lure her into his grasp. If he planned to pull something, she wanted to be ready. Emboldened by determination, she stepped over Jesus and headed topside. And she was quick about it.

Gato hurried along the companionway behind her. She could hear the soles of his shoes pounding the deck. It didn't matter that he was there or that he was following close behind, the thug could do as he pleased as long as he kept to himself. She cringed at the thought of his hands on her.

Was Salazar truly going to let her go?

She held onto the hope he would. And if he didn't, she would dive overboard and go for a swim. One way or another, she was getting off the boat.

When she reached the salon, she noticed Salazar and more of his thugs standing on the rear deck. She could see that much through the windows. It didn't stop her. She opened the hatchway and quickly stepped into the afternoon air. Gato was right behind her. She closed the door in his face.

"Put her in the Zodiac," Salazar ordered.

He hadn't bothered with small talk. She was glad of that. An armed man stood waiting for her. He motioned the barrel of his automatic rifle. Gato was there, too. She didn't hesitate. Gato followed.

"Where is Jesus?" she heard Salazar say as she stepped away.

She glanced back and saw Gato shrug. *Tell him*, she thought. *Tell that asshole one of his filthy pigs is curled up on the floor cradling his swollen balls.*

The gesture was all he offered.

No guts. Just as well.

With a feeling of satisfaction she hurried along the narrow companionway to the boarding ladder. The thought that ran through her head was that the nightmare was almost over. She was getting off the boat. Stopping a couple of feet short, she peered expectantly over the side.

A lump rose and lodged in her throat.

Gourde looked up at her from below as though he was expecting her. So did the other man seated in the inflatable. From their expressions, they weren't happy.

Fine.

She'd go with them if that's what it took to get to shore.

Then, she saw Gourde smirk.

CHAPTER 65

Jack backed off on the throttle. They weren't going to catch *Margarete*, not on the jet skis. He looked at Robert and saw him slow to a stop as well. No doubt he felt just as helpless.

There had to be something they could do, but what?

He wiped the salt sting from his eyes and mouth with his hand, and motored over to Robert. Cutting his engine back to idle, he floated next to him. Their water craft rose and fell with the swells.

"What's the plan?"

Robert huffed. "Get Kazuko off that yacht, of course."

"I know that. How?"

"Sure aren't doing it on these things."

Jack considered their predicament. "Ryan is coming with a boat. We'll use that to go after her."

"I don't know about Ryan. He may not even be able to get one."

"No faith in the man?"

"Not much."

"I don't think we should count him out."

"And if he doesn't show?"

"We're not giving up."

"No shit." Robert's eyes remained fixed in the direction of the yacht. "I'll never give up looking for her, not until she's safe in my arms."

Jack felt just as strongly about Kazuko. And he didn't have to tell Robert that. He knew it. So did Kazuko.

She'd know they were coming for her.

And now that Jack thought about it, what they would do when they caught up with the boat remained an unanswered question. They were no better off or any more prepared than they had been on shore. But as sad a fact as that was, they were doing *something*, regardless of how foolish it seemed. He felt good about that. It was better than standing idly by while Salazar sailed off to who knew where with Kazuko onboard.

He scanned the water behind him. If Ryan had a boat, he wasn't on his way yet. "You could be right about Ryan."

Robert scoffed. "I know I'm right."

Jack read the doubt in his friend's expression—the same doubt he had. He held onto the hope they were wrong. There wasn't much else they could do at the moment. Not with the yacht speeding away and a big ocean for it to vanish in.

It would be virtually impossible to find Kazuko once they lost sight of her.

And if they did locate her at some future date, it would be too late.

Too late . . .

He cringed at the thought. Then he noticed *Margarete* slow down. They were a good distance away, but the boat had plainly cut power.

He pointed. "Looks like she's stopping."

"I say she's stopped. Let's go." Robert didn't wait. He goosed the throttle.

Jack drifted a fraction of a second longer to make sure his eyes weren't deceiving him, then gave the engine gas. The jet ski roared forward.

They weren't done yet.

The ride was no less punishing, but they were closing on the yacht. The wind and salt spray lashing his face mattered not at all. He still did not know what they would do when they caught up to the yacht, but he knew there was no stopping Robert.

He'd hate to be the person who tried.

There was still a hundred yards of open water between them

and *Margarete* when he saw a Zodiac speed away from the boat. Almost immediately, a boil of foam erupted behind the yacht as the ship got back underway.

Salazar was on the move. But that no longer mattered.

The game had changed.

He steered toward the Zodiac and kept the throttle pressed tight against its stop. A big man sat at the tiller of the frail craft. A man and a woman sat in front of him. There was no mistaking the long, silky, black hair blowing in the wind. Nor the woman's honey-colored skin.

Kazuko.

And if he was right, Gourde was driving.

Jack put his jet ski on a collision course with the rubber boat. Robert had seen her, too. He was headed in that direction.

Two against two—the odds had improved.

But first, they had to catch up to them.

The Zodiac was quickly gaining speed. There was plenty of horsepower to push the small inflatable along. And the person driving wasn't wasting any time getting them to shore.

It was going to be close.

CHAPTER 66

Jack kept the throttle of his jet ski wide open. The Zodiac continued to pick up speed, but he and Robert were gaining on it. He could see Kazuko clearly now. And he could see Gourde. The man in front he thought he recognized from the fly-over at the mine. All three were looking in Robert and his direction.

And it wasn't casual interest. They'd been recognized.

Gourde and his partner knew they were being pursued. Kazuko realized it, too. She struggled with the two men.

A wildcat fighting to get free.

Jack expected her to jump at any moment. He kept the throttle buried to the stops. Robert was no doubt doing the same. They'd be there to pluck her out of the water when she dove in.

If she could break loose.

She was clearly having a problem fighting off her captors. Jack could see her struggle to the side of the Zodiac only to be pulled back into the middle of the boat by the two men. She kicked and thrashed, trying to wrestle her arms from their grasp. But she was no match for Gourde and the other man.

The men obviously intended to keep her in the boat all the way to shore. But what then? Drag her kicking and screaming up the sand?

Or worse?

Idiots.

All they had to do was let her jump overboard and the chase would be over. They had to know that. But then maybe they didn't. Action born on desperation. Maybe that's what it had been all along. It didn't matter. The men had chosen poorly. They'd pay dearly for what they were doing to her.

And for Salazar's men shooting Robert.

A rolling swell sent him airborne. He came down sideways and accelerated the rest of the way through a three-sixty. The next swell threatened to toss him from his seat. He goosed the throttle and righted himself.

Again, he went airborne.

He landed hard and kept control. Robert was off to the right. He'd managed to do the same. They were less than fifty-yards from the inflatable, and closing. Kazuko still struggled with the men to break free. She wouldn't give up.

Not ever.

The gap narrowed. Both men's eyes focused on him. There was no doubt now that they knew who he was and why he was there. He could see the hatred etched into their expressions. They obviously weren't armed or they would have been shooting.

He ached to get his hands on them.

There was no letting them go. Even if Kazuko managed to jump overboard, Robert would be there to pick her up.

It wouldn't take both of them, Jack thought.

He'd hunt down Gourde and the other man, even if it meant he had to chase them all the way back to the mine.

They weren't getting away.

Another swell sent him flying amid a trail of water and foam. They were nearing shore. In the shallower water, the swells were building closer together, more difficult to negotiate—for the Zodiac, too. He bit back his anger and kept the throttle buried.

All at once, the inflatable hit a wave and jumped wildly.

The men made a grab to hold on.

Jack saw them let go of Kazuko to keep from being tossed in the water. He held his breath. Her chance.

She didn't hesitate.

She hit the water and came up swimming.

Damn, she was fast.

In the heat of the chase, he'd forgotten what a great swimmer she was. She stroked hard in the direction of Robert. He'd seen her leap overboard and was slowing down to pick her up.

My turn, Jack told himself.

He didn't slow. Robert was with Kazuko. She was safe.

Gourde and the other man weren't so lucky.

Jack hoped they felt the wrath of God pressing down on them. Time was on his side. It had run out for both men in front of him.

If they knew fear, surely they felt it now.

He aimed his jet ski at the inflatable. He wasn't going to let them reach shore. They had their chance and blew it.

His gauged his timing and braced himself. Nothing stood in his way.

At the last second, he leaped, taking Gourde headfirst into the water with him as the Kawasaki slammed into the rubber boat with devastating force.

CHAPTER 67

Jack hit the water and lost his grip on Gourde. But the big man was already in motion. There was no way for him to stop what was happening.

They both went under.

It only took a second for Jack to get his bearings. Six feet of clear water separated them. Gourde flailed and kicked in a frantic struggle to reach the surface.

Jack remained confident in what he was doing. He was in his element. Exactly what he had wanted . . . and counted on. The big man was powerfully built, but he did not appear to be a good swimmer.

Now they were equal.

Jack didn't back off. He grabbed Gourde around the neck in an arm-bar chokehold and hauled him back under. There was plenty of fight in Gourde, and plenty of strength. He tightened his hold on the big man. Bull neck, powerful shoulders—it was like wrestling a floundering whale.

Gourde hammered an elbow into his ribs. Even under water, it felt as if he'd been struck by a speeding bus.

He felt his grip slip.

He pushed away. He couldn't let Gourde get hold of him.

They both kicked to the surface.

Jack took a breath and dove deep. He pulled off his shirt and shoes and looked up. Above him Gourde kicked and stroked crazily toward shore. A dozen feet away, the jet ski bobbed upside down. Next to it floated the tattered remains of the inflatable.

Both were a ruined mess.

He expected to see the other man's body floating mangled and bloody among the debris. It wasn't. But Gourde was there swimming as best he could.

Jack counted on the big man's desire to get to the beach overpowering his eagerness to fight in the water. Surprise and timing was everything. Make the asshole have to take a breath, suck in some water, get him coughing. He wouldn't be allowed to reach land.

Amid a trail of bubbles, Jack swam at him. He came at the flailing man from below and slammed his carefully aimed right fist into soft flesh at the base of the guy's sternum.

It was immediately obvious he hadn't missed.

He heard the big man groan amid a flurry of bubbles as he expelled air from his lungs. The urge to take a breath would come next.

He grabbed the waistband of Gourde's pants and pulled him under. The normal reaction of a drowning man is to kick and claw for the surface. Grasp anything within reach and hold on.

Total panic.

Jack knew what to expect and counted on it. But he also knew the danger of the situation. He had to stay in control.

Gourde kicked violently and lashed out with his hands. Jack was ready for it and backstroked away. He shot to the surface and took another breath. Gourde popped up a few feet away, coughing and gagging.

Jack ducked under. He could hold his breath a full two minutes if he had to. He didn't think it would be necessary.

On the surface above him, Gourde stroked and thrashed toward the overturned jet ski. He'd still be coughing, trying to catch his breath. His only thought would be to grab hold of anything that would keep his head above water.

He wouldn't make it.

Jack made another run at him, swimming as fast as he could.

A human torpedo on a collision course. And again he hammered a fist into the big man's midsection, adding the speed and weight of his body to the punch. An instant later, he pulled the man under by his waistband.

Gourde reacted with even more panic. Jack could hear the man's garbled cries as he desperately kicked and clawed for the surface, trying to not inhale.

Jack caught a knee to the side of the head and one to the ribs. Hard enough for him to want to back off.

Not in the plan.

He maneuvered himself behind Gourde and wrapped his arms and legs around the lower half of the big man's body. A bear hug that would drag him under and keep him there.

Jack squeezed as hard as he could and let his body sink. Gourde would not reach the surface. He'd pay horribly for what he'd done.

But Gourde wasn't going down easy. He was a wild man possessed with one thought, one goal: get to the surface and breathe. He kicked and clawed at the water. He grabbed and tugged at Jack's arms, and punched ineffectively at his head and shoulders.

Jack held on.

It took every ounce of strength he had to control the big man's violent thrashing. A minute, a minute and a half…he fought to control his own need to breathe.

Finally, Gourde's erratic movements slowed, and then ceased.

There were no more escaping bubbles from his lungs. No more garbled cries of panic.

Only deathly silence.

Jack released his hold and let the man drift, arms and legs played like a dead frog floating in a lily pond.

With any luck the sharks would make a meal of him.

If they don't choke on the meat.

Jack kicked hard toward the sheen of sunlight above; he needed oxygen, fast.

CHAPTER 68

Jack did not slow down at the surface. His head and shoulders erupted from the ocean amid spray and foam. He tilted his face skyward and breathed in. It seemed like he had been under forever.

Settling onto his back, he fanned his arms to keep himself afloat and took several more heaving lungfuls of air. Only then did he sink his feet beneath him and look around. There was one more person to concern himself with. The second man's corpse was not among the wreckage.

Not that could be seen from below.

He raised his head out of the water and scanned the surface for the man's body.

Nowhere.

Somehow he'd survived. But now it was his turn.

Jack steeled himself for what would come next. The fire of revenge had not been quenched by Gourde's death. And wouldn't, until both men answered for what they had done—not just to him, or to Robert or Kazuko, or even to the scientists who'd been murdered; they would have to pay for what they'd done to the people at Kaburi Landing, as well. And to the Mazaruni and all the creatures that perished in its depths.

The man would pay the way Gourde had.

With his life.

The whine of Robert's jet ski drew Jack's gaze toward the beach.

A swell rolled under him lifting him up. Robert and Kazuko were speeding into the surf on a direct heading for shore. Ahead of them, the missing man from the Zodiac raced north along the beach, moving fast on the hard sand above the tide line.

He'd gotten farther than Jack anticipated. He never expected him to reach shore alive.

But he was far from safe.

Robert would not let that happen. He'd get his payback . . . Kazuko, too. They'd have the pleasure of taking the asshole down.

And the ultimate pleasure of knowing Gourde floated with the fish.

Jack wasn't content to remain among the debris. The once-fine Zodiac was done for. The overturned jet ski would need a lot of work to get it running. There was no need for him to remain there.

Taking a deep breath, he swam toward shore. His confidence in Robert's ability to handle the fleeing man was undeniable, but he wasn't going to leave anything to chance.

The man was going down hard.

And neither Robert nor Kazuko would be hurt in the process.

Jack waded onto the beach next to the abandoned jet ski. His adrenalin pumped. Robert and Kazuko raced up the beach. They were forty-yards away—Robert sprinting for all he was worth over the soft sand a half-dozen steps ahead of Kazuko—narrowing the gap between them and the man desperate to escape his fate.

The guy wouldn't make it much further.

Jack joined in the race.

His legs moved, but with great effort. The struggle with Gourde had taken more out of him than he realized, and he could see at once he had no chance of catching them. Robert and Kazuko were moving fast, so was the man they chased after. It appeared he was running toward a dirt road and a wall of dense foliage beyond.

Thick enough to get lost in.

Or something else.

Jack tried to picture what lay beyond the forest canopy. They had not passed the inlet to the Essequibo River. The town of Parika, possibly—more likely the airstrip he'd flown into when he arrived in Guyana.

282

The helicopter.

The fleeing man veered toward the jungle fringe. There was still some distance between him and Robert. Kazuko was right there, too.

Jack pushed himself to move faster.

Get him before he reaches the jungle, he willed his friends.

The man might still get away.

All at once, Robert took on an unexpected burst of speed. And then he was on the man, clubbing him on the back of the neck with his fists.

Driving him to the ground.

Robert's momentum carried him forward, taking them both crashing to the sand in a tangled heap. He came up on top and hammered his right fist solidly into the man's face three times before he let up. Kazuko stood yelling at Robert to hit him again.

It wasn't necessary.

Jack got there and saw at once that Robert's punches had dazed the man. There was no fight left in him. Kazuko stood cussing. It looked as though she wanted to stomp him. And then she did: two solid blows to the ribs.

Jack put his arm around her shoulders to calm her.

"Asshole." She wasn't ready to let go of the fight.

"Calm down," he said. "The man's done for."

She looked at Jack. Fire glowed in her eyes.

"He deserves more," she said. Then she looked down the beach as if searching for Gourde. "That other sonofabitch, too."

"Don't worry about him."

She brought her gaze up to meet his. And in that moment, a silent look of understanding passed between them. He did not need to explain further.

She knew Gourde was dead. That *he* had killed him.

"You two," the dazed man muttered as Robert used his left hand to roll him into a sitting position.

"In the flesh," Jack said.

He and Robert stood over the man. Robert gasped to catch his breath. His right hand was still balled into a tight fist.

"Both of you should have been dead."

"Close but no cigar," Robert answered with a huff. "Now, I would advise you to sit there and not move."

"I'd listen to him," Jack added.

The glassy look of shock faded from the man's eyes, replaced by the dull sheen of resignation. He rubbed the blood from his mouth and looked at it on his hand, but made no move to stand.

He peered up at them. "So what now? You have no authority over me."

Robert stiffened. "Authority enough to kick your ass if I want to."

"And I'll help him," Jack said.

"Because of *her*?" The man tossed a nasty look in the direction of Kazuko. "I had nothing to do with her being on that boat. That was all Gourde's doing."

"You asshole." Kazuko raised the flat of her hand.

Jack caught her wrist before she could slap the guy's face. At the same time, he fought to control his own anger. He wished he'd let her smack him. He had that and so much more coming.

"And he worked for you," answered Jack.

"And it was his idea, not mine," the man insisted.

"Should have let me hit him," Kazuko said.

"I think you're right."

"I would have," Robert grumbled. "Even added one or two of my own in for good measure."

"Gourde's the one you want," the man protested. "Go after him."

"Your friend is waiting for you at the gates of hell," Jack said.

"You killed him?"

Jack could still feel Gourde convulsing in his grasp. He did not harbor the least bit of regret. Drowning was almost too good for him.

"He had an accident."

The man's shoulders visibly slumped. "I'm next, I suppose."

Jack studied the man. "Depends."

"On what?"

Jack turned to the sound of a vehicle speeding toward them on the road. A dusty green Land Rover with two people on board. He could just make out the face of the man driving.

"On them," he said.

"Ryan," Robert confirmed.

Jack nodded. "Looks like he made it after all."

CHAPTER 69

The Land Rover skidded to a stop. Dust billowed from the back and engulfed the SUV as the two occupants climbed out of the vehicle. Jack waved Ryan and Captain Arjoon over.

He'd expected Ryan to show up, just not in a car. He figured Captain Arjoon had been embarrassed into action. It didn't matter; they were there.

And in the nick of time.

Almost.

"That's not exactly a boat," Jack said when Ryan approached.

"I ran into Captain Arjoon out front of your hotel." Ryan tossed a sideways nod in the captain's direction. "He was on his way to see you."

"Impeccable timing, Captain," Jack said to Arjoon.

"We needed to talk," answered Arjoon. He looked at the man on the ground and scanned the ocean in the direction of the distant yacht. "We still do."

"It was his idea to follow along on shore," offered Ryan. "I take it this is one of the men responsible."

"One of them," Jack said. He silently watched Captain Arjoon produce a pair of handcuffs and shackle the man's hands behind his back. He added, "Another one is floating out there."

"Drowned?"

"You could say that."

Arjoon lifted the man to his feet. "What is your name?"

The man's gaze shifted from the police captain to Jack, and back to the Captain. "Billaud. I have done nothing wrong."

"Doubtful." Captain Arjoon shoved Billaud toward the Land Rover and followed close behind him.

Jack watched. He wondered if he would get what was coming to him. It was almost too bad he wouldn't be there to find out.

Almost.

He looked at Ryan. "He claims he had nothing to do with Kazuko's kidnapping, but he's at least responsible for poisoning the Mazaruni and the death of a dozen or more villagers. And he probably ordered the scientists killed."

Ryan looked at Kazuko. "You're all right?"

Kazuko visibly shivered and clutched her tattered blouse. Robert put his arm around her and pulled her close. Looking up at him with a smile, she snaked her arm around his waist.

"Fine now," she said.

Jack was happy to see her anger had subsided. He eyed the yacht fading in the distance, and stared at Ryan. "Seems your man is getting away."

Ryan peered out to sea. "He'll show up somewhere."

"And when he does?" Jack tossed Ryan a questioning glance.

Ryan smiled. "I'll be there."

"You're not giving up, then?"

"Not likely."

"Might think about it," Jack said.

"You could have a point." Ryan turned and stared pensively in the direction of the yacht.

Jack didn't press.

For a moment, he stood taking in the scene. Arjoon was busy with Billaud. Ryan was lost in thought. Robert and Kazuko held onto each other. Everyone was doing their own thing.

Exactly the way it should be, he thought.

He looked at his friend. "I'm going to pull that jet ski of yours on to the sand before the tide carries it away. Then I'm going to see if I can get the other one ashore. With luck, I'll get my deposit back."

"We'll help," Robert smiled. He looked at Ryan. "Wanna come?"

Ryan shook his head. "I'm going with Arjoon and see what Billaud's has to say."

Jack was happy to let Ryan go. He waited for Robert and Kazuko to gather themselves and the three of them headed toward the water. Jack was watching the waves when he spied a nylon bag roll ashore in the surf. He trotted ahead and retrieved the duffle as the tide began to suck it back into the face of the next wave. Robert and Kazuko caught up to him.

"What'd you find?" Robert asked.

Jack zipped open the bag and peered inside. "Drug money, would be my guess."

"Money?" Robert edged closer and craned his neck.

Jack reached inside the bag and pulled out a banded packet of hundred dollar bills. "Soggy greenbacks—a lot of them."

Robert gripped the edge of the bag and pulled it open enough to see the money inside. He held it so Kazuko could have a peek. Then, he glanced toward Arjoon and Billaud. "Asshole over there and Salazar must have made some kind of deal."

"My guess is Salazar bought himself some gold."

"A lot of gold by the look of all that cash."

"What should we do with it?" asked Kazuko.

Jack eyed Arjoon. A lot of people had been hurt or killed. Unimaginable damage had been done to the river's ecosystem. Perhaps the money could be used to help set things right.

"What do you say we to turn it over to Captain Arjoon?"

Kazuko looked from Robert to Jack. "Can we trust him?"

Robert shrugged.

Jack said, "Guess we don't have a choice."

"*Ho'oponopono*," Robert said.

"Making things right." Jack chuckled. "Seems to be a habit of mine."

CHAPTER 70

It was almost midnight when Jack stepped from the shower in his room at the Princess Hotel. The hot water left him feeling almost human. Bruises had formed where he'd been kicked and elbowed by Gourde. His muscles ached, but it was comforting for him to know Gourde had not died easy.

The price—Jack swore to himself—*for messing with me and my friends.*

Wearing a thin, white hotel robe and nothing else, he stepped from the bathroom and walked to the end of his bed where his clothes lay neatly folded. With some urging from Captain Arjoon the hotel laundry had been adequately accommodating.

All clean and tidy.

Jack did not mind that Arjoon had kept him up late answering questions. He'd expected as much. And he knew there would be more questions that needed answers. But for now the Captain had what he needed from them.

Billaud would remain in jail.

At least for now.

There were never any guarantees.

Jack toyed with the idea of switching off the lights and climbing into bed. Then he quickly dismissed the thought. He was beyond exhaustion, but the day's events had left him way too keyed up to sleep.

Robert and Kazuko—he was sure—were as exhausted as he was. He wondered if they were fast asleep in their room, or if they were as keyed up as him.

And then he thought about Pillai. She and Soukis were in Bartica. The police would be talking to them, too, and probably already had. He wished she was here, cuddled in his arms.

And as he thought about how good that would feel, he realized there was nothing he wanted more. He remembered how wonderful it was to take her, naked and wanting into his arms at the creek. Warm female flesh pressed tight against his.

It hadn't bothered her to strip in front of him. She'd been as eager as he'd been to scrub away the chemicals threatening to poison them. He'd tried not to look, but found it impossible not to stare. Their attraction to each other the first day they'd met had been immediate and undeniable. She was a smart, wonderfully brave, lady.

And she was beautiful . . . all of her.

In spite of his best effort to look away, he'd searched out every visible curve of her exquisite body. No imperfection could make him look away. Then, she had stood and turned her big, dark eyes on him.

Two denied lovers caught in an impossible situation.

For an eternity they'd stared at each other. And even now, closing his eyes, he could feel her gaze sweep the length of his naked body. It hadn't been enough. Not for him, or her. The two of them—lovers—alone in the jungle.

He took a deep breath and smiled.

A knock at the door jarred him from the bliss of his memory. Irritated at the untimely interruption, his first thought was that Captain Arjoon was there with more questions—something that couldn't wait till morning. But then the man didn't seem that dedicated. Whatever he had left to ask would surely wait until after he had a good night's sleep.

Tightening the belt on his robe, he opened the door. At once he cursed himself for having hesitated even a second.

Pillai stood there smiling at him.

She was the last person he expected to show up. The timing

was perfect.

She was perfect.

The thoughts that had been dashed away by the knock at the door, returned. He took her hand and eased her inside the room. "I didn't expect to see you for at least a couple of days," he said, his back facing the open door.

Pillai stepped close. "Kazuko called and told me what you did. I couldn't stay away."

"I'm glad you didn't."

She looked up at him. "I wasn't sure how—"

He placed his fingertip lightly on her lips, not letting her finish. She didn't protest.

And she looked at him exactly the way she had at the creek. Those alluring eyes melted his heart.

He gently brushed a stray strand of black hair from her forehead with his fingers, cupped the sides of her cheeks with his big hands, and kissed her long and passionately. And when he pulled away, he held her close a splendid moment longer.

"Remember?" he asked. "I promised you that next time it would be a king-sized bed and champagne."

"And I'll hold you to it," she said. "But you need to know we are not alone."

Jack reluctantly let go of her and faced the door. "You could have cleared your throat or something."

"What?" Robert laughed. "And miss all that?"

Kazuko edged Robert aside. To Pillai, she said, "Jack should have been the one to call you, not me. But then, he isn't always the sharpest knife in the drawer."

"I wanted to in the worst way." Jack felt his face heat with embarrassment. He needed to explain. "Captain Arjoon didn't exactly give me a chance to make a phone call until he was done with his questions. By then I was afraid you'd be sound asleep and I didn't want to disturb you."

He glanced back and forth between the two women hoping they understood.

"You're forgiven," Pillai said with a flirtatious wink.

Kazuko just smiled.

He breathed a silent sigh of relief.

"I've still got some making up to do," he promised. "Lots of it. And it will be my pleasure."

"Again...I'll hold you to it," Pillai said.

Flashing back on their romantic interlude at the creek, Jack looked forward to his king-sized bed. He turned his attention on Robert and Kazuko who stood smiling from the doorway. Something had brought them to his room.

"Okay," he said. "I know why Pillai is here. What has you two up so late?"

"We thought you might be hungry," Kazuko answered. She stepped into the room and took Pillai's hand. Obviously, they had become good friends.

Jack noticed Robert and Kazuko were dressed in new sets of clothes. Probably purchased in the hotel gift shop. That was what he should have done since his other clothing was in his room in Bartica. Pillai had changed into a fresh outfit, too. All three of them looked ready to be seen in public. He glanced at his freshly laundered work attire on the bed. They would have to do.

"It'll only take me a minute to dress," he said.

CHAPTER 71

The next day Jack was roused out of bed by the harsh ring of the phone on the bedside table. He glanced at the clock: 10 AM. He wanted to let it ring. He wasn't ready to get up yet.

"Hello," he mumbled into the receiver.

"Captain Arjoon here," the voice answered.

Jack sighed. "More questions already?"

"Only a couple."

Jack heard something in the tone of the man's voice that made him sit up. "I find that hard to believe. What's up?"

"Billaud got himself killed last night."

It took a second for what he was being told to sink in. He rubbed the sleep from his eyes, and said, "You couldn't have called with better news."

"I thought that would make you happy."

Jack was fully awake now. Arjoon definitely had his attention. "What'd the asshole go and do, mouth off to the wrong person?"

"Several wrong persons, apparently."

"Good for them. Hope he died slow and horrible."

"A broomstick shoved up his ass, so yeah, I'd say he did."

Pillai stirred on the bed. Her long hair spilled across her bare breasts. Jack smiled. "Where does this leave me and my friends?"

"Gerard Gourde's timely drowning simplifies matters a lot," he explained. "As far as the kidnapping goes, there's nothing to be done, not with him dead and Salazar in the wind. But there are the murders in Bartica. Even so, there are only a few details left that need explanation. We have the other men involved already in custody. They'll answer for their part in the killings, but they're eager to put the blame on Gourde and the man you killed inside the hut."

"I really didn't have a choice. Those men intended to kill us."

"Nothing we've found leads us to believe otherwise."

Jack felt a rush of relief. "So what happens to me?"

"Self-defense is not a crime in this country. You will be free to go after I'm done talking with you today. So will your friends. But I do think it would be a good idea for you to conduct your scientific research elsewhere."

"I'm sure that can be arranged." Jack paused in thought. "I do have a question you can answer for me. What about the money?"

Captain Arjoon laughed. "I was wondering when you would get around to that."

"Well?" Jack truly wanted to know.

"Let me put it to you this way. You are a very persuasive man . . . and maybe the most honest person I've met. This morning I spoke to Deputy Minister Sukhai at the Ministry of Health. She was quick to agree with me that there is no way to determine who the cash belongs to. So we decided the money will be turned over to the Ministry of Health to aid in the cleanup of the Mazaruni."

"That's wonderful news. When would you like to meet so we can wrap this mess up?"

"Can you be in my office in an hour?"

"One hour," Jack said, and clicked off the phone.

"More questions?" Pillai asked sleepily.

She was on her side, facing him. The top edge of the sheet lay draped across her hips . . . her exposed breasts were full, soft, and inviting. He snuggled in next to her and melted into the warmth of her cinnamon skin. His muscles were sore and his body still hurt in the places where Gourde had kicked and hit him. None of that mattered. Not with her in his arms.

He snaked his arm around her waist and held her close. "A few loose ends," he whispered. "But you don't have to be there."

"Can I tell you something?"

"Sure."

"You're a tough character. But I think you're a softy at heart."

He felt his face heat for the second time in only a few hours and kept it buried against her breasts so she wouldn't see him blush. "My compliments to your astute observation. Hopefully my secret is safe with you."

"What secret? Kazuko told me all about you. Warned me, too. I'm afraid you're an open book, Big Boy."

"I'm not that big."

"Really?"

"Well, maybe." They both chuckled.

CHAPTER 72

Late that afternoon, having read over and signed the detailed statements they'd given Captain Arjoon, Jack and his friends were free to go. They adjourned to the nearest bar for a celebratory drink. Ryan joined them. They crowded around a small table and Jack paid for the first round.

They were all in a party mood.

"So," he said to Ryan, "where do you go from here?"

"I'm not sure." He stared at the label on his beer bottle and picked at the corner. "I was thinking about following the advice a friend gave me and forget about Salazar. For now, anyway."

"Sounds like a good idea."

There was plenty of chatter in the bar, but for a long moment no one at their table spoke.

Ryan broke the silence. "That was one hell-of-a mess you got yourselves into."

"We didn't *get* ourselves into anything," Jack answered. "More like, it fell on our heads with no encouragement from anyone at this table."

"Still."

"We're all anxious to put it behind us."

"How about you?"

"Especially me."

"I meant, where do *you* go from here?"

"Captain Arjoon hinted that he didn't want me in his country, so I'll be leaving on the first flight out. My friends, too. Last night we talked about spending a week in Key West. The annual Hemingway Festival will be getting underway and I owe them the vacation they were supposed to have here."

Ryan chuckled. "This certainly was no vacation."

"Not even close. So, as I said, I guess that's where we'll go."

"What do you mean *guess*?" Robert said. "You bet your ass we're going."

Kazuko turned to Pillai, and smiled. "I do hope you've decided to join us. It'll be great fun. And Key West is nothing like this place."

Pillai peered knowingly into Jack's blue eyes; slowly her lips curled into a conspiratorial smile. "I suppose I can squeeze in a week of fun before I head home. Besides, Jack promised me something he hasn't yet fulfilled. I intend to see that he keeps it."

Jack recalled only making one promise. He furrowed his brow at her. "And what promise would that be?"

Robert and Kazuko looked questioningly at each other.

"Jack making promises." Kazuko chuckled. "I want to hear this."

"Makes two of us," Robert said.

Pillai swept her gaze over the people at the table and settled on Jack. He didn't need to look to know his friends' eyes also focused on him.

He felt his face heat for the third time.

"You promised me a king-sized bed, remember?" She winked. "The one in your room is a queen."

Jack had to laugh. "I did at that."

"Well?" Pillai arched her brow at him.

"Top of the list, I swear."

"Then I couldn't possibly turn you down."

For once, Jack wasn't blushing. "I can't wait."

They lifted their beers in a toast.

For the next few minutes, he sat with his back against his chair quietly looking at the women, thinking about the humiliation Pillai had endured at the hands of Gourde. And Kazuko. He hadn't been given a detailed account of what she went through aboard the yacht, but her torn clothing had been enough to give him an idea of what went on. He didn't need to know more. This wasn't the first time she'd proved to be worth her salt . . . Pillai, too, from what he had been told. Both women were strong and courageous. The emotional scars were there—he was sure—but neither woman was letting them show. He admired them for their fortitude and had the utmost respect for their character.

Ryan sucked down the last of his beer, pushed away from the table, and rose to his feet.

"Going already?" Jack asked.

"Wish I didn't have to, but there's some business I need to tend to that requires a clear head." He fished a twenty out of his jeans pocket and tossed it on the table. "The next round's on me. And who knows, maybe we'll see each other again."

"You never know," Jack said. He stood and offered his hand. "Take care of yourself."

Ryan accepted his hand and shook it. "Enjoy Key West."

"We will," Robert said, pushing his chair back. He stood and took his turn shaking Ryan's hand. "Thanks again for bringing the cavalry."

"Right. Like you two needed it."

"You tried, that's what counts."

"I suppose so." Ryan faced the women and offered them a friendly salute. "Kazuko, Pillai, it was definitely nice meeting you ladies. I just wish it had been under more pleasant circumstances. Unfortunately, that's rarely the case in my line of work."

The women stood and offered their hands as well.

"Next time it will be," Kazuko said.

"I look forward to it then." And with that he walked out of the bar.

"Back to celebrating." Jack signaled for another round. "Ryan's buying."

"Good." Robert reached for the twenty. "I like free booze."

"Wish we were flying out tonight," Kazuko said in a wistful tone.

"Another night won't matter," Jack assured her. "Robert and I will have you and Pillai on the first flight out of here in the morning . . . first class."

"What about our clothes?"

"I made arrangements to have them brought here." He smiled at Pillai. "Yours, too. I hope you don't mind. Soukis helped."

"Mind?" Pillai scoffed. "I'm happy to not have to go back to that town."

"I'll drink to that," Kazuko added.

"A week of cold beer, cheeseburgers, and Jimmy Buffet tunes." Robert raised his bottle. "Nothing can possibly go wrong there."

EPILOGUE

Jack tightened his seatbelt and peered through the window in the fuselage next to him. The plane banked on approach, and the Key West airport came into view. Beyond that, the broad expanse of deep-blue Gulf water, fishing boats, tankers, and all types of pleasure craft, powered and under sail—a 'V' of frothy white foam in the wake behind them as they cut a path through the water.

He'd tried to doze, but couldn't. His mind had replayed the events in Guyana a hundred times, every sordid detail. They were fortunate to be alive.

All of them.

He knew he'd be a long time forgetting the harrowing days he spent there.

The jet touched down with a minor shriek as its tires settled onto the runway. Jack focused his mind on more pleasant thoughts as the plane taxied to the gate. Seated in the front two rows, he and his friends were first to exit the fuselage. Robert headed for the car rental counter.

Jack, Pillai, and Kazuko were pulling their bags from the conveyor belt in the baggage claim area when he walked up to them.

"I'm driving," he announced.

"Only because you insist," Jack said. "You've got a car, I take it?"

"In the lot."

Fifteen minutes later, Robert was seated behind the steering wheel of a red and white Mini Cooper with a roof rack packed tight with their suitcases, driving them southwest on Flagler Avenue. Jack welcomed the blast of cold air from the vents on the dash.

"Could have picked a car with more leg room," he said, adjusting his butt in the seat.

"Be glad you're not squeezed in back here," said Pillai, from behind him.

"He'll owe us for this," Kazuko added. "They both will."

Robert grinned into the rearview mirror. "Small town, small car."

Jack had to chuckle. "If you say so."

He refocused his attention on the road. Having concentrated his research work in the Northwest Hawaiian Islands, he had never been to Key West. His only knowledge of the place had come from the internet in his room and the article he'd picked up at the airport. Ahead of them lay the southernmost point in the contiguous United States. And not too far from that was Duval Street, with its seemingly endless supply of bars, restaurants and nightclubs.

Party central . . .

"Our suites at the Pier House should be ready when we get there," he said, hoping to un-ruffle the girls' feathers. "We'll get settled in and then find us a bar on Duval Street, have some conch chowder and drink us some cold beer."

Robert negotiated the sub-compact around a pedestrian and fell in behind a slow moving car. "My sentiments, exactly. What do you say we skip the settling in part, dump the bags in our rooms and get us that beer you just promised?"

"Was that a promise?" Pillai asked Jack.

"Apparently so."

"Sounded like one to me," Robert said. He made a quick right turn onto White Street and braked hard to avoid hitting a car ahead of them.

"Take 'er easy, Hoss." Jack gripped the dash. "Correct me if I'm wrong, but you seem a bit uptight."

"Not really . . . well, yeah."

"And?"

Robert appeared to give thought to the comment. "Guess I

haven't quite gotten over what we just went through."

"I don't think any of us have," Kazuko was quick to point out.

"You can say that again," Pillai added.

Robert slowed, made a left turn onto Highway 1, and sped up. This time he took it slower. "That beer is sounding better and better."

* * *

Two days later, Jack rested his muscled arms on a table inside Sloppy Joe's and gripped his glass of beer: cold draft lager with not too much head. He lifted the brew to his lips and savored a refreshing swallow that did a lot to brighten his already great day.

Pillai sat next to him; nothing could make him happier.

He pointed at a photo gallery of Ernest Hemmingway hanging on the wall. "What do you ladies think of this place? Supposedly, it was Hemmingway's choice watering hole. There's even a drink named after him. If you look, it's on the menu: the *Papa Dobles*—his favorite—two and a half jiggers of white rum, the juice of two limes, and half a grapefruit."

"I'm sure he had many," Pillai said.

That was enough to make them all chuckle.

Jack curiously scanned the pictures of the famous author. At least two dozen photos framed the drink menu above the bar. "I read somewhere that he wrote the draft of *The Old Man and the Sea* in eight weeks."

Robert nodded. "That's right. It became a book-of-the-month selection and won Hemingway the Pulitzer Prize in May 1952, a month before he left for his second trip to Africa."

Jack was truly enjoying himself. Not many people knew it, but he'd always been a Hemmingway fan.

"If my memory serves me correctly," he began, "in 1954, Hemingway was almost killed in two successive plane crashes while on a sightseeing flight over the Belgian Congo."

"He survived?" Pillai asked incredulously.

"He did," Jack said. "He spent a few weeks recuperating and reading his own obituaries written after the public believed he had died when the second plane exploded on takeoff."

"Think how lucky he was," Kazuko said. "Two plane crashes."

"One crash when he was flying over the Congo," Robert explained. "And a second that occurred when he attempted to fly out to get medical attention for injuries suffered in the initial crash. You just can't trust the bush."

"You fly," Jack pointed out.

"A De Havilland Beaver." Robert grinned. "They don't crash."

"If you say so." Jack went back to his beer.

Sloppy Joe's was quiet with only a few mid-afternoon customers. It wouldn't stay that way long. The town was filling up. Somewhere up the street, Jimmy Buffet sang a tune about cheeseburgers and paradise and a big glass of cold beer. There would be a band playing to the evening crowd here: Barry Cuda and the Sharks. The place would be packed. Jack was content to sit there quietly enjoying his Land Shark Lager.

And so, it seemed, was Robert. After a whole three minutes he asked, "So what do you want to do next? Tuesday is the Hemingway Festival. That'll be fun. Until then we can check out the Mel Fisher Maritime Museum—see what a half billion dollars in treasure looks like. And then there's the Shipwreck Museum, one of Key West's top attractions."

"And there's Hemingway's house." Kazuko pointed out. "And about a thousand cats."

"That, too," Robert agreed after a millisecond's thought.

"We'll get to them all in time," Jack promised. Then he lifted his empty glass and added, "But right now I mostly just want to sit here and enjoy a couple more of these."

Robert appeared eager to comply. He waved to the bartender. "Another round."

They were halfway through a third beer and a litany of Robert's jokes when Jack heard his name called out. He turned and saw Ryan walking towards them. The last person he expected to see.

"Ryan," he said. "What brings you here?"

"I got word that Salazar made it this far before his boat sank."

"Now that's interesting." Jack glanced at Robert, and then looked at Ryan. "Thought you gave up on him?"

"Did, until I heard that his yacht tore the bottom out on a reef not far from here. I had to come and see it for myself."

Robert motioned to the table. "Care to join us? The beer's cold."

"Sounds good." He smiled at Kazuko and Pillai. "But I best be on my way. Just wanted to look you up and give you the news. Only took three bars to find you."

"What about Salazar and his goons?" Kazuko asked. "They went down with the ship, I hope?"

"The only survivor was a woman: Annett Flores, I think her name was. I know that must break your heart."

"That he and his crew of pigs are dead? No. But I am glad Annett made it."

"Good enough," Ryan said. "Be seeing you."

When Ryan was out the door and beyond earshot, Jack looked at Robert. "Wouldn't it be fun to dive the wreck and recover all that gold?"

Robert scoffed. "And have it turn out like every other adventure you get me involved in?"

Jack gripped his chest as if hurt by the accusation. "I'm shattered. What on earth are you talking about?"

Robert gave him a good long look. "You know what I'm talking about. Likely as not, you'd play Sir Galahad and we'd end up having to fight our way out of one nasty situation and then another." He shook his head. "In the future, I'll just refrain from joining you on any of your wild exploits."

Of course Robert had been joking, but Jack knew there was some truth to his friend's words.

The thought made him laugh.

ABOUT THE AUTHOR

William Nikkel is the author of five *Jack Ferrell* novels and a steampunk/zombie western featuring his latest hero, Max Traver. A former homicide detective and S.W.A.T. team member for the Kern County Sheriff's Department in Bakersfield, California, William is an amateur scuba enthusiast, gold prospector and artist, who can be found just about anywhere. He and his wife Karen divide their time between California and Maui, Hawaii.

www.ingramcontent.com/pod-product-compliance
Lightning Source LLC
Chambersburg PA
CBHW070830250626
47159CB00003B/718